more of you

Love You More ~ Book 2

laura pavlov

More of You Playlist

Go Easy ~ Matt Maeson
Way Down We Go ~ Kaleo
Novocaine ~ The Unlikely Candidates
Not Losing You ~ Maddie Poppe
Possum Kingdom ~ Toadies
Miracle ~ Chvrches
Violet City ~ Mansionair
Don't Give Up On Me ~ Andy Grammar

Love is composed of a single soul inhabiting two bodies.

Aristotle

one

. . .

Jade

MUSIC BOOMED behind the stage where I stood. The walls vibrated from the loud cheers coming from the audience. It was still hard to wrap my head around—how quickly Exiled's fanbase had grown. *"More of Me,"* the song Cruz wrote, had skyrocketed to number one on multiple charts. Their tour sold out within an hour of tickets going on sale, and we'd spent the summer traveling across the U.S. from venue to venue. I kept a journal of our travels, and Cruz and I tried to do one touristy thing in each new location we visited depending on time. He always made a point to find a library in each city for me to see. As much as he made fun of my nerdy obsession with libraries—he managed to find one everywhere we went.

The music for *"More of Me"* started to play, and my stomach dipped. It always did when he performed the song he'd written for me. Cruz liked me to sit on the side of the stage where he could see me during his shows, so I sat in a chair and wrote in my journal as I listened.

Things had changed dramatically in the last two weeks, and the tension was palpable when the band wasn't on stage. They did their best to hide the turmoil when they performed, but I had a front row seat to what was going on. Tory, Adam's now ex-girlfriend, used to sit with me during the shows, and I missed my partner in crime. Now I sat solo. She'd been gone for more than a week, and nothing was the same. Adam was miserable, even if he was too stubborn to admit it. The day she'd left was horrible. Adam told her to leave and she'd been inconsolable. We'd spent two nights at a hotel in Nashville, and Tory had stayed up late drinking with a few friends from high school who attended college not far from the venue. Cruz and I usually went to our room after the shows. Adam had been exhausted and turned in before Tory was ready to say goodnight to her friends. He woke up early the following morning and realized she hadn't come to bed. He found her in Dex's room with all her friends and a pile of white powder on the table, and apparently some on her face —and he'd lost it. Tory had never done drugs in front of me. I think she had too much to drink and got caught up in the moment. But Adam was not okay with it. He and Dex didn't get along before this happened, so things had gone from bad to worse. And Adam was Cruz's best friend, so Cruz and Dex's already tumultuous relationship was way past the point of no return.

The roar of the crowd pulled me from my thoughts, and I realized the music had stopped. I looked out onto the stage to see Cruz smiling at me. He motioned for me to come out there, and panic surged through my veins.

"Come on, baby. They want me to sing to you," he said, his voice sexy and raspy through the microphone.

I shook my head. My legs froze in place. The thought of going out there in front of all those people terrified me. The lights were flashing, creating all sorts of designs in my peripheral vision, and I heard my boyfriend say something to his fans about giving him a minute. There was laughter and whistling, as he jogged toward me. He pulled his headset off and a wide grin spread across his beautiful face.

"Everyone wants *more Jade*," he said, melting my heart just like he always did.

I laughed. He was ridiculous, but in the best way. Cruz Winslow made me feel like the most important person on the planet every time he looked at me. And it would all come to an end soon. This was the last show I'd be at for a while, as I was going back to school in a week.

"What are you doing? I can't go out there. I like watching you from here."

"Do you trust me?" he asked, his head cocked to the side, and his honey-brown gaze locked with mine.

"Always."

"Come on." He took my hand and led me onto the stage. I wasn't sure how my legs were moving, but they were.

I bit down hard on my bottom lip and used my free hand to grip the back of his T-shirt, tucking myself behind him. The cheers from the audience were deafening and I glanced over at Cruz's brother, Lennon. His gaze locked with mine and he winked. He really was a different person on stage. It's where he came alive. I'd grown so close to him, and he'd become more like a brother to me over the last few months.

"My girl's a little shy, but I told her you wanted a little more Jade, am I right?" he said, and the crowd went crazy in response.

"Yeah, trust me. I fucking get it. I can't get enough myself," he teased his fans, and the cheers and screams only grew louder. Luke came out of nowhere with a stool and Cruz helped me to sit down. I covered my face with my hands and tried to remain seated, but I wanted to sprint off the stage.

The music started again, just as it had when I'd been in my little cocoon just moments ago when he'd halted the show to come and get me. The audience quieted, and my boyfriend started to sing. He pulled my hands away from my face and looked only at me, and for a moment I forgot where I was. He sang to me often in the quiet confines of his room, and for the next few minutes, that's exactly where I convinced myself I was. Just he and I. He moved closer, stepping between my legs, and his hand caressed the back of my neck while he sang the last part of the song to me.

And she asks me…

Why would you want more of me?

She doesn't know just what I see.

Beautiful girl with eyes of jade.
Shines so bright can't find the shade.
Heart so pure even in her pain.
In the drought she is the rain.

When he finished, his eyes remained locked with mine. I wrapped my arms around his neck and settled my head against his chest, hugging him tight. He pulled me from the chair and my legs came around his waist, just like they always did. We just didn't usually have an audience whistling and screaming in the background. He carried me over to my hideaway beside the stage and set me down on the stool.

"You okay?" he whispered against my ear.

I nodded and pushed up to kiss him before he ran back on stage. Cruz had come into his own these last few months. He was convinced this wasn't his passion, but he was a natural. He'd written so many new songs as we traveled on the bus, and whether he believed it or not, he was an amazing singer and songwriter. We spent as much time together as possible, as we both knew things were going to change when I went back to school.

Telling Cruz that I'd decided to return to Northwestern in the fall was one of the hardest things I'd ever done. I'd chosen myself over him. And it certainly wasn't because I loved myself more than I loved him. I didn't. I loved him more than anything. More than I'd ever known possible. But I knew I was doing the right thing, even if my heart didn't agree. I needed to stay true to myself for *us*. For our future. But the thought of not seeing him every day—it did something to me.

He hadn't been fazed when I told him. He said he thought I was doing the right thing, and we'd make the most of the time we had together. He was hoping to walk away from Exiled next year and he'd move back to Chicago until I finished school. I didn't know how it would all work, and I wondered if him leaving the band would be more challenging than he thought. Exiled was an international sensation now, and AF records was scheduling a worldwide tour for them.

How would they just suddenly replace Cruz as the lead singer without it being a problem? He didn't seem worried, so I tried to do the same.

I'd been home to visit Dad twice. I talked to him and my two best friends, Sam and Ari every single day. They loved seeing photos of our travels, and I was enjoying this time away from the regular stresses in life. Luke hired me to handle all the social media for the band this summer, as it was an actual position they needed, and it allowed me to fulfill my promise to my father to work. Cruz didn't want me handling the merchandise during the shows, because he didn't think it was safe. He was as overprotective as my dad.

I pushed to my feet when they ran off the stage. It would only be for a few minutes and they'd go back out and perform another song or two for their encore. Dex walked by giving me one of his creepy smiles. He was a predator. In every sense of the word. He exploited others for his own benefit. He knew exactly what he was doing when he came between Tory and Adam. It was premeditated and malicious. He hated that I didn't give him an opening to mess with me and Cruz. He was the worst kind of narcissist, and his sudden taste of success and fame didn't help the situation. Adam ruffled the top of my head as he moved past me, and Lennon paused and kissed me on the cheek.

"Good job out there tonight, girl. You did it," he said with a laugh.

"I didn't have much of a choice," I teased.

"Move," Cruz snarled at his brother before he pushed me up against the wall and kissed me.

Lennon chuckled as he walked away, and my hands tangled in my boyfriend's hair.

"Hey," I said, trying to catch my breath when he pulled away.

"You mad at me for making you go out there?" he asked, nipping at my ear.

"No. You're impossible to be mad at."

"Love you," he said, leaning down to kiss me one more time before he ran back out on stage.

I stood and watched Cruz sing the last song in his dark skinny jeans, a ripped tee, and combat boots. His hair was a disheveled mess, and he was the most beautiful boy I'd ever seen. His chiseled jaw and full lips made him all the more appealing. But it was his honey brown eyes that always did me in. He glanced over his shoulder and I gave him a small wave. He chuckled as he sang, because for some reason, Cruz seemed to think I was funny even when I wasn't trying to be.

"Hey," Luke said, coming up behind me.

"Hi. Great show tonight." I turned to face him. I liked Luke. He was more than just a manager, and he always looked out for Cruz, which I appreciated.

"Yeah, they killed it. You gonna miss all this?" he asked.

"I am. I wish I didn't have to leave."

"Nah, you'll be fine. You're doing the right thing, Jade."

"You think so?" I asked as cheers and screams filled the space around us. The band was wrapping things up.

"I do. You two will be fine. I took care of that little favor you asked me for, and he's here. He set up in one of the spare rooms in back. He's supposed to be the best in town, and I checked his references and saw his work. Seems like a talented dude. But when Cruz loses his shit, don't blame me," Luke said with a laugh.

I leaned forward and hugged him. "I won't, I promise. Thanks for doing this. I'll meet him after the show."

"Anything for you," Luke said as Dex came running toward him and picked their manager up off his feet.

"Put me down, asshole." Luke pushed back and almost fell on his way down.

"I'd love to pick you up, princess, but I think it would piss off your broody ass boyfriend. What do you think?" Dex invaded my space.

"If you touch me, you'll be very sorry," I said, glaring at him.

"Oh yeah. What are you going to do to me, Jade? You like it rough, huh?"

I stomped my foot hard on the top of his and he stepped back with a laugh.

Cruz walked up and looked between us. "What's going on? Is he bothering you?"

"So protective. How are you going to watch her when she's gone?" Dex's smile resembled the Joker's. It made the hair on the back of my neck stand up.

"Shut the fuck up," Cruz said, taking my hand and leading me down the hall.

"Just ignore him. He wants to get a rise out of you," I said.

"He's such an asshole. I don't like him messing with you."

"I can handle myself. Dex doesn't scare me," I said.

He stopped in the back room and grabbed two water bottles. The guys no longer chugged a celebratory beer after shows because Adam wasn't speaking to Dex. Cruz didn't mind because he'd cut way back on his drinking this summer. I think he learned that he couldn't beat me at a single card game when he was drunk, but he claimed it was because he wanted to set a good example for his brother. I loved how much he cared for Lennon.

"You shouldn't have to handle anything when it comes to Dex. I swear to Christ, I'm going to kick that kid's ass someday. And I'm going to enjoy the hell out of it."

I laughed. "Hey, I have a little surprise for you. Will you come with me?"

"*More Jade*, I'd go anywhere with you. You need a little something right now?" He pushed me up against the wall and kissed me hard.

"Oh my God, no." It was difficult not to laugh through my words, as I forced him to look at me. "I don't need a little *something*, I get plenty of that."

"Then where are you taking me?" he asked.

I took his hand and led him into the room at the end of the hall. "I have a surprise for you."

"And clearly it's not sex. Just for future reference, baby—that's all I ever need."

I laughed as I pushed the door open. "Hi, you must be Skully?"

"I'm not into threesomes. I don't share," Cruz whispered against my ear.

The large tatted man stood and offered me a hand. "Yeah, you must be Jade."

Cruz glared at him. He was ridiculously jealous, even when there was no reason to be. I rolled my eyes. "This is my boyfriend, Cruz."

"Nice to meet you, man. Great show. Luke gave me the best seat in the house."

"Cool. Who are you and how do you know my girl?"

Skully laughed. He was much older than me and Cruz, probably in his mid-forties. He put his hands up and smiled. "Easy tiger. I'm a married man with three little hellions that my wife insists we keep. I don't have time for anything more."

"You do know you're ridiculous, right?" I said to my boyfriend. "Skully is a talented tattoo artist and I'm getting a tattoo."

"The fuck you are," Cruz said.

"Excuse me?" I crossed my arms over my chest, and Skully chuckled before walking away to give us a minute.

"Tattoos are painful, baby. I'm not watching someone hurt you."

Me and Skully both laughed at the same time. Cruz had gotten a few tattoos while we'd been traveling this summer, and his arm was fairly covered in ink. And he was telling me not to get one?

"I'm not a child, nor am I afraid of a little pain. I'm getting a small one," I said, taking his hand and leading him over to see Skully's work.

"Dude, I've been doing this for a long time. She's going to be fine. It's a small tat. If you think you can't watch though, you should step outside. I don't want you making her nervous."

I tried to cover my smile. Skully was not taking Cruz's shit, which I'd come to learn he actually liked.

"Fuck that. I'm not letting her do it alone. What do you want to get?"

"A small music note, on the inside of my wrist. A little something to remind me of you," I said, dropping down to sit in the chair next to Skully.

"That's sweet. And how did you find *Skully*? No offense dude, just want to make sure you know what you're doing before you touch her."

"I hear you, brother. Trust me, Luke researched the shit out of me, but here's some of my work." Skully handed him a binder full of the art he'd inked on people over the years.

"This is impressive." Cruz studied each page.

"Thanks. Mind if I check yours out?" Skully asked, quirking a brow as he glanced at Cruz's arm.

"Not at all." My boyfriend tugged his shirt over his head, and my cheeks heated as I took him in. He was stunning. Chiseled abs and strong muscles covered in beautiful colors with meaningful sayings and drawings.

"Nice work. Who did them?"

"I had them done at Dark Angel back home," he said.

"Yeah? I worked with the owner, Chris, for years. We trained together before I moved out west. Did he do this one? More Jade?"

"Yep. I drew it and he inked it." Cruz looked over at me and winked.

"Incredible work. The color is insane," Skully said, handing Cruz a piece of paper with the drawing of the music note.

"Yeah, I'm happy with it. All right, I'm being an asshole. You've got this. Sorry."

"I get it, brother." Skully winked at me.

Cruz bent down and took my free hand. Skully got to work and once the design was ready to go, he tested out the area on my wrist and asked if it hurt.

"Not at all. I'm good," I said with a laugh, looking over at my boyfriend who squeezed my hand and studied my every movement.

We talked as he inked the tiny music note on my left wrist, and Cruz started to relax. "That's sick, baby. I love it."

"I do too." I like that I'd have something to remind me of him forever now.

"Okay, let me just clean you up. You're a champ, Jade. This one's a different story." Skully jabbed his thumb at Cruz and we all laughed.

"I'm sorry for being a dick. Just can't handle seeing her hurt."

"Nah, man. I'm the same way with my lady. She makes you human," he said.

"She does." He kissed my wrist over the bandage and fought me when I paid for the tattoo.

"Let her win this one. She just tatted herself for you," Skully said.

Cruz put his hands up. "Okay, okay, I got it."

We jumped on the bus to head back to the hotel. Cruz never let go of my hand. Everything was about to change, and we were both feeling it.

Like a dark cloud that loomed above—we were preparing for the storm.

two

. . .

Cruz

WE HAD A FEW DAYS OFF. Fucking finally. It worked out well
with Jade getting ready to head back to school. I wanted to spend
some time with her before we started this long-distance nightmare. It
wasn't that I didn't think I could stay faithful to her. That wasn't an
issue. I didn't feel right when I wasn't with her. I liked taking care of
her, and I knew I'd be all over the fucking country these next few
months, so that wouldn't be an easy task. But I was fucking proud of
her for making the decision to return to school. Hell, I knew it was
the right thing for her to do. And when it came to Jade, I wanted that
for her. Even though it fucking sucked for me. It would be like
surviving without sunshine. Or oxygen. She was my fuel. My reason
to be better. And I had to let her go for now. The thought made me
fucking sick. The realization that the first thing I saw every morning
wouldn't be her face, that her smile wouldn't be the last thing I saw
before I fell asleep each night—It scared the shit out of me.

We'd planned a trip to Disneyland since we were out west, and
Jade and I had always wanted to go. We'd seen so much these last
few months, and this was something I knew she wanted to do. We'd
planned to go with Adam, Tory, and Lennon, but seeing as Tory was
no longer around, Adam didn't want to go. So now it was me, Jade,

and my third-wheeling, cock blocking brother. He had zero problem with it. Jade loved Lennon and truth be told, I loved how close they were. I wasn't big on rides, so I kicked back and watched the two most important people in my life behaving like they were five years old again.

The park was packed. We'd hired a guide to escort us around, per Luke's insistence. I hated lines and I hated crowds, so he thought it was a wise thing to do. I sat on a bench watching a kid have a meltdown two feet in front of me while his mom patiently reasoned with him. He didn't want to go on Dumbo, and I kind of felt bad for the kid. I didn't want to ride the fucking elephant either. His mom bent down in front of him and calmly told him they weren't leaving until he went on the ride. The little hellion took a minute to think it over and then asked if he could have a chocolate-covered banana if he did what she wanted. Fucking brilliant. His mom agreed, and he wiped the snot from his nose with the back of his hand. He was a dirty little shit, but he looked over at me and smiled and I couldn't help but smile back. I saluted him for his brilliant negotiation skills.

Another family walked by with two kids on some sort of leash licking their oversized lollipops. Jesus, it was eight in the morning and these kids were all sugared up. I understood it. What else could they do? It's not like they could light up a cig or slam a beer to deal with the chaos around them. This place was a fucking madhouse. Frantic parents, excited kids, and Disney characters smiling every which way you turned. Smiles and sunshine for miles. Everyone was dressed for the warm weather, donning shorts and tank tops. The smell of vanilla and waffle cones invaded my senses, as my girlfriend and brother jogged toward me.

"Come on, baby. You're going on Dumbo with me once," Jade said.

Dumbo was her favorite movie, so go fucking figure, we had to come to this ride first. She and Lennon went on the ride together, while I watched and took a few pictures as they went by. Jade had Minnie Mouse ears on her head, a red Disney t-shirt, and jean cut-off shorts, and somehow managed to look sexy as hell.

"Come on, dickhead. Go on the ride with your girl," Lennon said as he placed his stupid Mickey ears on my head.

"I prefer to watch." I returned the ridiculous ears to my brother's head.

"Please, please, please." Jade put her hands together like she was praying. I was a sucker for her, and she knew it. She preyed on my weakness, and damn if she didn't win every time.

"Fine. Let's go ride the elephants," I said.

She bounced up and down before taking my hand and leading me to the ride.

"Are you having fun?" she asked, wrapping her arms around me, and hugging my middle.

I kissed her, hard and fast. "Yep. I love seeing you so excited."

"I'm so glad we're doing this together."

"Me too."

Our guide waved us forward and we stood off to the side, waiting our turn.

"I can't believe I have to go back to school in two days. I'm not ready," she said.

"You're ready, and you're going to kill it."

"So, we haven't really talked about what will happen? I mean, obviously we'll visit one another, and FaceTime every day—but how do you feel about everything? You know, is it going to be hard for you to be faithful while we're apart?"

I laughed. "There's no one I want but you. It won't be a problem for me. How about you?"

Her head tipped back, and she smiled. "Yeah, I don't think you need to worry about me. I held out for you for nineteen years."

"That's right, baby. You remember that when all those nerdy dudes try to tell you differently," I said.

"And what about all those hot chicks who throw their panties at you on stage?"

The guy waved us through, and Jade led me to one of the ridiculous elephants. We passed two very small kids before finding the one she liked.

"Nasty panties don't do it for me."

I climbed in and she slipped in in front of me, settling between my legs and leaning back, she looked up at me. "So then, what does it for you?"

"*More Jade.*"

She laughed as the ride took off. I saw my brother below filming us and I flipped him off. Jade's smile spread across her face, and for a brief minute I just took it all in. She'd changed my life so much. Who'd have thought I'd be at Disneyland laughing on a Dumbo ride with the love of my life. But here I was. Lennon was healthy, Exiled was on tour, and Jade was my girl. I couldn't ask for more. My dad was off my case, at least for now. We'd exceeded his expectations thus far, so he'd backed off. Mom had even come to a concert and spent some time with Jade.

"Put your hands up," Jade shouted, her body shaking with laughter.

I rolled my eyes and held my arms up. As if it were fucking challenging. The tiny human wearing a diaper in front of us had her little hands in the air. As usual, Jade saw the light in everything. And we were making memories, both big and small ones. Together.

When we got off the ride, she jumped up on my back and slapped my ass. I laughed. Couldn't help it.

"You liked it, didn't you, asshole?" Lennon said when we approached him.

"It was fine."

"You loved it." Jade leaned forward and kissed my cheek.

"I love *you*," I said.

"Okay, let's hit Pirates of the Caribbean next." Lennon led us toward the ride.

"We have to stop at the gift shop up here before we go on that ride," Jade said to our guide, still riding piggyback.

"For what?" Lennon asked.

"Duh, *swords*," my girlfriend said.

"Swords?" I looked around the store and Jade slid down my back until her feet touched the ground.

"How else would we fight pirates?" she said, dragging me down the aisle with the plastic weapons.

"You're fucking kidding me, right?" I asked when we got to the counter.

"Do I look like I'm kidding?"

"Unfortunately, you don't."

We'd avoided all attention so far this morning, and I was fucking thankful to have a day to exist outside of Exiled. We got on the small boat and Jade and Lennon both crouched down on each side of the row we were seated in. I sat on the bench in between them acting unamused, but I was completely enthralled with the scene before me. They were both ridiculously childlike. It was endearing and my fucking heart squeezed, which pissed me off. There was a musty, chlorine-like smell in the air, and the dimly lit space was brightened by hanging lanterns as our boat moved forward. The people around us laughed as they watched Jade and Lennon act as if they were in full battle with the pirates. My girl crept over to me and looked up, with those big jade eyes.

"*Cover me.* Lennon needs back up," she whisper-shouted, and the lady behind me laughed so loud it echoed off the dark walls.

"I got you," I said, shaking my head.

The rest of the day flew by. We went on every ride that Jade and Lennon had on their list, including the log ride which we got soaked on. We ate junk food and only got recognized a handful of times. I couldn't complain. The fans were the reason our tour had been successful, so I'd always be grateful for their support. Lennon ate that shit up and loved signing autographs and posing for pictures. I kept an arm wrapped around Jade as we made our way out of the park, and she and my brother talked a mile a minute about their favorite rides. I knew if I could freeze time, I'd have it stop right now. In this moment.

———

We dropped down on the Northwestern blanket at our favorite spot at Oak Street beach. I didn't want to say goodbye to her. But we'd be fine. There was no other option. I'd flown back to Chicago with her and would fly out early in the morning to get to our show in Seattle.

I was pushing it arriving two hours before we went on stage, but I wanted to take her back to school and get her settled. I knew she was struggling with her decision and I needed to know she'd be okay.

"Do you remember the first time I brought you here?" she asked.

"Of course. Your sexy ass belted out Shining Star. It's forever embedded in my brain."

"Oh yeah, that was *real*, sexy," she said with a laugh.

"You have no idea."

"I can't believe you have to go back tomorrow." She moved closer to me, and I pulled her on my lap. My chest rested against her back and I wrapped my arms around her.

"It'll be fine. Stop worrying."

"You're not worried?" she asked.

Hell, I was terrified, but I wouldn't tell her that. "Nope."

My fears weren't about one of us being unfaithful. Jade and I were solid. My fears were more about her dreams taking her away from me. That we wouldn't be moving in the same direction and life would get in the way. A person could never come between us, because Jade was it for me. And I was it for her. There was no question. We just fit. Always had. But life had a way of fucking things up, and its track record with me wasn't great. But I'd do everything in my power to make sure we got through this.

"How do you know?"

"Because I know we're meant to be together. I have something for you," I said, slipping her off my lap so I could reach in my pocket.

"You do?" She faced me, brushing the hair back from her pretty face.

"Yeah. It can mean whatever you want it to," I said, handing her the box with the petite platinum band covered in tiny diamonds.

She gasped. "What do you want it to mean?"

"I knew you would be mine the day we met. *You* are my home. I can be myself when I'm with you. Only with you. So, this ring can symbolize whatever you want it to. For me, it's forever—in whatever capacity you'll have me. You're my family. My future. My everything."

Her mouth turned up in the corners and her gaze filled with tears. "You're my family, my future, my everything, too."

"Love you, More Jade."

Tears sprung from her pretty green gaze and ran down her face. "I love you."

I pulled her back on my lap and hugged her close to me. Damn, this girl had found a way in and now I didn't know how to exist without her. She slipped the ring onto her ring finger on her left hand. Exactly where I wanted it.

"You like it?" I asked.

"I love it. So, it's sort of a swanky promise ring?"

"Sure, if that's what you want it to be. What's a promise ring?"

"It's a promise to stay together," she said, nuzzling her nose against mine.

"Hell, yeah, it's a promise ring then."

"What if I had said I wanted it to be an engagement ring?" Her head fell back in laughter.

"Then I'd say take me to the courthouse."

She turned in my arms and studied me. "You'd marry me today, Winslow?"

"I'd marry you right now. Right here. Whenever you're ready. But I'll get you a better ring when you give me the green light," I said.

"I'd marry you right now if I weren't nineteen, and you weren't traveling the world on tour with a rock band, and I wasn't a pre-med in college." She laughed, running her fingers through my hair. "But I know I'm going to marry you someday."

"Good. I'm counting on it."

She buried her face in my neck and I felt her wet tears against my skin. Her body trembled and I held her as she cried. We were entering a new chapter, and it wasn't one I was looking forward to.

three

. . .

Jade

"JADE, WAIT UP," Brayden called out from behind me.

He was in four of my five classes this semester. I intentionally sat in the middle of the room when I spotted him up front on the first day of class. I knew Cruz didn't like him, and I didn't want to send any mixed signals to Brayden. We'd gone to dinner a few times last year before Cruz and I had started dating, but we'd never been anything more than friends.

"Hey, what's up?"

"Not much. Brennan's class is killing me. The first three weeks have been crazy, right?" He wore a black tee and faded jeans. His dark hair was wavy and a little longer in the front and cropped in the back. Brayden was a nice guy, and he knew that Cruz and I were very much together. But I always got the feeling he wanted more, and it made me hesitant to hang out with him for fear of sending the wrong message.

"Yeah, the workload has been insane." I shifted my backpack on my shoulder as we walked through campus. The weather was still gorgeous, and I would enjoy every last second of it before the temperature dropped.

"I heard you got the research position with Professor Callahan. That's impressive."

"Yes, she's amazing. I was thrilled she was looking for an assistant," I said. Elaine Callahan was a brilliant emergency medicine doctor, and she'd chosen me to work with her on a paper she hoped to publish in the future.

"So many people applied for it, you should be proud she chose you," he said, a genuine smile spread across his face.

"Yeah, I was thrilled when I got the call. How about you? Are you working with anyone this semester?"

"Yep, I'm working at the lab with Professor Watson. It's a good gig for me. He works around my schedule."

"That's amazing. I've heard he's great to work with," I said.

"He's a cool dude. But, he's also a perfectionist, so I need to be on my game. A letter of recommendation from him would be helpful when I apply to med school."

"Definitely," I said, pausing when we walked into our anatomy classroom.

"So, what's the deal this year? You can't sit by me anymore because you have a boyfriend? We can't be friends?"

Well, that was direct.

And super awkward.

"No. Of course we can," I said as I took my seat and he sat in the chair beside me.

"Good. I know Cruz can be pretty possessive over you."

One sure-fire way to get on my bad side was to talk crap about my boyfriend. I didn't like it.

"He's not any more possessive over me than I am of him. It happens when you're in love," I said, meeting his blue gaze. I didn't want there to be any confusion about where Brayden and I stood or how solid Cruz and I were.

He held his hands up and laughed. "Okay, okay, I'm sorry. Wrong word choice."

I nodded and pulled out my pens and notebook. My phone vibrated and I saw the text from Cruz.

CRUZ

Missing you bad today, baby.

My heart squeezed. I missed him terribly. After spending every day together over the summer, the separation was painful. I was flying to Florida this weekend to see him. I couldn't wait. It would be complicated to do it often with my new research position, because Professor Callahan expected me to work weekends occasionally. But I'd gotten this weekend off, and I couldn't wait to see him. Our goal was to never go more than a month apart.

I miss you more. Are things any better with Adam and Dex? I met Tory for coffee this morning and she's still devastated about their breakup. I wish he would give her another chance.

CRUZ

Dex is an asshole, and I don't think he's ever going to change. Adam doesn't want to be around him any more than he has to. So, yeah, that's been fun on a tour bus with limited space. I think he'll forgive her eventually. He's been in a bad mood since the day she left.

How about you? Have you been in a bad mood since the day I left?

CRUZ

You know me. I'm always in a bad mood, but I'm a much bigger asshole when you aren't here. Can't wait for this weekend. Ponch will text you the times later today.

Flying on Cruz's dad's plane made everything easier. Aside from saving money purchasing a ticket, I didn't have to arrive hours early and I could study the entire time.

> Can't wait. Having dinner with Dad tonight, so FaceTime me after your show. I don't care if I'm sleeping, I'll wake up so I can see your face. Class is starting. Love you.

CRUZ

> Love you more.

Class started and I took notes for the next hour and a half. Brayden asked me to study later and I was happy to have a valid excuse for not meeting him. I was meeting my father for dinner right up the street from my house.

———

Sept. 24th

Dear Journal,

Last night I went with my roommate to the Sydney Opera House and it was amazing. I'm experiencing so many new things each day. Australia is such a beautiful country and I'm so thankful for this experience. I am surprised that I'm a bit homesick at times. I really miss Jack, but we write often, and he has been so supportive. Yesterday was our one-year anniversary and I was excited to speak to him on the phone. Did you ever think I'd be celebrating special dates with a boy? Who has time for that, right? Turns out… I do. He's amazing. He finished all his coursework and was accepted into the fire academy. He's one step closer to doing what he wants to do. He's so passionate about it too. Of course, I don't like the idea of him running into burning buildings, but I have to support his dreams just like he supports mine. It's called compromise, apparently, and I'm learning how to do it. Ha Ha. Not my strength, obviously.

Okay, I need to go pick out a cute outfit for my day trip to Bondi Beach. What? Yep, there's something new to find each day in Sydney. And I plan to see it all.

Ciao for now,

J.E.

I chuckled before I closed Mom's journal. She was so driven at my age, and I loved reading her love story with Dad. I'd asked him if he wanted to read her journals too, but he didn't. He said the memories were still there for him, and that's how he wanted to remember them.

I hurried out the door and walked a few blocks to meet Dad at our favorite Italian restaurant. He was waiting outside for me, and we hugged before walking inside. We took our seats and ordered dinner.

"You look skinnier than usual. You eating enough?" Dad asked. Never one to mince words, he said exactly what he thought.

"Yes. I'm eating plenty. Just busy with classes and research." I stabbed the spaghetti and twirled it around my fork.

"So, what's happening with Cruz. You're going to see him this weekend, right?"

"Yep. Flying to Miami for two nights. They're performing there, but I can spend the days with him at least, and I'll study during the shows," I said, twisting the promise ring around my finger. It comforted me in a way. Made me feel closer to Cruz even when we weren't together.

"Is he still trying to find a replacement? Seems like they've gotten pretty big time overnight. I don't know how they're going to be okay with him leaving." Dad reached for another piece of garlic bread.

I hated this topic. Deep down I knew he was right, but I didn't want to think about it. Right now, I was having a hard time, because I hadn't seen my boyfriend in a few weeks. I tried to keep a smile on my face the best I could and focus on school, but I was struggling. I didn't sleep well being away from him. I occasionally got online and looked at pictures of him in the media. Cruz had become a well-known rock star over the summer, and everyone wanted a picture, a comment, a moment with him. There'd been a few photographs with girls hanging on him as he walked inside the venue. I knew logically they were just grabbing on to him, he wasn't asking for it, and he had his head down and just continued walking. But it still stung. That tinge of insecurity always crept in when I thought about how many girls wanted to be with him. What made *me* so special? And I wasn't there. There was a lot of speculation online about our relationship. The hashtag #CRADE had gone viral. People had said we'd broken up, some believed we were on a break, some thought we were still together but had an open relationship. I tried to tune out all the noise and just focus on what was true. But it wasn't easy. I knew Dad heard things and probably worried, but there wasn't much I could do to stop the gossip.

"I don't know. He's going to try, that's all I know."

Dad set his fork down and studied me. "You okay? Is all this getting to you?"

"No. I'm fine. Just tired."

"Well, for what it's worth, I think you did the right thing, Jady bug. You know, coming back to go to school. I know it's tough, but you'll get through it," he said.

"Sure."

The rest of dinner was quiet and uneventful. Dad changed the subject, and we stopped talking about what would happen with Cruz and Exiled, and I was thankful for the reprieve.

When I got home, I studied for a couple hours before slipping into the tub. Once I dried off and pulled my jammies on, I climbed into bed. I slept with my phone beside me so I wouldn't miss Cruz's call. There was a text from Ari letting me know she would be sleeping at Jace's tonight. I envied her having her boyfriend here at school with her. I wished Cruz were here with me too. I dozed off with dreams of my beautiful, disheveled, sexy boyfriend.

My phone buzzed and startled me from sleep. My hand searched around the bed for my phone. It was two o'clock in the morning. I'd been out for a while.

"Hey," I said as I waited for FaceTime to show me his handsome face.

"Hi, beautiful. Sorry to wake you." His voice was raspy and tired. His words slurred a bit, so I knew he'd been drinking. I saw the bags under his eyes, and he pulled the baseball cap from his head and tossed it on the nightstand in the hotel room.

"Don't be. I wanted to talk to you. It's late there, almost four in the morning, right? The show ran long?" I asked, rolling on my side and propping the phone against a pillow so I didn't have to hold it.

"Yeah. We had a few drinks after. I don't have a reason to hurry back to my room anymore," he said, scrubbing a hand down his face. His tone was all tease, but I heard the sadness, and I understood it. Hell, I felt it. I didn't like that he was drinking so much more now, either, but I had to choose my battles.

"Are you having trouble sleeping?"

"I don't know," he said, and I pushed to sit up, holding the phone in my hand again.

"Talk to me. What's going on?"

"It's harder than I thought it would be, you know. Us being apart. I miss you. I don't sleep much, and the days are long when you aren't here," he said. His honey-brown gaze was filled with emotion, and a pain settled in my chest.

"I know," I said, my voice breaking on a sob. "I hate it."

"Please don't cry, baby. It'll be fine. And I get to see you this weekend."

I swiped at the tears streaming down my face. "I know."

"I drank too much tonight, so I'm feeling sorry for myself. Don't worry. Everything will be fine," he said, setting the phone down while he yanked the T-shirt over his head and dropped his pants. He climbed into bed and grabbed the phone again.

"I miss sleeping with you." I wiped beneath my eyes.

"I know. I fucking wish you were here with me right now."

"Me too," I whispered, and I slipped back down beneath the covers.

"You going to be able to sleep?" he asked.

"I don't know."

"Close your eyes, baby. I'll sing to you. That always settles you," he said.

And that's exactly what he did. I set the phone down beside me and closed my eyes, and the sweet sound of Cruz's voice singing the lyrics he'd written just for me lulled me to sleep.

———

"Why can't Jace be a rock star?" Ari asked as we drove down the highway toward the hangar. She and I were really happy that we were no longer living in the dorms and we loved having a house of our own.

"Please. Be thankful your boyfriend isn't touring all over the globe, with girls throwing their panties at him. I'd love if Cruz were still here going to school with me."

"I guess you're right. But you get to jet set off to concerts to meet up with your hot superstar boyfriend. It's kind of sexy, come on," she said.

I could see how people would think that. It sounded exciting and romantic. But it wasn't. I had to share Cruz with the world, and this weekend would be hectic for him. He had two shows, which meant late nights and lots of people. Alone time would be hard to come by.

"Sure. But there's something to be said about just living a normal life, too."

"Just remember, it's not forever. Soak this shit up, girl. Before you know it, he'll be back here by next summer."

I twirled the ring on my finger. "Yeah, I hope so."

"You worry too much. So, are you meeting him at the venue? You get in just an hour before the show starts, right?"

"Yep. He said there'd be a car there for me. I can't wait to see him."

"I bet. I know it's been tough on you. I told Jace he has to sleep at our house from now on. I don't like you being there alone," Ari said.

"Now who's worrying too much?"

My phone vibrated and I saw a text from my best friend Sam.

SAM

Hey J-bird. You on your way to Miami? Be safe. Text me when you get back. Dinner next week?

Yes, on my way now. Definitely down to meet for dinner next week. Miss you.

Sam knew I was struggling. He'd been thrilled when I decided to return to school after spending the summer with Cruz on tour. But he understood how difficult it was at the same time.

"Who's that? Cruz or Sam?"

I laughed. "It's Sam. Just telling me to be safe."

"He's like a built-in big brother, huh?"

"Definitely. Thanks for driving me. Sorry I've been such a dud this semester."

"Stop it. I know your class load is crazy. What pre-med tries to graduate in three year's? You're insane. And brilliant. You're doing all this research and you have a long-distance boyfriend. I'd say you've got your hands full. But when you get back, we need a girl's night out. You deserve to have some fun."

"Okay, I'm in. I could use a little fun," I said with a laugh.

We pulled in front of the hangar and I hugged Ari goodbye, hurrying inside to meet Ponch.

The flight was uneventful, and I finished most of my homework before he called me up to assist him with the landing. I loved getting to ride co-pilot. It was crazy to think I'd flown for the first time last year, and now I'd been on a plane more times than I could count. Ponch always let me ride co-pilot and it made the time fly by quickly.

"You excited to get there?" he asked. Ponch was Cruz's favorite pilot, and the only one I'd ever flown with.

"Yeah. I hate being apart from Cruz."

"Just remember, it will be a small blip in the big picture of life. Sonia and I spent three years doing the long-distance thing when we were young. Here we are thirty-five years later. It seems long right now, but you won't even remember this time apart. You've got your future to look forward to," Ponch said with a wink.

"That's true."

When the plane touched down and we came to a stop, I hugged him goodbye. We agreed to meet Sunday evening to fly back to school. I didn't even want to think about returning. That meant saying goodbye to Cruz. I saw the car sitting on the runway and slipped my backpack on my shoulder, pulling my suitcase behind me. When the back door opened and Cruz stepped out, I dropped all my stuff and started sprinting toward him. He wasn't supposed to be here, and I couldn't get to him fast enough.

The air left from my lungs when I slammed into him. I wrapped my legs around his waist and buried my face in his neck, and his arms came around me, hugging me tight.

"What are you doing here?" I said, my words labored and breathless.

"I couldn't wait to see you." He kissed me, and all my worries melted away. All the anxiety, stress, sadness—it all dissipated. Just like that.

"Don't you have a show in less than an hour?" I asked, slipping back down to my feet.

"Tough shit. They can wait. We aren't far from the venue. It'll be fine. Dex had a temper tantrum, but Adam and Lennon both thought I should come." He took my hand and led me to the car, and the driver grabbed my bags.

He pulled me onto his lap and wrapped his arms around me, in lieu of a seatbelt. I knew better, but I just didn't care. I needed this right now. I ran my fingers through his unruly hair and studied his features.

"I'm so happy to see you," I said.

"Me too. One month down."

"One month down," I said against his mouth.

He kissed me again and then trailed his lips down my neck. I tipped my head back to give him better access. I reveled in his touch. His hands slipped beneath my blouse and roamed around my stomach before teasing me over my bra. I gasped as my skin heated and he nipped at my ear.

"God, I missed you, *More Jade*."

"Missed you too," I said as the car came to a stop.

"Damn, we're here." He looked down at his phone when it vibrated. "Shit, it's Luke. Apparently, word's out that I'm not here yet, and there's a crowd at the back door. Fucking Dex probably leaked it. Keep your head down and stay right in front of me, okay?"

I nodded, before glancing out the window. My stomach dipped as I took in the large group gathered outside. Two people came close to the car and banged on the window, and I jumped back, slipping off his lap and onto the seat. The windows were tinted so they couldn't see inside. Cruz appeared visibly uncomfortable, and the driver turned to face us.

"Security is on their way out, Mr. Winslow. I'll lead you both in, and they can flank each side of you," the large man said.

"Thanks, Eddie." Cruz reached for my hand. "I'm sorry about this. It gets a little crazier with each show."

"I can see that," I said, reaching for my backpack.

"You can leave everything in here and Eddie will take it over to the hotel for you. Just bring what you need with you for now." Cruz looked out the window. "Okay, here they come. Keep your head down, Jade. Stay right between me and Eddie, okay?"

"Okay," I said. My heart raced and I sucked in a deep breath.

Someone knocked on the door before pulling it open. Eddie was there, reaching for my hand. I ducked out of the car, and Cruz held on to my arm. Two security guards flanked our sides, but several hands reached out and tried to grab my hair. What the hell was this? The screams were deafening, and flashbulbs lit up the dark sky. We hurried inside, and I looked back to make sure the door had closed behind us.

"You okay?" Cruz whispered against my ear, still urging me forward.

"Yeah."

"Thanks guys," he said before we stepped into a room and he shut the door.

He turned, pinning me to the door, holding my hands above my head. His mouth covered mine and he kissed me. My arms dropped back down, and my fingers tangled in his hair.

"Fucking finally alone, and now I have to go out there in a minute. But we're out of here as soon as the show ends, and we have the whole day together tomorrow."

I stroked his handsome face. "Okay. I'll be watching you the whole time."

"Where I can see you, right?"

"Where you can see me," I whispered.

He was more energetic than usual, but his adrenaline was always up before a show. Or maybe it was from the crowd that had pawed at us while we tried to get inside.

Someone pounded on the door and Cruz pulled me back before he opened it.

"There she is," Lennon said, rushing over to hug me.

"Hey there. I missed you," I said.

"Missed you too. And this one's been a mopey asshole. Thank God you're here. I heard the crowd out back was a little crazy?" Lennon dropped down to sit on the couch.

The room was small, with a couch and a coffee table, cement floors, no windows and a mini bar. I noticed rooms without windows now. Ever since the fire, I'd search the space I was in for an exit strategy. Cruz and I had barely made it out alive when The Dive had gone up in flames last year, and I was more aware than ever now. Note to self—this room didn't have a window.

"A mopey fucking asshole?" Cruz rolled his eyes at his little brother.

The door flew open again and Adam and Luke came through, rushing me one at a time for a hug. Adam lifted me off the ground and spun me around.

"Thank God you're here, Jade. I can't take much more of this sad sack," Adam said, flicking his thumb at my boyfriend. Everyone laughed. Except for Cruz. I made my way over to him and wrapped my arms around his middle, resting my head on his chest.

"I hate to break this up, but there's a rowdy group out there tonight and I don't think it's wise to keep them waiting." Luke rumpled my hair. "I have a chair for you beside the stage, Jade."

Dex walked in and his gaze locked with mine. "Welcome back, princess."

No one laughed. You could cut the tension with a knife. There'd never been any love lost between Dex and I, but obviously he was at odds with everyone now. His gaze was bloodshot, and he was ridiculously thin. His skinny jeans barely clung to his narrow hips. His brown hair was long and disheveled. Dark circles rimmed his eyes and his cheeks were sunken.

Cruz intertwined his fingers with mine and tucked me beside him as we made our way out of the room.

"I can't wait until I have you to myself," he whispered against my ear.

"Me either."

I dropped down on the stool, and he kissed me before jogging out on stage.

I took him in. He was mesmerizing. Damn. It was hard to believe he was my boyfriend sometimes. He commanded the attention of everyone in the room, and the venue was packed. He was sexy and confident.

And he was mine.

four

. . .

Cruz

THE CROWD WAS MORE aggressive than any we'd faced before. Several people had managed to get on stage, and the energy was palpable. Luke didn't look pleased as he argued with a security guard off to the side of the stage. I kept an eye on my girl whenever I could, and she smiled and waved every time I caught her gaze. It was the most at peace I'd been in weeks. Having her here settled me. It grounded me in a sense. I'd been running on empty lately and somehow her presence made everything better. This was the first night I wasn't drunk at a show since the day she'd left. Somehow living in a haze when she was gone made everything more tolerable. Time moved faster and I didn't have to think about how much I fucking missed her.

We got our asses off the stage after the last song, and the crowd was abnormally loud as they shouted for an encore.

"Jesus, they don't have enough security here. This is a shit show," Luke said as he paced in the hallway.

I lit a smoke and pulled Jade beside me. Dex grabbed a bottle of Jack and chugged it. That about summed him up these days. Nothing was in moderation. He was out of control and everyone knew it. Lennon slammed a beer and Adam paced alongside our manager.

"Dude, I don't even know if we should go back out there. Did you see how aggressive they were in the front row. I know they're fans, but it's like a crowd full of stormtroopers out there," Adam said.

I laughed, but Jade looked up at me with concern, twisting the ring I'd given her around her finger. "It's fine, baby. They're just excited. It's your call, Luke. We can go back out, or just call it done. But I think we may need to start traveling with our own security. This is out of control."

The crowd grew louder—the tone thunderous.

A dude walked up and pulled Luke off to the side. They argued back and forth, and I'd never seen our manager so disheveled before. He ran his hand through his hair and his arms flailed around as he spoke. I didn't know what it was about, but I knew we needed to make a decision soon. The chaotic vibe had me on edge. Someone either needed to entertain them or get us the hell out of the building.

"Okay, we're going back on. Two songs and we're out of here," Luke said, and he didn't look happy.

"Quit being a bunch of pussies. We're fucking rock stars. Let's act like it." Dex slammed back another swig of whiskey and handed the bottle to Luke. He was such an asshole, and now he thought he was our moral compass?

I kissed Jade. "Sit tight. I'll be right back."

We led with *Angel Mine,* which I'd written for Jade this summer. I'd sang it to her in private, but this was our first time doing it live. It was a slower ballad, and I hoped it would settle the crowd.

It did not.

Dex decided to take it upon himself to start the music for *Money Talks,* which would have been my last choice for an out of control audience, but we went with it. It was a harder rock song for us, and a crowd favorite. The audience sang along, and we finished strong.

"You guys have been great. Thanks for having us, Miami," I called out.

I looked over my shoulder at Jade who moved to her feet, ready to get the hell out of there, when I saw movement in my peripheral. A group of people stormed the stage, and everything blurred.

A rush.

Chaos.

A fucking shit show.

I stumbled to stay on my feet and shook some crazy ass chick off my back. People swarmed the stage, running and screaming. Security scattered about trying to gain control, but it wasn't happening. I searched for my girl as people flooded the side of the stage, trying to make their way in back.

What the actual fuck?

I ran toward where Jade had been sitting, shoving people out of my way as I tried to maneuver through the crowd.

"Jade," I shouted, but it was impossible to hear over the pandemonium going on around me.

Jade was smart. She wouldn't sit there waiting to be trampled.

I scanned the area. Jade wouldn't run away if she thought I was in trouble. I searched the stage and spotted her. Of course, she'd gone after me. Charged right into the madness.

Some dude had his arm around her, trying to help her to her feet when I stormed in and grabbed her. "Thanks. I've got her."

He put his hands up and I nodded. What the fuck was she thinking running into a fucking shit storm?

I shielded her and led her off to the opposite side of the stage. Sirens sounded all around which meant the cops were there. Thank fucking Christ. These security guards were in way over their heads.

"In here." I pushed open a random door and closed it behind us.

It was a broom closet, but it would do for now.

"Are you okay?" I assessed my girlfriend before wrapping my arms around her and pulling her to me.

"I was afraid you got trampled," she said breathlessly against my chest.

I pulled away and looked down at her. "So, you thought you'd run out in the middle of that and look for me? Seriously, Jade? You could have been crushed."

"You think I should have left you?"

I shook my head in frustration. "Fuck yeah, that's exactly what you should have done."

"Sorry to disappoint you, but that's not who I am." She crossed her arms in front of her chest. She was rocking dark skinny jeans and a white blousy top. Her dark hair fell in loose waves over her shoulders. It was a little disheveled at the moment and sexy as hell. But it was her mesmerizing green eyes that always got me. Every fucking time.

"You could never disappoint me, baby," I said, pulling her against me.

The chaos was dying down outside and I heard someone call my name. Jade looked up at me and I put my finger up for her to remain there. The last thing I needed was some crazy fan charging her.

I cracked the door open and found Luke outside, manically calling my name.

"Dude, we're in here. Everyone okay?"

"Fuck, we couldn't find you. Yes, come on out. Is Jade with you?"

"Of course," I said, leading her out.

"Let's get out of here. The car's in back."

We followed him out and cops were scattered everywhere. It looked like a fucking war zone. I kept Jade in front of me and guided her to the car.

Police officers surrounded the waiting limo and we slipped inside. Lennon, Adam and Dex were all there.

"Jesus dude, where were you?" Lennon said, the fear in his voice impossible to miss. His left eye was swollen, T-shirt ripped, and his hair disheveled.

"I went to find Jade and pulled her in a closet. What the fuck happened?"

"I don't know, but I think my fucking arm is broken," Dex said, cradling his right arm. It's the most sober he'd sounded in months.

Jade moved closer to him. "Can you move it?"

He grabbed a bottle of whiskey from the back of the limo and handed it to Adam to take the lid off. "No."

Adam opened it and handed it back to Dex. He took a long swig before turning his attention back to Jade. "I can't move it at all."

"I have some ibuprofen in my purse. It's pretty swollen. This will help with the pain." She handed him a couple orange pills and he chased them down with the bourbon.

"Do you think it's broken?" he asked her.

"I mean, I'm not a doctor, so I don't know, but it doesn't look good. It's really swollen between your shoulder and your elbow. You may have broken your humerus."

"Jesus. I'll have a doctor come to the hotel. I'm not about to take you to a hospital and risk word getting out and have these crazy ass fans show up there." Luke dialed his phone and spoke to someone about the situation.

I leaned back and intertwined my fingers with Jade's.

"You okay?" I whispered against her ear.

"Yeah. That was scary though. Has that happened before?"

"No. The shows have been getting crazier, but nothing like this," I said.

Luke set his phone down. "Okay, the venue just canceled the show tomorrow. They can't provide proper security and too many people got hurt tonight. They aren't risking a repeat of what happened. A doctor is meeting us at the hotel to check Dex's arm out. Is anyone else hurt?"

We all said we were fine, and Luke called ahead to the hotel to make arrangements to have us brought in through the back door. We remained quiet as the shock of what had happened set in. I led Jade to our room, and she dropped down on the bed.

I went to the mini bar and downed a small bottle of whiskey. The cool liquid took the edge off. "I'll order some room service. You must be starving."

She reached for something on the nightstand and studied it. "Since when do you take Adderall?"

"Since I don't sleep well, and I'm tired all the fucking time."

"You saw a doctor for this? Isn't it for ADHD? Who gave this to you?" she asked.

"Baby, I'm starving. Can we order first and then I'll explain it to you?"

"Sure. I'll take a grilled cheese." She continued to study the prescription bottle and started googling on her phone. Fuck. I didn't want her to make this into a thing. It helped me get through the day right now.

I called room service and placed our order before sitting down beside her on the bed. I pulled her down to lie with me, so we were facing one another. "I was going to tell you about it when you got here. It's not a big deal. I saw a doctor and he prescribed them to me."

"When did you start taking them?"

"The week after you left. I just haven't been sleeping much, and we've been so busy. I can't afford to be tired all the time," I said.

She ran her fingers through my hair. "I don't sleep well when we aren't together either. I just don't like the idea of you taking something every day."

"Well, I won't need to take them now that you're here because I don't plan on getting out of bed. With the show canceled tomorrow night, we can spend the whole weekend together," I said, pulling her into me and wrapping my arms around her.

"That was crazy tonight. I'm still in shock about how out of control it was. Do you think Luke will hire your own security from now on?"

"I'm sure he's on the phone with my dad now, and they'll figure it out. I'm sorry you had to be here for that though. I tried to get to you as soon as I figured out what the fuck was happening," I said, brushing the hair back from her beautiful face.

"I tried to get to you, too."

"I know you did." I kissed her hard. I'd missed her so much and I didn't want to let her go anytime soon.

Room service interrupted us, and I got up to let them in. Once they left, Jade and I set up a picnic in bed, and we ate and talked for hours.

"It's so late." She yawned.

"Oh no, you can't go to sleep yet," I said, rolling her on her back as I settled above her.

"Trust me, I have no intention of sleeping."

My mouth crashed into hers. Needing, and wanting, and

claiming her. Her fingers tangled in my hair, and I pulled her up, lifting her shirt over her head, pausing to take her in.

"So, fucking beautiful," I said, as she unhooked her bra and let it fall to the bed. Her dark hair tumbled around her, and she looked like an angel with the light from the moon coming in through the windows and shining down on her. Surrounding her like a halo. I yanked my T-shirt over my head and propped myself above her.

"I love you," she whispered.

"Love you more," I said.

I kissed her, making my way down her neck. I wanted to worship every inch of her. I cupped her perfect tits and she moaned.

"I've missed you so much," she said.

My lips continued making their way down her body and she arched into me, begging for more. I pushed up and reached over to the nightstand for a condom. I rolled it on as she watched. Her jade eyes big and curious.

I settled between her legs and took my time, teasing and taunting her.

"Cruz, please," she said against my mouth.

I slowly pressed forward, inch by inch until I filled her. We moved together and her gaze locked with mine. Nothing had ever felt so good. This girl was a part of me. I needed her the way I needed oxygen. Like she was a fucking necessity. She set the pace, moving faster—her need fueling me. I couldn't hold back any longer, my restraint weakened, and she cried out my name as I went over the edge right alongside her. Panting and breathless, I pulled her to lie on her side facing me.

I'd never get enough.

I'd always need more Jade.

five

. . .

Jade

"THANKS FOR STAYING SO LONG TODAY," Professor Callahan said when she stepped in her office. I'd been here all day, doing research and making calls.

"No problem. Slowly but surely, we're getting there."

"So, I wanted to talk to you about something. Two physicians I work with have offered to meet with us next weekend and share all their findings on a similar project. The only day they could set aside to meet was Saturday. I know that's Halloween weekend, but I'm hoping you can make it work. I think this will be a key component to utilize in our finalized paper. Do you think you could be here?"

My heart sank. Cruz had made sure not to schedule any shows on Halloween, which was the sweetest gesture anyone had ever done for me. Making it a part of his contract so he could always be there for me. Unfortunately, the label had no problem scheduling shows the day before and the day after Halloween in freaking California. So, we'd planned for me to come spend the weekend with him. We'd made it another month, and I couldn't imagine waiting any longer to see him.

"Yes, of course. I'll be there," I said, swallowing over the lump in my throat. I was lucky to be here. I couldn't tell her I wanted to go see my boyfriend instead. Cruz and I would have to wait another week to see one another, and I'd muscle through Halloween on my own.

"You're the best. I'm very impressed with your work ethic, Jade."

It turns out when you have a long-distance boyfriend, the only thing that gets you through the day is throwing yourself into your work.

"Thank you so much. I'm thrilled to be working with you, Professor Callahan."

"Please, call me Elaine. I read through your resume a bit more this morning. Looks like you're on track to graduate in three years. That's impressive. I'd like to make this a long-term position through next year, if you're interested."

"Of course, I'm interested. That would be amazing." The idea of working with her until I graduated thrilled me. She was a big name in the medical field, and she also taught at the medical school here at Northwestern. A letter of recommendation from Elaine Callahan would be an awesome addition to my resume when I applied to medical school.

"Sounds great, Jade. I'll see you next week?"

"Okay, thank you."

I checked my phone as I started the long walk back to my house. There were thirty-four missed texts and fourteen missed voicemails. My heart sank. I opened the first one from Cruz.

CRUZ

Call me. There's a story going around that I was with some chick. It's obviously not fucking true. I don't even know who she is. She's saying she spent the weekend in Miami with me. I was with you the entire time. She's making this shit up, baby. Call me.

CRUZ

Baby, call me. None of this shit is true. People fucking suck.

CRUZ

You know me, Jade. I would never do that.

My stomach twisted. I tried to calm my breathing as I continued reading.

ARI

Are you okay? This skank is making it up. She claims it was on the weekend you were in Miami. It's all bullshit. Cruz keeps calling me because he can't reach you. He's a wreck, Jade. You need to call him.

CRUZ

I need to know you believe me, baby. Please call me.

SAM

Call me.

SAM

This girl is full of shit. You know that, right?

LENNON

Please call my brother. He's losing his shit. You know this isn't true. This girl just wants her two minutes of fame.

CRUZ

Call me, More Jade.

I stopped reading. I wanted to search the internet for the story that was clearly going viral, but instead I FaceTimed my boyfriend while I walked. The weather was changing, and the temperature had dropped. My hoodie wasn't going to cut it much longer.

"Baby, you know this is a bunch of shit, right?" he said when he answered. He looked tired. His hair was a rumpled mess like he'd been tugging on it for hours.

"I haven't seen anything. I've been with Professor Callahan. I just got out."

"Some crazy bitch that apparently Dex knows, is claiming that when the concert got canceled in Miami, she holed up in a room with me all weekend. Dex was with her that weekend. Not sure how the guy pulled that off with a broken arm. I was with *you* the entire time. She's making this shit up. And she's telling anyone who will listen," he said.

I closed my eyes for a second. Breathed. Wondered how this was even my life. I was dating a guy that people wanted to be with so badly, they'd sell stories to the press about fictitious weekends. I didn't know how to fit into this world, and I was starting to feel like an outsider watching it all take place.

A sob escaped and I put a hand over my mouth to try to stop it. It wasn't like I believed any of it was true. I trusted Cruz. We talked all day, every day. Our bond was unbreakable. But the realization that so many people wanted to come between us was a hard pill to swallow. The thought of my father and my friends seeing this story and wondering if my boyfriend was unfaithful to me—it bothered me. It bothered me so much. It shouldn't, but it did. I didn't want to have to convince people that my boyfriend loved me. I wanted them to know it. I knew it. But this girl had just put doubt out into the world, and I hated her for that. Hated being in a position that allowed it. Hell, it even invited it.

"Baby, please don't cry. This is all a bunch of bullshit."

I held the phone down for a minute, twirling the ring on my finger. I needed to get myself under control. I wasn't going to let some crazy girl come between us. I wiped my eyes and sucked in a long, slow breath before holding the phone back up. Cruz's honey brown gaze was wet with emotion. He held a cocktail in his hand and took a long swig. That was a whole other issue I didn't know how to deal with when I wasn't there.

"I'm okay. I know it's not true," I said. My bottom lip betrayed me as it trembled with my words.

"There is no one I want but you."

"I know," I said. My voice barely above a whisper. I didn't feel like having this conversation out on the street with people walking past me.

"You believe me, right?"

"Yeah. Let me call you when I get home, okay?" I said.

"Jade. Don't hang up like this. I need to know that you're okay. We're going to be together next weekend."

"I can't come next weekend," I said. As the words left my mouth, I lost it.

This was hard. So much harder than I'd ever imagined. Every day I questioned my decision to come back to school. Wondered if it was going to cost me the boy I loved most in the world. I didn't know how to fight against so many obstacles. I cut through the park and found a bench to drop down and sit on.

"Why can't you come? Ponch can fly you out whenever you want." His frantic tone made my chest squeeze.

"Professor Callahan needs me to be here next Saturday to meet with some of her colleagues, and Halloween is on Sunday. I have to be in class at eight in the morning Monday. There'd be no way to go to California and be back in Chicago that fast. We'll just have to wait until the following weekend." Sobs escaped me, and I looked at him through my tear-streaked gaze.

"Okay. I get it. Please don't be upset, baby. I'm so sorry I'm not there with you right now."

"I think I'm just tired. I'm overwhelmed with my classes, and it feels like everyone is against us being together. It's hard enough being apart. Why would someone make this up?"

"Because people are assholes. But it's all a bunch of bullshit. Fuck her. I don't even know this chick, which pisses me off. And she spent the weekend with Dex. So why the fuck doesn't she just say she was with him? He's probably behind it, but he's MIA right now and not taking our calls, so I can't ask him. He's a fucking piece of shit. I would never do anything to hurt you. You know that, right?"

I closed my eyes for a minute. This was too much. It was all too much. Now it might even be more personal than a crazy girl making up a story. His actual bandmate might be behind it?

"I know you wouldn't hurt me," I said, my voice low. Tired.

"What can I do, baby?"

"Quit the band and move here," I said. I didn't laugh. There was no tease in my voice. I was dead ass serious. I didn't want to be apart. I didn't want to do this anymore. I wanted him with me.

"Baby, I'm trying. Luke has his feelers out. He doesn't want to bring it up to the label until after Christmas. But he's on the lookout for a new lead singer. I want to be there for you. More than anything."

I shook my head. I wasn't this girl. I didn't beg my boyfriend to give up his job to be with me. I'd never been an insecure person, but I was so out of sorts. School was tough. Long-distance relationships were a nightmare and throw in the fact that my boyfriend was growing more famous with each passing day, and it was hell.

"I know you are. I think I made a mistake coming back to school." I swiped at the tears streaming down my face. I pulled my knees up on the bench and rested my chin there.

"You didn't. We're going to be fine. You just need to trust me, okay?"

"I do," I said, pushing to my feet and continuing my walk home.

"Tell me something good about your day," he said.

I laughed. Cruz had a way of calming me. "Well, Professor Callahan asked me to continue working with her through next year. Until I graduate."

"That's fucking awesome. You're such a rock star, baby."

"One rock star is enough in this relationship," I teased. "How about you? Did you take your final this morning?"

"Yep. One down. A few more classes to go. I just don't want to do more than one at a time, because our tour schedule is so tough," he said. Cruz would finish his courses online and have his degree by the end of the year if all went well.

"That makes sense. I'm proud of you for doing it. Are you getting any sleep?" I asked.

"I'm trying."

"Me too. You don't have a show tonight though, right? Maybe you can catch up on some sleep."

"Why don't we FaceTime and fall asleep together," he said, and I smiled.

"Sounds like a plan. I have a few hours of homework and I'm

going to do my anatomy reading in the tub and multitask." I laughed. "I'll call you when I get in bed."

"How about you FaceTime me from the tub?" He quirked a brow.

"Well, that would be an awful lot of multitasking, wouldn't it?"

We both laughed as I walked up the steps to my house.

"All right, I'll talk to you in a little bit. You sure you're okay?"

"Yep. I'm good," I said, walking in the front door.

"Okay. Love you, baby."

"Love you more," I said, before ending the call.

I dropped down on the couch and read through the rest of my texts and cleared my voicemail. There were several more messages from Cruz, Ari, Sam, and Brayden had even sent a text saying he hoped I was okay. It irritated me, because I got the feeling, he was just waiting for my relationship with Cruz to fall apart.

I clicked on the internet and typed in Cruz's name.

Endless articles popped up regarding an interview with *Farrah Clearwater*. I clicked on her picture and cringed. She was pretty. Blonde hair, big boobs, blue eyes, and unusually plump lips. She claimed that she and Cruz were holed up in a hotel room in Miami the weekend I'd been there. She got pretty graphic about all the sex they'd had and how he'd told her he was done with me. I fricking hated her. Why would someone go out of their way to do this? She'd had a fling with Dex. Wasn't that enough of a claim to fame? Why drag Cruz into her crazy story?

Our meetings with Professor Callahan's colleagues lasted longer than expected. Professor Wilden and Professor Black were both brilliant, and they had years of research compiled on the vascular changes that occur in patients with dementia. We'd be compiling our own data as well, and together, I knew we would have a lot of resources to offer. It had been a productive day.

"Thanks for staying all day, Jade. I hope you have some fun plans for tomorrow. I'm sure there are a lot of Halloween parties on campus, huh?" Elaine said with a wink.

"Yeah, we'll see. I think I'll probably get caught up on homework and sleep." I smiled. I'd learned my lesson last year. I had no intention of going out this year. I'd planned to be with Cruz and now that wasn't happening. He was performing in California tonight, so I'd talk to him after his show. He had to be in Seattle to perform on Monday, so he had one day off in between. He'd intentionally taken Halloween off in his contract so that he could be with me, but we hadn't thought out the logistics and how to make that work if he was across the country. I would fly out to see him next weekend, and I'd get through tomorrow just fine.

Dad and I were going to have breakfast. He wanted to make sure he saw me. Last Halloween had been an epic disaster, and I'd learned my lesson about trying to ignore the day that Mom passed away. This year I'd allow myself to grieve. It had been a crappy week. Farrah's story was finally dying down, but she'd put enough doubt out there that everyone had an opinion. I'd set all my social media settings to private because I was getting endless messages from strangers giving me advice about my relationship. Some were telling me to hang in there. Others were telling me that Cruz and I would never last. One even told me that I was too plain to date him and that she fully intended to sleep with him when he performed in Canada. She said she was just giving me a girl code heads up.

What kind of girl code is that?

One girl thought I should consider getting a boob job if I wanted to keep a guy like Cruz around. All in all—I was done with the messages and set all my accounts to private. I blocked anyone I didn't know well. I rarely got on social media anyway, so it was for the better.

Cruz had confronted Dex, and he admitted to sleeping with the Farrah girl. He denied being the one who told her to make this story up, but he also argued that this had been good press. He claimed that it didn't look good for the band that Cruz had a serious girlfriend, and it was for the better. Cruz said they'd gone to blows and ended up being torn apart by Luke and Lennon, and he'd FaceTimed me after with a swollen lip. He said Dex took a pretty good beating, and I didn't feel bad for him in the slightest. Adam still wasn't speaking to Dex, but he'd finally reached out to Tory, and hopefully they would eventually patch things up. They were at least talking now, so that was a start.

I waved goodbye to Elaine before trudging out into the damp Chicago weather. The sky was gray, and rain fell from above, leaving puddles scattered across campus. I pulled my hood up and made my trek home. I'd never been so exhausted, and I was looking forward to having a day off tomorrow.

When I walked in the house, it smelled like garlic and basil.

"Ari?" I called out.

"Hey, girl. I'm making us dinner," she said from the kitchen.

This was a first. Ari didn't cook, nor was she usually home on a Saturday night?

"What's all this?" I asked, dropping my backpack on the dining chair, and pulling my hood down. My hair was damp, nose ice cold, and I rubbed my hands together to get warm.

"I just wanted to do something special for you. I know you've been working so hard, and I thought a good homecooked dinner would be nice to come home to."

"You just scored some major BFF points," I said, giving her a hug and snagging a cucumber from the salad.

"Good. You deserve it."

She insisted I sit down at our cute white round table in the kitchen, which she had already set with white plates and yellow linen napkins. She served me a plate of ravioli, salad, and garlic bread, and I forgot about my crappy week for the next hour.

six

. . .

Cruz

I WAS EXISTING on no sleep, a lot of booze and a couple Adderall a day to keep me going. I texted Jade's best friend Ari when I got on the plane and spent the next four hours writing lyrics for our new album. I thanked Ponch for flying me on such short notice and agreed to meet him in eight hours to fly to Seattle. Was it crazy to go to Chicago when I could only stay for eight hours? Probably. But I didn't fucking care. My girl was struggling, and she needed me. She wouldn't say it, but I knew her. I'd made a promise to be with her on Halloween this year, and it was one I intended to keep. She was the one person I didn't want to disappoint.

I had a rental car waiting for me at the hangar and I drove over to Jade's house. I talked to her this morning after she'd finished breakfast with her dad. They both had a tough time every year on this day, so I was glad she spent some time with him. She told me she was going to do homework the rest of the day, but Ari kept me posted and said she'd been in bed since she'd come home from breakfast.

On top of the fact that today was the day her mom had passed away fourteen years ago, it had been a shit week. Dex had some skank sell a story to the press that she'd been having an affair with me. Why would my bandmate do that to me? Because he was an asshole. Always had been. And when you mixed in a little fame, and a shit ton of drugs—the guy was out of control. Jade had been with me the entire weekend in question, so it wasn't like she believed it. But it didn't mean it didn't bother her. Having people tear apart our relationship online sucked. None of it was true. It's an odd phenomenon to have complete strangers write about what's going on in your life. I was still adjusting—and I felt like Jade was pulling away a little more each day. Trying to protect herself in a way, which I understood. But I loved her so goddamned much I needed to be with her.

I pulled up at her house and Ari opened the door the minute I jogged up the porch steps.

"I'm glad you're here. She hasn't eaten since breakfast. I've checked on her a couple times, but she's been sleeping all day. I heard her sniffling, but when I tried to talk to her, she just acted like she was asleep," she said, and her concerned gaze had me hurrying inside.

"Okay. Thanks for looking out for her. I'll make sure she eats."

"Thanks for coming, Cruz. I think it's exactly what she needs. Text me if you need me. I'm going over to Jace's tonight to give you guys some privacy," she said, wriggling her brows.

I laughed. "Okay, crazy ass. Talk to you later."

I got out my phone and ordered a pizza. It was her favorite, and I was starving too. I walked down the hall into her room. It was dark, but the moonlight coming through the gap in her curtains provided enough light to make out her silhouette beneath the covers. I kicked off my shoes and climbed into bed with her. My chest pressed against her back and my arms came around her. Her hands came over mine, and she sniffled.

"You're here," she whispered.

"Of course, I am."

She turned in my arms and faced me. Her eyes were puffy and her nose red. I used my thumbs and wiped away the tears running down her cheeks.

"You have to be in Seattle tomorrow though?" Her voice trembled.

"And I'm in Chicago tonight."

She buried her head in my chest and hugged me. "I'm so glad you're here."

"Me too."

I just held her, stroking her hair the way I knew she liked it and telling her how much I loved her. The doorbell rang and she stilled in my arms.

"It's just pizza, baby. Come on. You need to get up and eat something. And then you and I are taking a bath together." I jumped up to go grab the door.

"You don't like baths," she said as I made my way to the door.

"I know. But you do."

I brought the pizza to her room and got her to eat a slice. I managed to down half the pizza on my own. She sat back on the bed and dark circles rimmed her pretty eyes. I pushed up and walked to the bathroom to start the tub, pouring in whatever bubbles she had sitting on the side of the bath.

"You're really taking a bath with me?"

"Yep. There isn't much I wouldn't do with you," I said, dragging her out of bed and leading her into the bathroom.

She dipped her hand in the water. "Ooh, perfect. It's nice and hot."

"I know just how you like it, baby," I said, lifting her T-shirt over her head.

I dropped down to my knees and kissed her stomach before sliding her panties down her body. Goosebumps covered her skin and I fucking loved the way she reacted to me. To the way I touched her. Kissed her.

I stood and yanked my shirt off and she pushed my joggers down and blushed when she noticed my overly enthusiastic erection. "You get in first, and then I'll sit in front of you."

I laughed. I loved when she took charge. I stuck my foot in and howled. "Jesus. It's fucking lava."

Her head fell back in laughter, and I was so fucking relieved to hear it, I was willing to sustain third-degree burns in this tub to make it happen.

"It only feels that way when you first get in. You'll get used to it fast. I promise."

I dropped into the water that was far too hot for any normal human and reached for her hand. She settled between my legs and I adjusted myself, so I wasn't stabbing her in the back with my over-achieving boner. My desire for her had never wavered since the day I'd met her.

"I'll have to trust you on that."

"Ah, this is nice," she said, settling her head against my chest. Her hair was pulled up in some sort of messy knot on top of her head.

I wrapped my arms around her, and my chin rested on her head. "Feeling better?"

"Yes. I can't believe you flew here for just a few hours. That's crazy. You're going to be exhausted," she said, tipping her head up to look over her shoulder at me.

"There's nowhere else I want to be. I knew today would be tough for you." I traced my finger over the tiny music note on her wrist.

"I don't get it, honestly. It's been fourteen years. I don't know why it's still so hard." Her hands covered mine.

"I don't think there's an expiration on grief. I think this day will always be tough for you."

"Maybe you're right. It's just been a crappy week, you know?"

I tensed at her words. I hated that my shit affected her. "This Farrah bullshit pisses me off."

"Yeah. I mean, I know nothing happened. I just hate that everyone wonders. I shouldn't care what anyone else thinks. In the big picture, I honestly don't. But it's weird having so many people think they know what goes on in our relationship, you know? Does that make sense?"

"It does. It's bullshit. It's the part of this business that I don't like. And I fucking don't want to be around Dex anymore. I really think he put her up to this."

"Why? What does he have to gain? Why wouldn't she just say she was with Dex? He's in the band too," she said.

"Dex is a manipulative fuck. He doesn't like that I have a girlfriend. Hell, he's just jealous. But either way, he's a vindictive dude. He won't admit he put this chick up to it, but he does say that the attention is good for the band."

"He's so messed up. I think he's very jealous of you," she said.

"Maybe he wants what's mine? He's been trying to come between us since we first met, right?"

The thought made my stomach twist. How far would this fucker take it? He'd already done some messed up shit.

"How are he and Adam?"

"Not good. Adam wants him out of the band. The problem is that he and Lennon know I'm trying to get out. They can't afford to lose both of us. Replacing one member will be challenging enough," I said, leaning down to kiss her neck.

Her head tipped to the side to give me better access, and her breaths came faster. "Does Luke have any leads?"

"He does, actually. There's a dude in New York he's met with a few times. His band fell apart a year ago, and he's a kickass vocalist. The only downside is he doesn't write music, but Luke thinks they might let me continue to write the lyrics after I leave."

"You're going to be impossible to replace. You're so talented," she said, leaning back to kiss me.

"Not true. I'm an average singer at best," I said.

"Why do you do that?"

"Do what?" I asked.

"Sell yourself short? You're an amazing singer and songwriter. The label wanted you, they see your talent. You're the only one who doesn't."

"Baby, I know I'm a talented fucker at a lot of things. I'm not suffering from low self-esteem. But, I'm not the best singer. Yeah, I write some kickass songs, which are all inspired by you, by the way. And you know what I'm fucking best at, right?" I thrust my hips beneath her.

She laughed. "Hmmm… what are you best at?"

"Giving you all the orgasms," I whispered against her ear.

Her head fell back in a fit of giggles, and damn if I didn't love making my girl laugh. "You're so cocky."

"Am I though?"

"Well, you are talented in that area, I'll give you that. Not that I have anyone to compare you to," she said. Her tone was all tease and she looked over her shoulder at me, biting down on her bottom lip. And I fucking loved that I was her first—*everything*.

"Trust me when I tell you, no one could love you the way I do. Nor could they rock your world like I do."

"Is that so?" She flipped over in the tub like some sort of fucking mermaid and pushed up on my chest, her lips teasing mine as she laughed against my mouth.

"It is so." I pushed to my feet and lifted her up with me. Water sloshed over the tub, and Jade's laughter filled the space.

"You're insane."

"No argument there," I said, wrapping her in a towel. I dried my body quickly and picked her up, laying her down on the bed. With the white towel wrapped around her, she looked like a little cherub. Green eyes shining up at me and her cheeks flushed. Absolutely fucking stunning.

"I wish we could stay right here forever. No school. No grieving. No band. No Dex. No Farrah. No lies. Just you and me," she said.

My chest tightened, and I sat on the bed beside her, pulling her on my lap. "It's always you and me, baby. We just have to tune out all the noise. And it's just you and me."

She buried her face in the crook of my neck, and her warm breaths tickled against my damp skin. I wrapped my arms around her, holding her close. It's what she needed right now. I was still caught off guard that I knew exactly what this girl needed. I'd never cared about anyone's needs but my own. Until Jade.

"I'm so glad you're here."

"Me too."

I held Jade like that until she fell asleep in my arms and I laid back on the bed with her against my chest. And it's the best sleep I'd gotten in weeks.

———

Our show in Seattle provided much better security, but that didn't stop Luke from hiring a security team of our own as well. We got on the tour bus to head to Montana for our next show. The tension with Dex was building, and I made an effort to keep my distance. The Farrah bullshit had died down, but it still caused Jade a shit ton of stress which pissed me off. Adam had been in a perpetual bad mood since he and Tory broke up, but she was actually flying with Jade to Montana this weekend to see him. He was in better spirits since he'd agreed to see her again. And I couldn't wait for my girl to be here. My short stint in Chicago wasn't long enough at all.

I was thankful that I had my own room on the bus. It was just part of the deal to get me to agree to go on tour. I needed my space from these guys, as well as a place to focus on my classes when we were in between gigs. I was determined to graduate by the end of this year, but I wasn't sure how attainable that goal would be. Our tour schedule was insane and much busier than any of us expected with all the travel and the shows. I was working on a new song, and I sat back on my bed and jotted down some potential lyrics.

I liked writing. More than I realized. I liked seeing my words come to life on stage. There was a power in the message I was sending out, and I'd be lying if I didn't admit I enjoyed it. But being apart from Jade sucked, and this lifestyle was taking a toll. I was drinking and smoking way too much. I'd become dependent on Adderall to make it through the day. It took a shit ton of whiskey to get me buzzed lately which wasn't a good thing. I needed to find my exit strategy. Lennon was kicking ass. He was in his element. I did the right thing agreeing to do this, for my brother's sake.

My phone buzzed and I saw my father's name across the screen. He'd been less annoying lately because I was doing what he wanted. When things were going his way, he was much easier to deal with. But when I left the band, all that would change. Unconditional love did not exist in my father's world.

"Hey," I said when I answered the call.

"You aren't seriously thinking of walking away from everything you've built, are you?"

I knew he'd fight me when Luke talked to him about it. He knew

I wanted out from the minute I signed my contract with AF records. But now that Luke had his feelers out, he would push back. Typical Steven Winslow move. He was like a child having a tantrum when things didn't go his way. Most people backed down because he had a big bark and he never stopped when he wanted something. It's probably how he'd won Mom over.

"You knew this was coming. Luke's just putting his feelers out. I told you I'd give it twelve months."

"Even after you've come this far? Jesus, Cruz. You're a household name now. People are talking about you. Exiled has skyrocketed under your leadership," he said.

"That's not true. Adam and Lennon are fucking rock stars. Hell, even Dex is talented as hell even if he's an asshole. Don't put the band's success on me. It cuts down the other guys. *This is not my dream.* It's not something I want to do forever. You knew that going into this."

"I assumed you'd wise up when you realized how many doors this would open for you," he said.

"Doors I never wanted to walk through."

"Your face is splashed across tabloids everywhere. That doesn't appeal to you?" he said.

He was fucking serious. My dad lived for fame. Good or bad press worked for him.

"Not even a little. That's not something I'm seeking. Never have. Never will."

"So, the money doesn't appeal to you? Because from where I'm sitting, you sure seem to live the high life pretty well."

And there it was. No one loved to wield their power around more than my father.

"Well, I was raised with it, so obviously it comes naturally for me now. But the truth is, my trust fund from grandfather is completely separate from the trust you have set up for Lennon and me. So, if you want to wave that around and threaten to take it away because I want to pursue my own dream, go for it. I'll make residuals on the music that Exiled releases while I'm in the band. I also plan on getting an actual job when I stop touring, so I'll have income of my own as well. I'm not worried about it."

Dad let a rush of air go, and I pulled the phone away from my ear for a minute. He was pissed because his money card had been played and it wasn't working. My mother's father set up a trust for my brother and I years ago, and the interest alone made us a shit ton of money. But the private planes and lush lifestyle came from my dad's income, one he wanted to wield over me. But I didn't give a shit. I didn't need it. I had more than enough, with or without his help. And with the success of Exiled, I was putting away a lot of cash, and I'd benefit from doing this for years to come.

"I guess you've got me there. I can't force you to do anything now, can I?" He didn't hide his frustration.

"I'm not trying to stick it to you, believe it or not. I'm just trying to live my life. I don't want the same things that you do. Why is that so bad?" I said, surprising myself at the logic behind this conversation. My dad and I usually just yelled and screamed, and that's how we communicated.

"I just don't understand how anyone could walk away from what you've created. You're on the verge of being an international star. Everyone will know who you are everywhere you go. If you walk away, then what?"

Jesus. The man was warped. I don't want the level of success where I have to rent out a fucking theater to see a movie—I mean, who in their right mind would want that shit?

"The people I care about will know who I am. Why the fuck do I care what the world thinks of me? That doesn't appeal to me. Never has. Why can't you respect that?"

"You're so much like your mother. She was just like you when she was your age, you know. She didn't want any of this. She always wanted it to just be her and I. And now look at her, she's hosting parties for the most famous people in Hollywood."

I ran a hand down my face. He really was delusional.

"Jesus, Dad. Listen to yourself. You didn't let her live her life. You forced yours onto her. She never wanted any of it. And you're so proud of what she's become, because you aren't seeing what you've done."

"What have I done, son? Given her a life most people dream of?" he said.

"No. You gave her the life you dreamed of. Where is she during these fabulous parties? She's locked in her room, downing Ambiens like they're candy. That's not a happy woman. Sure, she loves you, which is why she does it. But what about her? If you love her so much, shouldn't you contribute to her dreams? It's all about you and it always has been." It actually felt fucking good to have a civil conversation with him. Even a brutal one. I wanted him to hear me. To understand my resentment. To fucking wake up and see what a selfish prick he was.

He laughed. "You've always had a flair for the dramatic. Trust me when I tell you that your mother, my wife, has everything she wants. She's a supportive wife, nothing wrong with that."

He never listened. Never saw anything beyond himself. He's what made me realize how important it is that my girl chases her own dreams.

"If you say so."

"Anyway, this was about you, not me. My life isn't up for debate. Yours is. Once you make this decision, you won't be able to take it back. Are you sure it's one you can live with? Walking away from all this?"

"Yep. I'm sure."

I'd never been surer of anything in my life.

seven

. . .

Jade

I HADN'T SLEPT much in days, and here I was, getting off a plane in Las Vegas. Traveling so much was making school more of a challenge. I was chronically sick. I'd been on antibiotics twice for strep throat. I was drowning trying to balance my classes and my boyfriend's touring schedule. Next week was Thanksgiving and I was looking forward to some downtime. Cruz would fly home and we'd spend time with my dad.

"I'm so glad we're here together," Tory said, scooching her stool closer to mine as we sat on the side of the stage.

"Me too. I'm so happy you and Adam have patched things up."

"Well, we're getting there. That asshole Dex keeps trying to cause trouble."

"What is he doing?"

"He keeps making jokes about the night my relationship blew up in my face. I don't know what his problem is. I hate that guy," she said.

"Yeah, I'm not a fan. I don't know why he messes with you and Adam. No one wants to be around him. You'd think he'd figure that out." Dex definitely seemed to thrive on ruining everyone's relationships. The guy was as insecure is they come.

"Well, Adam said they can't really get rid of him with Cruz wanting to leave at the end of the year. They're kind of stuck with him."

My pulse picked up at the mention of Cruz leaving the band. I couldn't wait to get away from this lifestyle. In the beginning, it was fun and exciting, but this world was toxic. Between Dex, Cruz's father, the stories in the press—I was over it.

"Yeah, I guess replacing two band members would be tricky. He knows that too, so I'm sure he feels like he's in a position of power," I said.

"How are you handling the whole long-distance thing? I'm sure it's tough with your classes?"

"It is. And I miss him when I'm at school. But we're making it work. What about you guys? Do you have a plan?" I asked, assuming things were back on track for her and Adam.

"Adam wants to take things one day at a time, so I don't really know. He doesn't think I should tour with them because of what happened before. You know that's not me, Jade. I don't even know what I was thinking," she said, her eyes welling with emotion. "I guess I just wasn't thinking."

I squeezed her hand. "Hey, stop beating yourself up. You made a mistake. You owned it, and you've learned from it."

"I know. I just love Adam so much and I want to get back to where we were," she said, sniffling as Cruz glanced over at me from the stage.

My stomach dipped. It didn't matter how many times he looked at me, he always got a reaction. His honey-brown gaze locked with mine, and I smiled. Tory left to go use the restroom and I watched my boyfriend move across the stage. He'd become such a confident performer, even as the size of their audience had grown. A girl jumped up on stage and my heart raced. They had a lot of security there, so I didn't know how she pulled that off. I moved to my feet and stood at the edge of the stage to see what she'd do. She moved behind Cruz and started grinding up against him. My blood boiled. I was seething. Luke sent one of the guys out there to get her off stage, but the crowd went crazy. Cruz glanced over at me and I didn't wave, nor did I smile. I wondered what happened at all the shows I couldn't attend. I'm sure he did his best to shield me from it all, but it didn't mean I wasn't bothered by it. Girls were offering themselves up on silver platters as they shouted crazy things at my boyfriend. I'd never been a jealous person, but I'd also never been in love before Cruz.

I decided to go use the restroom as Tory walked my way. "Where are you going?"

"Bathroom," I said, but it came out more, huffy than I meant it to.

"What happened?"

"Some girl just got up on stage and dry humped my boyfriend. You know, a typical day at the office," I said with a laugh. But I was pissed.

She smiled and studied me. "Don't let that get to you, Jade. Did they get her off the stage?"

"Yeah, after she had her thirty seconds of fun."

"I know it sucks, but you know he can't do much about it," she said.

"I know. I'm fine. Just going to use the restroom. I'll be back out in a little bit."

"Okay."

I took my time. Checked my texts and emails. Calmed myself down. When I made my way back out to the side of the stage, the show was coming to an end. Cruz ran out and pulled me off the stool, and I wrapped my legs around his waist. I didn't look at him and tried my best not to smile.

"Are you mad, baby?" he teased.

I rolled my eyes. "What would you do if someone dry humped me in front of you?"

"I'd beat the shit out of him."

I met his gaze and shrugged. "It is what it is."

"You know I only want you, right?"

"Yes."

Dex gripped Cruz's shoulders, interrupting the moment. "Time to go back out there."

Cruz glared at his bandmate and set me on my feet. "I'll be right back."

"Okay," I said, and Tory laughed and shook her head at me.

"You two are so dang cute together."

"Baby," Cruz said over his mic from the stage.

My stomach dipped and I shook my head at him. I was not going out there this time. The crowd was huge, and I didn't want to be scrutinized.

"My girl doesn't like big crowds. And she definitely doesn't like when girls jump on stage and grind up against me. She's the only one that gets to do that," he said to the crowd, and they cheered even louder. "So, how about I sing the song I wrote for Jade now."

Damn, I loved him so much, I had a hard time staying annoyed with him for very long.

I listened as he sang *More of Me*, and he looked over at me several times. When he finished singing, he jogged over to me and kissed me before returning to the stage for one more song.

And that was why I was willing to go through hell to make this work. Because I needed to be here for him. He was worth all the effort.

———

"I can't believe we have a midterm tomorrow. It's the day before Thanksgiving. Who does that?" Brayden said. His tone was more of a whine, but I understood it. The library was pretty dead tonight, because everyone was leaving to go home for the holidays. Most classes were canceled tomorrow, as it was the day before Thanksgiving. Cruz would fly in tomorrow after my test, and we'd have five whole days together. Exiled had a break in their tour, and it couldn't come at a better time. I tossed a lozenge in my mouth to coat my ever-present sore throat.

"I know. It sucks, but at least we'll be done for a while," I said.

"That's true. What are you doing for Thanksgiving? Are you going to see Cruz?"

"He's coming home. My dad and I have a tradition of cooking together every year, so we'll go to my house," I said.

"All that travel has to be tough on you guys, huh?"

"Yeah, but we make it work," I said.

"We sure as shit do." A harsh tone came from behind me as two hands settled on my shoulders. I turned around to see Cruz, and he wasn't happy.

"What are you doing here?" I said, jumping up to hug him.

"I came early to surprise you. Is there anything else you want to know about *our relationship*?" Cruz hissed at Brayden.

"Dude, we were just studying and making small talk," Brayden said, putting his hands up in defense.

"Sure, you were."

I tossed my books in my backpack. Cruz looked like he was about to lose his shit. His hands gripped the back of the chair, and his knuckles were white.

"Okay, I'll see you tomorrow for the test. Sorry," I said as Cruz glared at him.

"Why are you apologizing to him? He knows exactly what the fuck he's doing." Cruz pointed at Brayden.

My heart raced and I grabbed his hand and led him out of the library. I was fuming.

"What the hell was that," I said, my tone loud and angry once we were outside.

"Are you kidding me? That asshole wants you," he shouted and pointed his finger at me. Thankfully, campus was fairly desolate, not that I really cared at the moment.

"Really? You're mad because you think *one* guy wants me. That bothers you, does it?" I stormed off, walking ahead of him.

"You're fucking right it bothers me."

I whipped around and he almost slammed into me. "*Everybody wants you, Cruz.* Girls jump on stage and grind up against you *in front of me.* They throw their panties and their bras at you. I've had to change all my social media accounts to private because I get so many messages from girls telling me that I don't deserve you. That I'm not pretty enough. My boobs aren't big enough. I'm not sexy enough. Do you have any idea what it's like to date you? How scary it is to love someone that everyone wants to take away from you? But I don't make a scene every time it happens because—I'm not a *whiney vajayjay*."

Cruz stared at me with his mouth gaping open. "Did you just call me a *vagina*?"

I rolled my eyes and started walking again.

"Baby," he said, wrapping his fingers around my bicep.

"Don't *baby*, me. You're such a hypocrite." I turned to face him.

He laughed. The sky was gray, and the air was chilly. I zipped my coat all the way up and tucked my hands in my pockets.

"You really think I'm a vagina?"

"I said whiney vajayjay." I tried to hide my smile.

He quirked a brow and tugged me close to him. "I'm a whiney vagina asshole, aren't I?"

"You are."

He kissed the top of my head. "I hate that guy."

"He didn't do anything. He's actually seeing someone."

"I don't care what he says. He wants you."

I tipped my head up to meet his honey-brown gaze. "Did you not hear anything I just said?"

"I blacked out after you called me a vagina." He laughed. "I'm kidding. I heard you. I can't believe you didn't tell me you were getting messages like that. You can't keep things like that from me."

"What is it that you think you can do about it?"

"I'd respond to every single message and tell them to fuck off. You're the prettiest girl I've ever seen. With the best boobs. And you're sexy as hell, especially when you're angry," he said, his lips grazing mine as he spoke.

"Is that so?"

"It is," he said, nipping at my bottom lip.

"I'm glad you're here." I pushed up on my tiptoes and kissed him.

"Me too."

———

"You two cheated. How do you win every time?" Sam said, tossing the cards across the table. I'd known Sam my entire life. Literally, we'd grown up together because our parents were the best of friends. He'd never been a good loser.

"Don't be a sore loser. We're just *that* good," I said.

"Why don't you call him a vagina?" Cruz asked, and Sam sputtered the water he just guzzled all over the table.

Cara, Sam's girlfriend, and I both laughed.

"Why the hell would she call me a vagina?" he said, reaching for a napkin.

"The hell if I know. She called me some sort of vagina yesterday."

"I called you a whiney vajayjay, which you are sort of being right now," I said, trying to cover my smile.

Uncle Jimmy, Sam's father, walked in to grab a beer. "Hey, I've heard of this vajayjay. Maria, what's that cocktail your sister said we needed to try? Was it a vajayjay?" he shouted, so she'd hear him in the living room.

My jaw hit the ground and Sam, Cara and Cruz fell over in a fit of hysterics.

Sam's mom, Aunt Maria, walked in the kitchen. "What so funny? No. It's called a Moscow Mule. What the hell is a vajayjay?"

"I'm begging you both to just drop it. Get yourselves a Moscow Mule and call it done," Sam said. His face was bright red, and his eyes were wet from laughter.

"These kids and their fancy cocktails. It's hard to keep up," Uncle Jimmy said, following his wife out of the kitchen.

"If my dad says vajayjay one more time, I'm going to lose my shit," Sam said.

"He also mentioned *cock*—tails," Cruz said with a smirk.

I smacked him on the shoulder, and we all lost it. I shook my head and started gathering all the pieces to Sequence and piling them in the box. Cruz got up and poured himself another cocktail. I didn't want to keep track of what he was drinking, but he was putting back a lot of whiskey lately. It concerned me. But I didn't want to start a fight when I only got to spend a few days at a time with him.

The apartment smelled like turkey and pie. I loved being home. I called Dad in to start carving because the pop up in the bird showed it was ready. Cara helped me get the side dishes onto the platters that I'd set aside.

"Did you see that pamphlet on the counter I set out for you, Jady bug?" Dad asked when he plugged in the electric knife.

"Oh, yeah. I haven't had a chance to look at it yet."

"It came in the mail yesterday and I read through it. Sounds like an amazing opportunity." He carved as he spoke, and I handed him the platter to put the meat on.

Cruz glanced over at me and reached for the pamphlet sitting in front of him. "What's a medical brigade?"

"It's this club I joined on campus. They go to Honduras, Nicaragua and Ghana—areas with limited access to healthcare. It's pretty cool. They set up sustainable health initiatives. Things we take for granted like running water, and dental care. Restrooms with showers and resources for basic hygiene. They build water systems and provide services at local schools for the kids. It's really amazing."

"That's a great group to be involved with," Dad said.

"Do you want to do it? How long would you be gone?" Sam asked.

My gaze locked with Cruz. "I might do it down the road."

"They have a brigade over Christmas break," Cruz said, studying the brochure.

"I know, but I'm going to be with you on tour. I can do it next year when you're back home. Maybe you'll even want to go with me?"

Cruz and my father exchanged a look, but I couldn't decipher what it meant. My boyfriend stood and wrapped his arms around me. "You know I'd support you if you want to go this year."

"I know you would. But we've been apart enough. I'm not going to take away the little time we do get to be together."

He kissed my cheek and whispered against my ear. "I love you."

"Love you more," I said, turning in his arms to kiss him.

"Get a room for God's sake. There's food in here," Sam said, and Dad's head tipped back with a chuckle.

"You're really on one today," I said to my best friend, and everyone laughed.

We had an amazing dinner, and we played our usual game where we went around the table and answered the questions that I'd placed under each plate. Platters still covered the table, with remnants of food lingering. Frank Sinatra sang in the background, giving me that warm holiday feel. Sam, Cara, Uncle Jimmy, Aunt Maria, Uncle John and his wife Aunt Teresa sat on one side of the table. Their two littles, Sienna and Piper, Uncle Vinny, his girlfriend Emma, Dad's best friend Sara, Dad, Cruz and I all sat on the other side. Everyone I loved most in the world minus Ari and Lennon were all here. Lennon went to Mexico with some friends, but he'd FaceTimed Cruz and I twice today saying he wished he'd stayed and joined us.

"Let's hear yours, Cruz," Sam said to my boyfriend.

Cruz lifted his plate and opened the folded paper in his hand. "Name something or someone you were proud of this year?"

He winked at me before speaking. "Honestly, it would probably be when you decided to return to school after the summer. Yeah, it fucking sucked for me—uh, sorry, I mean it sucked for me." He paused and everyone laughed. Dad sat at the head of the table with his hands folded as he listened intently to my boyfriend. "But I was so fuck—shit, I did it again, sorry. I was so proud of you for making the right decision."

I sighed. I still doubted the decision I'd made, but it made me want to burst that he was proud of me for making it.

"Thanks," I whispered.

"You're the last one, Jady bug," Dad said.

I lifted my plate. "What is the best gift you've ever been given? That's easy. The song you wrote me. *More of Me*. And, the bag full of Office Max supplies was a damn close second."

Everyone chuckled and Cruz pulled me close to him. His breath smelled like whiskey, but I didn't even care. He just *got me*. Always had. He understood my joy of all things office supplies and he'd bought me a giant bag filled with sticky notes, highlighters, and every office supply one could dream of last Christmas.

"I wish you could write me a song," Cara said to Sam.

"I don't have a clue how to write a song."

"It's not as hard as you think. If you have the inspiration—you can write a song," Cruz said, looking down at me.

"Then I guess you're going to have to help me write a song," Sam said.

I smiled up at Cruz.

Maybe I'd write a song for him, too.

He was all the inspiration I'd ever need.

eight

. . .

Cruz

THE MATTRESS BOUNCED and I rolled over. It was still dark outside. It couldn't be morning yet. I'd been up late writing music after spending Christmas Eve at Jade's father's house. My sleep routine was so fucked up I never knew if it was day or night anymore. The time zones we traveled to were always changing, and I'd lost the ability to sleep during normal hours. It probably didn't help that I took Adderall like it was candy and used Xanax to balance me out. It took the edge off, and I was always on edge, except when I was with Jade.

The label wanted more songs. Word was out that I was trying to leave the band. Finding a new lead singer wasn't the issue—I was a stronger songwriter than I was a singer. AF Records wanted to suck every last bit of lyrics out of me that they could. My brother and Adam were on edge because Dex was out of control, and they feared it would all blow up when I left. Jade was supportive and understanding. I was fucking lucky to have her. She didn't pressure me about it, because she knew I was getting pressured by everyone else. I had until this summer to get this figured out. That was the deal. I gave them a little over a year, and time was ticking. But we hadn't expected Exiled to grow as fast as it had. We didn't know we'd be going on a worldwide tour, which would start in January. It meant a lot more traveling, twice as many shows, and less time with my girl. I'd lost my anonymity. Privacy was now a luxury, not the norm. I was still figuring out who I was, but the whole fucking world had something to say about me now. I was doing my first big interview with Rock the World magazine in a few weeks, and I didn't have a fucking clue what we'd talk about. An entire day had been set aside for it, as there would be a photo shoot with the band and an interview with me after. Most days I felt like a hamster running on a wheel that led nowhere. And I was falling into a pattern of survival that scared the shit out of me. Drinking too much and numbing myself with prescription meds that I was trying to justify I needed. Then more booze to compensate for the massive hangover that greeted me each morning.

The mattress bounced again, and I peeked one eye open. She was a vision. Jade wore a white hoodie, pajama bottoms with candy canes all over them and a Santa hat on her head. Her cheeks were flush, lips full and turned up in the corners, and green eyes that I dreamed about when I actually slept. She'd become my pulse, my grounding force, the only thing in my life with any normalcy. I had no home anymore. Jade was my home.

"Why are you awake, baby?" I mumbled, pulling her down to lie with me.

"Oh, no. Did I wake you?" she whispered.

I laughed. "You weren't trying to?"

"Nope."

Her body vibrated when she laughed, and I wrapped my arms around her.

"Why are you bouncing beside me on the bed and staring at me?"

"Was I?"

"You were," I said, kissing her mouth hard.

"It's Christmas morning. I'm excited to give you your gifts."

So fucking sweet. This girl was everything good in my life, and I was holding on as tight as I could. There were times that I felt her slipping away. When we'd been apart for weeks on end. When stories came out in the press about me that were unflattering—rumors of other women. They were all untrue. There was no one I wanted but her. And then she'd come visit or I'd come here, and it was like no time had passed. Like nothing had happened. Like we were unbreakable. I hoped we were. Because she was it for me.

"What time is it?"

"Hmmm… I don't know? Five eighteen?"

I laughed even louder now. "Only you would be up this early."

"We could open gifts and then go back to bed? We don't have to be at Dad's until eleven."

I rolled her on her back and settled above her. "There's only one thing I want."

I tickled her sides and she squirmed and laughed.

"Presents first," she said. Her smile beamed and I looked down at her and studied every feature. I pushed the dark hair back from her face and traced her bottom lip with the pad of my thumb.

"Okay, let's go." I leaned down and kissed her before pushing up.

She clapped her hands together and ran out in the living room. Her roommate Arianna had gone home for the holidays, so we had the place to ourselves. Hell, I had my house down the street that was also empty. But Jade had a Christmas tree set up and the whole house looked like a winter wonderland. I wasn't used to the holidays being like this. My family decorated, sure. It was over-the-top, but there was no warmth. No excitement. And we didn't wake up early to exchange gifts. There was nothing traditional about the Winslows.

I dropped down on the couch in front of the tree. There were a few packages that she'd wrapped, and I'd brought mine in the shopping bags they'd come in. I wasn't much of a wrapper, but I liked shopping for Jade. There wasn't anyone I liked buying for more than her.

She formed a pile of packages and dropped down on the floor near my feet.

"Who should go first?" she asked, tucking her hair behind her ear.

"Ladies first, right?"

"Well, I don't see any ladies in here, but I guess I'm the next best thing." Her head tipped back with laughter. "Is there one that I should open first?"

"Nope. You choose."

She picked up a package from Neiman's and shook it. "This one's quiet. Let's see what's in here. Never had anything from Neiman Marcus. My boyfriend is a big spender, huh?" She wriggled her brows.

I laughed. "Sure, he is."

"Ooooh, I love this." She jumped to her feet and tried it on. "This is so nice. Thank you."

She ran off to her bedroom to look in the full-length mirror. I'd gotten her a blazer because of all the research she'd been doing. I knew she'd be presenting at some point and needed that classy, professional look.

"This is gorgeous. How did you possibly find a blazer with a hoodie zipped inside it?" she asked, bounding back out to the living room.

"I asked my mom if she knew of a jacket that wasn't too fancy. One I thought you'd actually wear. So these have different inserts you can zip on and make it dressier or more casual. The hoodie zips off and it can just be a jacket."

"You know what I love most about it?"

"What?"

"That you know me so well. I'm going to live in this," she said, zipping up the hoodie and wearing it over her jammies.

I laughed. That got more points than I'd expected.

"Okay, your turn," she said, handing me the first package.

I unwrapped it and pulled out a large brown leather photo album. I opened the book to find the first picture Jade and I ever took together. It was a selfie that we'd taken the day we'd gone to Oak Street beach. Her hair blew back in the wind as she laughed, and I had a ridiculously cocky smirk on my face. Beneath the photo she wrote in pink script: *This was the day I officially fell for you.*

I turned the page and took in photo after photo of our adventures over the last year. Each one had script beneath it. There were pictures of our first date, our travels on the road, and several selfies of moments that were important. The day I gave her the ring she wore on her finger, Thanksgiving, her first trip to meet my parents. She was documenting our story.

"This is incredible. By far the most thoughtful gift I've ever received." A lump formed in my throat for some unknown reason. Because Jade Moore had turned me into a sappy pussy.

"You love it?"

"I love it," I said, turning each page and taking my time to read each memory.

Jade moved to sit beside me on the oversized chair, as we looked through the book and reminisced.

"I thought it might help if you had that on the road with you. You know, to feel close to me."

"It will. Thank you," I said, as I pulled her on my lap and kissed her.

"Oh no you don't, Romeo. There are more gifts to open. Don't try to distract me with your moves."

We both laughed as she got to her feet and grabbed the large package with her name on it. "What's this?"

"Open it and see," I said.

She pulled out the hard case carry-on with wheels. Jade traveled a lot to come see me, and she lugged this duffle bag everywhere she went. She needed something easier to carry.

"Wow, this is *so swanky*. Ooh, la la, it even has wheels."

"Yeah, it will be a little easier for you to lug all your shit with you, right?" I asked.

"I don't know what *shit* you're referring to, Winslow. But yes, it will make traveling easier." She stood up and pulled it all around the living room while wearing her blazer. "I look like a professor, don't I. I've got my fancy jacket and my cool wheeling bag."

I rolled my eyes and laughed. I could get Jade a spiral notebook and she'd make it out to be the best gift in the world. My family didn't even open gifts like this. We all opened at the same time, and there was no discussion or back and forth involved. No big shows of gratitude or excitement.

She sat back down and gave me my next gift. It was a cardboard, rectangular booklet, with little envelopes and pouches on each page. The outside said: LOVE COUPONS. My head fell back as I read each page. She wrote out each custom ticket for things like breakfast in bed, massage by Jade, Shining Star rendition on the beach, weekend getaway, dinner of my choice, bubble bath together. My favorite one was the one that said: Get out of the doghouse free coupon. Beneath it, she wrote: you are allowed one idiotic mistake, no questions asked. It's a free pass.

"Thank you. I can't wait to use these. I plan to use every single one."

"I figured they'd come in handy." She wriggled her brow.

She reached for the next box and opened it to find a black frame with three openings. I'd developed my three favorite photographs of us together in black and white. I'd had fun choosing and editing the pictures I liked best. My brother had taken all three photos of us, as he'd become a decent photographer on the road. He mainly focused on landscape, but Jade and I had asked him to take a few along our travels. The first one was Jade rolling her eyes, mouth wide open with laughter, while I took a vampire size bite out of her neck. The next one was a candid. We didn't realize Lennon was taking it at the time, and she was riding on my back at Disneyland with her ridiculous Minnie ears on her head, and I was smiling, which was a rarity in itself. She had a grin spread clear across her face as she looked down at me. The last one was of Jade sitting on my lap, smiling at the camera with me staring in awe at my girl. They all captured our relationship really well, which was why I chose them.

"Oh my gosh. I love these," she whispered, studying each cut out in the frame.

"Me too. I have copies of them on the tour bus now too."

She shook her head and smiled. "You're full of surprises, Winslow."

She handed me the last package. It was heavy and I tore the paper off and tossed it on the floor. I pulled out The Collin's Big Book of Art—from cave art to pop art.

"I've wanted this for a while. How'd you know?" I asked, flipping through the pages.

"I didn't. I just did a little research on the best art history books out there. This one came highly recommended."

I leaned forward and kissed her before pushing to my feet.

"Where are you going?"

I opened the closet door and reached in the back for her last present. It was an oversized Office Max bag filled with all the silly paper supplies she loved. I carried the bag over and set it down beside her.

"I knew you'd know what it was in the bag, so I hid this one."

"My God, Winslow. You sure know the way to a girl's heart," she said, digging into the bag and pulling everything out.

"I try."

She dumped out the sticky notes, highlighters, pens, markers, sharpies, stickers, whiteboard markers, index cards in rainbow colors, and so much more. I basically went down the aisles and filled the cart with everything they had.

"I'm in heaven," she said, organizing piles by paper goods, markers, and other supplies.

Once she sorted her piles, she pushed to her feet and came to settle on my lap. She straddled me and ran her fingers through my hair. "And now for the big finale."

I laughed. "Are you teasing me, by offering up your body?"

"No tease here," she said.

I pushed to my feet, wrapping her legs around my waist and carrying her back to the room. I dropped her down on the bed and settled above her.

"Thanks for the best Christmas. I love you," she said.

"You aren't going to insist on wearing the blazer right now, are you?"

She quirked a brow. "It does give me the studious look, doesn't it?"

"I can't get enough of you as is. I'll take you exactly how you are, More Jade," I said. I lifted her up and pulled off her jacket and her sweatshirt. "Jesus, you're like a little hot pocket all bundled up."

She smiled and arched her back so I could slide down her pajama bottoms and her panties. She pulled the Santa hat from her head and tossed it aside. Her hair was spread out all over the white bedding and I just took her in for a minute before I ripped the T-shirt over my head and pushed down my boxers.

"So, fucking gorgeous," I said.

I kissed her hard. Her breathing came out in little pants and I fucking loved it. My lips traveled down her neck, kissing her slowly. Moving down her body, I took my time tasting and worshiping her. I settled between her thighs, burying my head where I knew she ached to be touched. I looked up at her and watched as she squirmed and moaned, and I took my sweet time. She cried out my name with her release, and there was nothing more satisfying than pleasing her.

And I only wanted more.

nine

. . .

Jade

WE ARRIVED in New Orleans for New Year's Eve. Exiled was performing at a sold-out arena. I'd never been to Louisiana, so I pulled out my journal and wrote about everything I'd seen that day. We'd spent the day in the historic French Quarter. We'd taken a double decker bus, per my begging Cruz, and had an amazing tour of the city. It was getting more difficult to be out in public with him. Even with a hat and glasses, people recognized him everywhere we went. The paparazzi was real, and they loved to snap pics of Cruz any chance they got. It was wearing on him, though I could tell he tried to hide it from me. He said it was no big deal, but I didn't believe him.

We'd argued about the prescription I found for Xanax in the bathroom at the hotel. He was already taking Adderall to handle his hectic schedule, and now he was taking anti-anxiety medication to take the edge off. I obviously wasn't a doctor yet, and I didn't pretend to know everything, but, if you need all these medications to deal with life, perhaps you needed to change your reality. He didn't want to hear my input about it, because he said it was temporary. As was the increase in his drinking, apparently. And he just kept saying there was light at the end of the tunnel, and he ended the conversation every time I brought it up. I didn't like it. When he was in Chicago, and it was just me and Cruz, he kept things tame. But being here with him at his shows, he wasn't himself. He was edgy and short tempered. Not with me, but with everyone around us.

We arrived at the show, and Tory and I sat on the side of the stage like we usually did.

"Does it seem like things are getting crazier, or is it just because it's New Year's Eve in New Orleans?" Tory asked me, leaning close so I could hear her.

The guys were out on stage, mid-performance, and the crowd was rowdy.

"Yeah, things feel different every time I come. The paparazzi are relentless, sticking their cameras in their faces. The fans seem more aggressive with each show. I mean Miami was insane, but that was due to poor security. Now, even with all the security, they are so aggressive," I said.

"Yeah. Cruz does not seem happy about people shoving cameras in *your* face," Tory said.

She and Adam were back together, and I couldn't be happier. I liked having someone to watch the shows with and Tory had become a good friend.

"He's ridiculously overprotective." I laughed.

They finished the show and jogged off stage. Cruz picked me up and I wrapped my legs around his waist, and he spun me around, it kind of became our routine when I was there. "So glad you're here, baby. It's always better when I can look over and see you."

"Time to get back out there. This crowd is nuts," Luke said.

Cruz set me down before taking the bottle from Dex and slamming whiskey. I watched the liquid move down his throat. He wiped his mouth with the back of his hand and his gaze locked with mine. I wasn't smiling anymore. I couldn't fake it with him.

"You worry too much," he whispered against my ear, before kissing me hard and running back out on stage.

When they finished their last song, we all made our way backstage to get our things. Cruz lit a cigarette and grabbed my backpack for me.

"What a kickass show," Dex said, passing around a bottle of whiskey.

I took a small sip and passed it to Tory. It was New Year's Eve after all. Thankfully it was almost midnight, so we'd made plans to go back to Jackson Square for the countdown.

Cruz guzzled from the bottle before passing it to Adam. Adam and I exchanged a look, but I quickly looked away. Cruz would not like me and Adam discussing this. Even though I disagreed with what he was doing right now, my loyalty would always be with him.

We made our way to Jackson Square. The streets were filled, and though people recognized the guys, they just offered them booze and cheered as we walked by.

Cruz pulled me close and leaned down to talk against my ear. "You having fun, baby?"

"So much fun."

Music blared in the streets and Tory and I danced. Luke went to get us all drinks, and when the countdown began, Cruz reached for me and held my back to his front as we yelled out with the crowd.

"Ten, nine, eight, seven, six, five, four, three, two, one…"

He turned me around and covered my mouth. My body swayed against his as fireworks went off around us. I pulled away to look up as the sky lit up like a painting against the dark background. Pinks, oranges, and yellows broke off into large designs above. It was stunning. Cruz wrapped his arms around my middle and rested his chin on my shoulder as we watched together.

Dex dragged us to a bar where we had another round of shots. I didn't want to overdo it, as we were in a new city and I wanted to explore more tomorrow before I flew home. I skipped the last few rounds of shots and so did Tory and Adam. *Cruz did not.* But it was New Year's Eve so I wouldn't nag him tonight.

People made their way out of the bar, and Adam suggested we head back to the hotel. Cruz intertwined his fingers with mine and we stepped out to the street.

"Well aren't you a hot piece of ass," some drunk guy said as he walked our way, staring directly at me. I ignored him.

"What the fuck did you just say?" Cruz turned around and shouted at him.

"You heard me. When she dumps your ass, she can come warm my bed," the jerk said.

The guy's friends appeared pretty wasted from the looks of it, but they made an effort to shut him up. They tried to pull him away, but he pushed them off. "Leave me the fuck alone. I can hit on whoever the hell I want. She'd be lucky if I let her fuck me."

Cruz dropped my hand and dove on top of him. It was one big blur. The street light above shone right on them, as my boyfriend flailed his arms like a wild animal. The sound of people cheering and fists hitting bones filled the air around me. Cruz punched the guy in the face a couple of times before Luke and Adam pulled him off. Dex stood there laughing and Lennon moved to stand beside me. The whole thing was ridiculous. The guy was a drunk asshole, but Cruz should have just walked away. I swiped at my face when I realized tears were streaming down my cheeks. People had gathered around to watch the show. It pissed me off. What was the point? We were having a good night.

Cruz stood over him and spit on the ground, before taking the bottle Dex offered him and tipping his head back to take a long pull. The other guy was lifted to his feet by his friends who supported him as they walked away. I heard him shouting, "fuck you" as they dragged him off.

I turned and stormed away. This was not how I wanted to spend my New Year's Eve. I could walk to the hotel. It wasn't far from here, and I needed some space.

"Jade. Baby. Stop."

I ignored him and kept walking.

He jogged up beside me and laughed. "You can't be mad."

"I sure as hell can be if I want to be."

"He disrespected you," he said.

"It's New Year's Eve. He's drunk. Be the bigger person."

"Not when someone talks to you like that," he spouted, and he didn't hide his anger.

"You wouldn't have reacted like that if you weren't drunk. You don't just get to punch everyone who pisses you off."

"Ah, of course that's what this is about. You think I drink too much. I shouldn't be taking any medications either, right? Do you have any fucking clue the pressure I'm under?" He stopped in the middle of the street, his voice loud and his face red.

I put my hands on my hips. "No. Because you keep telling me everything's *fucking fine.*"

His eyes doubled in size when I dropped the F-bomb. Good. That's the way it was meant to be used. For effect.

"Because you have enough goddamn stress to deal with. I'm trying to handle it. Handle you. Handle my brother. Handle the band. My father. My fucking life."

I poked him hard in the chest with my finger. "You don't need to *handle me.* I can handle myself."

"Is that so? Like you just handled that guy? Like you handle Brayden every time he fucking hits on you?"

"*Oh my God.* You're insane. This isn't about that guy, nor is it about Brayden. You're deflecting. This is about you being out of control."

"Me being out of control? I'm the only fucker in control. I'm the one holding everything together," he said, his words slurring.

"That's not how it looks from where I'm standing."

His face hardened. He looked angry. He studied me before he spoke, "What's this about Jade. You want to pick a fight with me? Is this your idea of foreplay because you want me to fuck you?"

My hand came up before I could stop it. I slapped him across the face. Hard. I turned on my heels, tears streaming down my cheeks as I walked to the hotel. Thankfully, he'd given me a room key when I'd arrived at the concert. I felt him behind me the whole way as I made my way down the sidewalks of New Orleans. He didn't speak and I never looked back.

When I stepped on the elevator, my gaze locked with his as he approached, and the doors shut before he could get on. He looked —broken.

I slipped the key in the door and latched the swing bolt above once I stepped inside. I leaned my back against the door and slid down to sit on the floor. I heard something knock on the other side of the door and I guessed it was Cruz's forehead.

"Jade," he said, his voice calmer now.

"Go away. I don't want to talk to you right now."

"Baby. I'm sorry. I fucked up," he said through the door.

We'd never had a fight like this. Sure, we argued. We disagreed. But he'd never spoken to me like that, and I didn't like it. I knew he was spiraling, and I didn't know how to stop it. Didn't know if I could.

I stood and looked through the peek hole and saw him sitting on the ground. I slowly opened the door and looked out.

"It's your room. I can't stop you from coming in. But I don't want to talk anymore tonight. You're drunk and I'm tired," I said.

He pushed to stand, losing his balance in the process. He stumbled in the room and went straight to the mini bar.

Unbelievable.

I watched him with disbelief.

He grabbed a few mini bottles of vodka and a beer and dropped down to sit on the couch. He had a suite with a living area and a bedroom. He opened the vodka and drank it down before popping open the beer.

"You can have the bed. I'll sleep out here," he said. His words weren't completely coherent, but I heard him well enough.

I reached for my suitcase which had been brought up earlier and pulled it into the bedroom and locked the door behind me. I dropped down on the bed and let the tears fall. I didn't know the boy sitting out in the living room. He was a stranger. I'd never felt so distant from Cruz and it terrified me.

I washed my face and changed into my pajamas before slipping into bed. Alone. Not the way I saw this night going. But lately everything in my life was unpredictable. And I hated it. I cried until exhaustion won over and I gave in to sleep.

A knock on the bedroom door woke me, and I sat up. I was disoriented until memories from the night before flooded me. My heart sank and a heavy feeling settled in my chest. Light was coming through the crack in the drapes, so I knew morning had arrived.

"Baby, please open the door." His tone was hesitant. Remorseful.

I moved to my feet and unlocked the door, before turning to climb back in bed. I slipped beneath the comforter and pressed my back against the headboard. My gaze locked with his, and I saw the hurt and devastation. The look in his honey brown gaze mirrored my feelings.

"Jesus, Jade. I'm so fucking sorry." His eyes welled with emotion as he walked toward me and dropped to sit on the edge of the bed.

I nodded. I didn't even know what to say. I didn't know how we got here. The tears picked up where they left off last night as they slid down my face. Like paint running down a canvas with nowhere to go, leaving trails of despair in their wake. I pulled my knees up and wrapped my arms around them, resting my head there.

He just watched me, until two tears overflowed from his eyes, catching me by surprise.

"I don't know what's wrong with me. I'm losing control of everything," he said, scrubbing a hand over his face.

"Come here," I said, my voice breaking on a sob.

He had his arms around me within seconds. My face nuzzled into his neck, relishing his warm skin. We sat that way for a while before I pulled back to look at him. I took in a few long, slow breaths while I tried to regain control.

"I'm really worried about you," I said, my voice hoarse and tired.

"I don't want you to worry about me. I'll figure this out, I promise. I'm sorry I got in a fight with that asshole, although I can't promise I won't defend your honor again. It was stupid. But I'm most sorry for the way I spoke to you. I don't know why I said that. Why I get so fucking pissed off." He pulled me onto his lap and wrapped his arms around me. He turned my face and kissed my cheeks, my chin, my nose, my eyelids. Every square inch he could reach.

I smiled. "I think mixing alcohol with the prescriptions your taking is dangerous. I googled those medications, and I think you need to double check with your doctor to make sure that they can be taken together."

"I promise I'll talk to my doctor about it this week. And, I'm going to cut way back on the drinking," he said, hugging me tighter.

"Okay." I turned in his arms and studied his face, running my fingers down his cheek. "I love you. You know that, right?"

I felt like he needed to hear it more than ever right now.

"I do. I love you so fucking much."

He kissed me, so gently, before tipping me back on the bed and settling above me. He didn't do anything more. He just kissed me for the longest time until I moaned against his mouth. He pushed back and looked down at me with a cocky smirk.

"What do you need, baby?"

"Everything."

And that's exactly what he gave me.

———

On the plane ride home, I sat beside Tory who was sound asleep. Cruz and I had had the worst fight we'd ever had, but we'd talked about it and I hoped he would follow through on his promise to talk to his doctor. I reached in my bag for Mom's journal.

Jan 1st

Dear Journal,

I'm excited for the New Year, and I just made a long list of goals that I hung on my bathroom mirror so I can look at it every day when I'm getting ready. It feels so good to be back home, and I landed a dream internship at NBC this semester. I'll be working at the station today (interns get to work on all the days non-interns want to be off), and I'm trying to rally because I was out late last night.

I went out with Jack and a few of our friends. He acted like a jackass, which I informed him is very fitting seeing as his actual name is Jack. I wanted to drink champagne, and he wanted tequila. All the guys drank way too much and Jack's friend, Ollie got into a fight, which meant we all got kicked out of the bar we were at. I've never been kicked out of a place in my life. Jack argued for twenty minutes with the bouncer about our "rights". I was over it.

So, I called a taxi and tried to head home on my own. My stubborn boyfriend jumped in the other side of the cab and insisted the driver take us to Oak Street beach. We found a nearby grocery store and Jack bought a bottle of champagne which we hid in a bag and took with us to the beach. We rang in the New Year together, staring at the water, drinking champagne.

He's such a stubborn ass, but I love him. Even when we fight. I love him. I can never stay mad at him long, because the truth is, he's the best guy I know… when he isn't being a jackass. Okay, have to get to work… ah, the life of a future reporter.

Ciao for now,

J.E.

I smiled at my mother's words. It's funny, I could never imagine my parents fighting, or getting too drunk—I forgot they were young once too.

But Mom and I had one thing in common.

We both loved our boyfriends even when they acted like jackasses.

ten

. . .

Cruz

"LONG FLIGHT, HUH?" Luke said as we made our way to the car.

"That's an understatement. Seventeen fucking hours," I said, lighting a smoke as we walked.

"You know you need to quit that shit. Your voice is going to take some abuse with so many shows back to back right now," Luke said.

Fuck. I'd cut way back on the booze. I'd barely had anything to drink in the last three weeks since New Year's in New Orleans. Now he was going to ride my ass about smoking?

"It's fine." I snubbed out my cigarette when we got to the car.

"So, I've got two guys I'm meeting with when we get back to the States. They're both talented. One is a damn good vocalist, but the other dude is a decent singer and he writes as well, so we'll see. You sure you want to leave all this?" Luke laughed and held his hands up.

"Yeah. I'm sure."

"I hear you. Just not going to be easy to replace you. You're more talented than you think," he said.

I rolled my eyes and got in the car, pulling out my phone to text Jade. This would be our longest time apart, as it had been three weeks since I saw her last and I wouldn't be back in the States for another three weeks. Her schedule was too busy to come here, and it was too far for either of us to travel for a weekend. And it fucking sucked. The last time I saw her we'd ended things okay, but it had been our first real fight, due to me being a complete asshole. Now I'd have to go six weeks without seeing her.

> Just landed in Australia. Long fucking flight. What did the doctor say? Is it strep again?

Jade had been sick on and off for months. I knew it had a lot to do with the fact that she was pushing herself too hard between school and visiting me. We were both drowning this year and doing what we could to hold things together.

MORE JADE

> So glad you're there. Yeah, I went. I have mono. It's such a bummer. I'm praying I didn't give this to you. How do you feel?

I laughed. Jade had fucking mono and the first thing she did was worry about giving it to me.

> I'm fine, baby. I'm worried about you. Should you go stay at your dad's? I wouldn't mind ditching this tour and coming there to stay in bed with you.

MORE JADE

> I can't go to class until the fever's gone. The doctor said I shouldn't travel for a few weeks, and probably just need to take it easy for a while. With you out of the country, I wasn't going to travel anyway, so it's fine. I just hope I don't miss too much class. Elaine said I can do the research from home for the next week. You don't know how badly I wish you were here.

> Me too. Miss you so much. I'll FaceTime you when I get to the hotel. I love you.

MORE JADE

Love you more.

I hated being so far away.

We got to the hotel and grabbed some dinner before heading to our rooms. It was the middle of the night here. How in the hell was I supposed to go to sleep now? I was so off on time. Dr. Grove gave me a prescription for Ambien for times like this. It wasn't something I would take daily. For fuck's sake, the last thing I wanted was to be dependent on this shit like my mother. I popped one in my mouth and wanted to wash it down with a bottle of whiskey because that would really knock me out. But I'd been really working at cutting back on the booze, especially the hard stuff, and I wanted to FaceTime my girl before I went to sleep. Tomorrow would be a long day. I guzzled some water before settling on my bed.

"Hey," she said as her pretty face came into focus.

"I thought you were supposed to be resting."

Jade sat in the middle of her bed with books and papers spread out everywhere around her. She wore a white hoodie and black leggings. Her hair was in a messy knot on her head, and her face was bare of makeup. Stunning. She looked pale and dark circles rimmed her eyes. She'd been running herself into the ground.

"I am resting."

"I think resting means that you lie down and take it easy," I said with a laugh. I rolled on my side and propped the phone on a pillow.

"I have midterms coming up. Plus, I have a ton to get caught up on for Elaine. I'm presenting next month at the University," she said.

"You are? When? I want to be there."

"Can you? You'll be back from Europe by then, and I would love if you were here," she said, pausing to look at me.

"I'll make it work. Text me the date and I'll send it to Luke. He said he has two guys he's looking at to replace me. Both are pretty good prospects. We're more than halfway through this long-distance bullshit."

"How do you feel about that? You know, leaving? Are you ready for the slow life again?" She laughed.

"I'm so ready."

"Take lots of pictures of Australia for me, okay? Keep your eyes out for kangaroos."

I chuckled. "I will. You feeling okay? How's the fever?"

"It's fine when I take Ibuprofen, but it spikes back up every six hours. It'll pass. My professors were all okay with me skipping class for a few days, and then I'll just take it slow. How about you. Is it hard adjusting to the time change?" she asked.

"No. I'm pretty tired." I wasn't going to tell her about the Ambien because she'd worry. I had this shit under control.

"Okay. Get some rest. Your next three weeks are going to be crazy busy." Her green gaze was wet with emotion and my chest squeezed. I hated how much I'd hurt her lately. The distance. My lifestyle. My drinking. The fact that I couldn't be there for her when she needed me. I was fucking failing as a boyfriend and it sucked.

"Are you okay?" My voice strained as the words left my mouth. This girl was my weakness.

"Yes. Of course. Just miss you."

"Miss you too. I always need, *More Jade*," I said, quirking a brow when her gaze locked with mine.

"That's what I want too, you know."

"What?"

"*More of you.* All of you. Not to have to share you with the world," she said, swiping at her cheeks as a few tears streaked down her pretty face.

"You have all of me, baby. Only you."

"Okay. Get some rest," she said as she blew me a kiss.

Our call left me unsettled. I was going to fuck up the best thing in my life, it was inevitable. My eyes grew heavy, and thoughts of Jade filled my head as I drifted off.

———

When I performed on stage in front of thousands of people, I didn't have a care in the world for those few hours when people screamed my name and sang along with me. Sang along to the songs that I wrote. It was powerful and I'd grown used to the attention. Craved it. Thrived on it. But I'd also become a slave to it. To the energy it required of me.

We were in London and this was our last show before we'd head back to the States. It had been a long three weeks, and I was spent. I'd dipped into the booze a little more tonight because we were celebrating a successful string of shows here. I was feeling good. The audience sang the lyrics to *More of Me* right along with me, and I wished Jade were here to see it. She'd be pissed that I was buzzed, but it had been weeks, and I'd cut way back. I needed to have some fun tonight.

The crowd yelled and screamed after the last set, and we extended the show a few more songs. I was beat by the time we walked backstage. We'd taken the tour bus here, and we'd partied on our way over tonight. I grabbed my bag and stepped on the bus to head back to the hotel. Adam quirked a brow at me after he glanced over at Dex and Lennon. They'd invited a couple chicks to ride along with us. We had one big suite with separate bedrooms back at the hotel, which Luke usually booked when Jade and Tory weren't joining us on tour. Made it easier to keep us in check, I guess.

"Great show, Cruz," one of the girls said to me.

I nodded. "Thanks."

"Does he have a girlfriend?" another girl asked Dex.

I walked back to my room on the bus, because I didn't want to be around this shit right now.

"Yeah. The dude's practically a married man. But don't worry about him. I can take care of all of you," Dex said before I closed my door.

I called Jade from my room, but it went to voicemail. I wanted to talk to her. I fucking missed her.

When we arrived at the hotel, Dex invited everyone up to the suite.

"Great. This ought to be fun," Adam said, when we squeezed on the elevator. Luke looked annoyed when all five girls followed us on.

"Yeah. Apparently Dex thinks he can handle all these chicks.

Lennon doesn't look too pleased," I said so just Adam could hear me, and we both laughed.

"So, you both have girlfriends. Are you sure about that?" The tall blonde chick with enormous tits batted her lashes at me.

"Yeah, we're fucking positive." I glared because I didn't need to be reminded that my girl wasn't here. I hadn't seen her in six weeks, and I was horny as hell and in a perpetual bad mood.

"Doesn't mean you can't have a little fun. No one needs to know," she said.

"Hey. Not happening," Lennon said. Hell, my brother would kick my ass if I ever fucked around on Jade. Which would never happen.

"Party poopers." She pouted like a fucking toddler.

I rolled my eyes and stepped off the elevator and into the suite. Luke went to the room next door, and Adam followed me into my room. I grabbed an Ambien and some whiskey from the mini bar and downed it. It would be the last night I'd need to take it, because I'd get back on a normal time schedule once we were back in the States tomorrow.

"I thought you weren't drinking the hard stuff?" my best friend said.

"I'm not. Just having an off night. What are you, my babysitter now?"

He laughed. "Jesus, you're a moody fuck sometimes."

"Just ready to be home."

"Yeah, me too, brother. I'm going to go FaceTime Tory. I'll check back on you later," he said, pulling my door closed.

I tried Jade again. Voicemail. Fuck. I needed to see her face right now.

I reached for another bottle of whiskey and downed it. They barely held a few ounces of alcohol, and I was in the mood for a pity party. I took out the last few mini bottles and dropped them on the mattress, before turning on the TV and getting my buzz on.

I was feeling good. And tomorrow we'd head back home. Just a few more days before I'd see my girl.

My door swung open and Lennon stood in the doorway.

"You want some pizza, dickhead?"

I laughed. My brother was a little shit, but he was fucking funny when he wanted to be. "Yeah, I'm starving."

"Jesus, dude. What did you do? Rob the mini bar?" He picked up six or seven little bottles and tossed them in the trash.

"Whatever. You're one to talk."

"Come on. Let's get some food in you," he said.

I grabbed my phone just in case Jade ever decided to call me back and dropped to sit on the couch. Two girls sat on Dex's lap and one was sidled up next to Lennon. The other two chicks sat at the end of the couch. One being the voluptuous blonde that looked like she'd drop to her knees and suck me off if I gave her the go-ahead. I grabbed a plate and tossed on a few slices of pizza before devouring them.

"You have a big appetite, huh? I'm Courtney by the way," she said. I had to give it to her, she didn't give up easily. She had her tits pushed up and they were spilling out of her tube top, and she wore black skinny jeans. She had a decent body, I'd give her that. But she wasn't Jade. She had zero chance.

"Yep. You do know nothing's going to happen here, right?"

"Yeah, yeah, I get it. You have a girl back home and you don't want to mess that up. That's actually pretty refreshing. But I'm kind of stuck here while I wait for them, so just making small talk," she said, thrusting her thumb at her girlfriends.

Well, that was honest. No harm in a little conversation. The other blonde beside her passed me a bottle of tequila and I took a swig. It burned going down.

"Thanks. Where are you from?" I asked while I went back to eating my pizza.

"We live in New York. Came to see the show."

"You came all the way here to see us? Why wouldn't you wait and see us back in the States?" I said.

"We did. We've seen you guys perform almost a dozen times in the last six months. We travel all over." Courtney said, and her tits bounced when she spoke.

I chugged a little more tequila and washed down my pizza. "Damn. You're like super fans."

"I think you mean groupies," Courtney's friend said, and she hiccupped no less than ten times as she said it.

I was relaxed. The Ambien had set in. I'd never mixed it with booze before, and the combo packed a nice punch. The other two girls were practically dry humping Dex right in front of us, and my brother sat in the chair beside me with some chick on his lap. Courtney and her hiccupping girlfriend started asking me all sorts of questions about Jade. I liked talking about her. I propped a pillow on the couch and stretched out a little, answering all their nosy ass questions.

"So, a doctor and a rock star. That's hot. It doesn't bother her with you on the road, traveling all the time?"

I certainly wasn't going to tell them that my time with Exiled was coming to an end. That was something we wouldn't share with the fans until the time came.

"We support one another, and she trusts me," I slurred.

"Wow. Doesn't that get *hard*—oops, no pun intended." Courtney paused to laugh. "Doesn't it get lonely being away from her for so long?"

"Fuck, yeah it does."

I polished off the rest of the bottle, wanting to make my way to my room, but I didn't even know if I could walk that far. My phone rang on the coffee table, and I tried to feel around for it.

"Grab that for me. It's Jade," I said, my words barely audible. Fuck, I didn't even recognize the sound of my own voice.

"Hi Jade, I'm Courtney. We're hearing all about you right now," I heard her say to the phone. Jade must have FaceTimed because she held it up and talked to it.

I laughed when I tried to reach for it and fell off the couch.

"Oh, hi. Is Cruz around," Jade said, and she didn't sound happy.

"Baby, I'm just telling them how much I love you," I shouted from the floor as I laughed some more.

"Who's there, Courtney? Can you turn the screen around so I can say hello?" Jade asked.

I pushed myself back up, crawling onto the couch. Courtney was literally narrating the scene, and if I had my shit together, I'd grab the phone from her. But obviously I was a drunk fucker and the Ambien was winning this battle.

"That's Asia and Brit sitting with Dex. And that's my friend Shanna with Lennon. And this is Victoria next to me, and we're just talking to Cruz. He told us you want to be a doctor. That's cool, right?"

"Sure. I think so. Can I talk to Cruz for a minute?" Jade's voice was calm, but I knew she was pissed. Hell, this place looked like a fucking orgy.

Lennon jumped up when he realized what was happening. He grabbed the phone from Courtney and kicked me in the shin to pull it together. "Shit. Jade, hey. What's up?"

"Looks like you guys have quite the party going on there, huh?" she said.

"Cruz is beat from the show, so he was just chilling here on the couch." Lennon moved to sit beside me, trying to force me to sit forward before he handed me the phone.

"Baby, I miss you," I said, taking the phone from my brother. It didn't even sound like I was speaking English. I was so fucked.

"Yeah, it looks like it."

"It's the first time I've gotten a little drunk. I tried calling you, but you didn't pick up," I said. This was her fault. I was lonely and so what if I got a little fucked up. I covered my mouth when a loud burp escaped. Courtney laughed loud, which made me laugh.

Jade stared at me. "Cruz, I need to go."

"No, baby, I'm not done talking."

"Well, there's a nurse here and she needs to take my blood." Her voice was stone cold, and Lennon grabbed the phone back from me.

"Jesus. Are you in a hospital gown?" Lennon said as he studied the screen.

"Yeah, my fever wouldn't break so they admitted me. It's just a complication from the mono. I'll be fine. But I need to go." The devastation in her voice sobered my ass up. I ripped the phone out of my brother's hands.

"I'm so sorry, baby. I'll be there in a few days. I love you," I said.

She disconnected the call. She didn't have anything else to say to me.

"Fuck," I shouted and threw my phone across the room.

"Trouble in paradise," Dex said when the phone missed hitting him in the head by a hair.

He had no idea.

eleven

. . .

Jade

I SHOVED a notebook in my backpack and turned when someone knocked on the hospital room door.

"You know you didn't need to go and make a scene in class just to get me to come visit," Sam said with a laugh.

I hugged him and stood there a little longer than usual, closing my eyes. For the first time in days, I was starting to feel like myself.

"Well, you know how much I love being the center of attention." I dripped sarcasm and pulled away, twirling the ring around on my finger.

I'd been admitted to the hospital yesterday morning. I'd fainted on my way out of anatomy class in front of a room full of people, and someone had called 911.

Could anything be more mortifying?

I was fine by the time the paramedics arrived—and by fine, I mean I was able to sit up. They insisted on taking me to the hospital because my fever had spiked, and my heart rate was low. To say I was out of sorts was an understatement.

I'd been battling mono for nearly a month. Every time I thought I was on the mend, I took a step back. I hadn't felt good in weeks. I started every day behind the eight ball. I struggled to keep up with my classes, my research project was way more time consuming than I'd anticipated and worrying about Cruz had become a full-time job.

It all came crashing down on me last night as I sat in this sterile room listening to the monitors beep, as the fluorescent lights from the hallway shined in through the crack in the door. My father had rushed from the firehouse, abandoning his shift and slept quietly in the chair beside my bed, I'd humiliated myself collapsing in class, all while my boyfriend was drunk in London lying on a couch with a bunch of girls who'd answered my call. Because he was too drunk to sit up and have a conversation with me. There were limits—and I'd hit mine.

Loving Cruz Winslow was like chasing a tornado. Watching a destructive storm spiral out of control like a freight train with no destination. Always just a little out of reach, leaving pieces of my heart in its wake.

"Don't beat yourself up, J-bird, it happens to the best of us." Sam walked over and dropped down to sit on the chair beside the bed.

"Oh, yeah? When have you ever seen someone faint in class?"

"I can't even keep track. They're dropping like flies at my school," Sam said. He attended art school in the city.

"Sure they are. Well, it was a wake-up call. Things are going to change."

"Is that so?"

"It is," I said, pulling my backpack over my shoulder, ready to go.

The nurse had released me just before Sam came to pick me up. I'd insisted Dad go to work, he'd already missed a full shift yesterday. My phone beeped for the millionth time today.

CRUZ

What time are you getting released? I'll be there tomorrow.

Now.

Yeah, I was sticking to one-word responses. Had been since our lovely FaceTime call last night. Things needed to change. Cruz had been drinking heavily for a while, and it had shown itself in New Orleans when we were together for New Year's. Obviously, things hadn't changed. This cycle we were on wasn't healthy.

I wasn't healthy and neither was he.

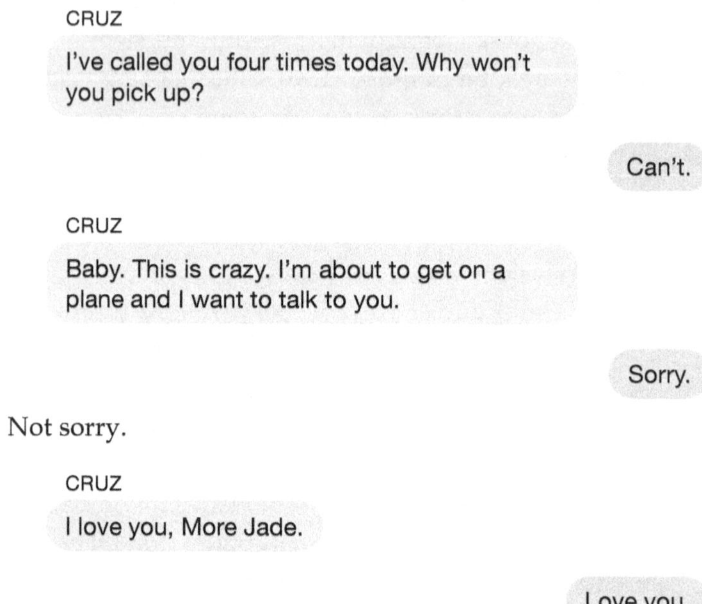

Not sorry.

I'd give him those two words. I could never deny him that, because I loved him so much. Maybe too much. Even if we were facing some serious challenges. Which we were.

I slipped my phone in my back pocket and followed Sam out to his truck.

"Was that Cruz?"

"Yep," I said as I buckled my seatbelt.

"You're mad, huh?"

"I don't even know if I'm mad. *I'm tired.* And while I was being admitted to the hospital, he was partying with some random chicks. Yeah, I guess I am mad," I said, crossing my arms over my chest.

"I get it. But the dude is on tour, what do you expect? You honestly think he's going to quit drinking now? He calls you, I don't know, maybe eight thousand times a day. Pledges his love to you at every concert. I mean, I don't think he's fucking around on you if that's what you're worried about."

"You're defending him?"

"I'm not defending him, Jade. I'm just calling it as I see it," he said.

"I don't think he's cheating on me. It's not that."

"So, what is it?"

"It's too much. All of it. I'm losing myself because I'm trying so hard to keep us together. To make sure he's okay. I can't control what he does when he's far away," I said.

"You shouldn't be controlling what he does when he isn't far away. That's not healthy for either of you. He's a grown-ass man."

He was right, and I hated it. Hated being this girl. Controlling and needy. It wasn't me. None of this was me. Maybe I didn't know who I was anymore.

"I know. But he doesn't have limits like you, and I do. He's never been given them. So, I worry about him. Constantly. And I just can't keep this up. I'm drowning." The tears started to fall, and Sam pulled in front of my house.

A light layer of snow still covered the ground, and the air was chilly. Typical for February. I used the sleeve of my sweatshirt to swipe at the tears rolling down my face.

"Jade, you're one of the strongest people I know. If you think it's too much—*it's too much.* Doesn't mean you can't be there for him. It just means you need to set some boundaries for yourself. You're trying to graduate in three years, you have one of the toughest majors out there, and you still think you can travel all over the country and keep it all together. So, you don't see each other as often, doesn't mean you can't stay together. Let him manage his own life. He should be anyway. Cruz is a smart guy. He does have limits, trust me. He's just someone who pushes the envelope. If you let him fall, he'll figure it out. It's like you're trying to micromanage him from a distance, and it's not going to work. He'll stop drinking when he's ready. You can't quit something for someone else. You know that. Let him figure this out." Sam's blue eyes shined as he looked at me.

"And what if I lose him in the process?" I whispered.

"Then he was never yours."

I sighed. He was right. I needed to take a step back. Let go a little bit. I was holding on so tight for fear he'd slip away—and it wasn't working.

"Well, I don't think I have much of a choice. I'm the one who decided to come back to school. I made my bed, now I have to lie in it."

"You made the right decision. Stop blaming yourself. All this shit would be going on if you were there. It's better that you're removed from it. You are where you should be. And he'll come back to you J-bird. I've seen the way he is with you. The kid is crazy about you. So, chill out a little. Stop running yourself into the ground. You're twenty years old. Life's not supposed to be so hard yet, right?"

I laughed a little. "Right."

"Want me to come in and hang out for a while?"

"No, I'm fine. I need to go call Elaine and email my professors to see about make-up work. But thanks for getting me. Love you, Sam."

"Love you too," he said, hugging me goodbye.

I made my way through the front door and into my bedroom. I grabbed all my laundry and tossed it in the hamper. It was time to clean up my room and my life.

I slept a whole eight hours last night and got my make-up work for my classes organized. Elaine was super understanding about our research and insisted I take the rest of the week off as we were ahead of schedule according to her. I was presenting a portion of our research next week and she wanted me to focus on that for now. Cruz was coming today, but I still hadn't spoken to him. He sent me his flight info and said he had a ride from the hangar. He knew I had class, so I told him I'd meet him at the house this afternoon. We needed to talk. It wouldn't be easy because when I saw him, when we were together, all of my problems always melted away. My judgment was clouded when it came to Cruz. Always had been.

I attended a medical brigade meeting on campus after class. A bunch of people had gone on the holiday brigade over winter break, and they were sharing their stories. Listening to them talk about the experience made me eager to contribute myself.

I walked outside with my friend, Jessica. We'd met in this club a few months back, and I really liked her. She'd tried to convince me to go with her over winter break to Honduras. I'd been traveling with Cruz at the time.

"How are you feeling? I heard there was a lot of hoopla when you dropped to the ground like a ton of bricks in class," Jessica said with a laugh.

My cheeks heated. I dreaded going to anatomy tomorrow. Everyone would be whispering and staring, and I wasn't looking forward to it.

"I know. It's so embarrassing. I'm feeling a lot better. No going out or traveling for me for a while. I need to just get over this virus and take it slow."

"I'm teasing you. Don't be embarrassed. You push yourself too hard," she said.

Jess was tall with long blonde hair. She was gorgeous and kind. I liked her a lot, and we'd gotten to know one another over the last few weeks.

"Thanks. I'm fine. So, are you going on the summer brigade too?" I asked.

"Yes. I talked to my parents and they've agreed to let me go for the whole summer. I know you're going to be traveling with Cruz, but what if you just come for a couple weeks? It would be great if we could do it together."

"I definitely want to go next year. Cruz will be living here again, so I'll get to see him all the time. He's still touring this summer and I promised I'd travel with him those last few months," I said. So much for stepping back. I was still planning my life around him. I didn't know how not to.

"I get it. I mean, the brigades are life changing and all, but touring with your hot rock star boyfriend is hard to turn down."

Two arms wrapped around my waist from behind and startled me. I knew it was him before I turned around. Jessica stood there gaping, and I realized people were watching us and taking pictures on their phones.

"Hey," I said, turning in his arms to face him.

He kissed me and then pulled back. "Hey yourself."

"I didn't know you were coming here."

"Well, since you won't pick up your phone to talk to me, I decided to just show up because I couldn't wait to see you," Cruz said, studying me.

That's right. I'm supposed to be mad at him, I reminded myself.

"This is my friend Jessica. She's in the medical brigade club with me."

"Nice to meet you, I've heard a lot about you. You just went to Honduras over winter break, right?" he asked, reminding me that he really did listen to what I told him.

"Yes. It was an amazing experience. By the way, I'm a huge fan." Jessica's face reddened, and she looked over at me nervously. Trust me. I got it. He was gorgeous, and his presence was a lot to take in.

"That's cool, thank you. I know Jade wants to go on a brigade, too," he said.

"Yeah. I hope we can go together," Jessica said. "Well, I'll let you two catch up. Text me later."

I waved goodbye and turned to see people holding their phones up as they watched us. I forgot how invasive people could be when it came to Cruz. And being here at school, was mild. Nothing like when we went to his shows. But it was still an invasion. I wanted to be mad at my boyfriend in private. I glared at the girl standing the closest to us and started walking.

"They aren't following us anymore, so I'm guessing that's not the reason you still aren't speaking to me?" Cruz said, moving beside me and intertwining his fingers with mine.

"I'm still mad at you." I glanced over at him, and he smiled. My stomach did little flips like the traitor it was.

"I know you are. I'm sorry, baby. I had an off day. I fucked up and got drunk. But you know how much I love you. You don't think I want anyone else, do you?"

"It's not that. You said you were cutting back on the drinking. Do you not remember what happened in New Orleans?"

We walked up the steps and into the house, and I dropped down on the couch.

"Of course, I do. And I *have* cut way back. I swear, Jade. It was one bad night." He pulled me onto his lap and wrapped his arms around me. "Do you know how worried I've been? You won't talk to me. You barely answer my texts. I've been going out of my fucking mind."

"That was sort of the plan," I said, turning to face him and trying to cover my smile.

"Oh yeah? You enjoy torturing me, don't you?"

I leaned down and kissed him. Slow and soft. "I actually don't. But you need to understand what this is doing to me. I'm stressed all the time. I haven't felt well in a long time. I shouldn't even be kissing you right now. You could get this, you know."

"I don't give a fuck if I get it." He pushed the hair back from my face and ran the pad of his thumb over my bottom lip. "I don't want you to be stressed, baby."

"I don't either. This is harder than I thought it would be. And when that girl answered your phone, I was in the hospital—and I don't know, I was so angry, Cruz. I don't like feeling this way."

"What way? *Jealous*?" He smirked.

I rolled my eyes. "Maybe. If that's what you want to call it. I don't want to worry about you getting drunk and doing something stupid."

"Baby, it doesn't matter if I'm drunk or sober. I don't want anyone else. Ever."

He kissed his way down my neck, and I pushed off his lap so I could face him.

"We need to figure this out. Things need to change. It's not a joke, and I can't talk about it if you're kissing me," I said.

His honey-brown gaze searched mine before his lips turned up in the corners. "Tell me what you need."

I leaned back against the couch. What did I need? I needed a boyfriend who wasn't traveling all over the world. I needed a boyfriend who was here with me. But I couldn't have that. Not yet.

"I need to know you're safe. You can't be out of control drunk, Cruz. I know you have a lot of pressure, but we've already seen how it can spiral. I can't fly to concerts as often as I did this past semester. With my research and my courses, it's just impossible to keep up. And I—I just don't know where I fit in your life now." My voice cracked as the words left my mouth, and tears ran down my face. It was the truth. That really was at the core of this. I didn't know where I fit in his life anymore. I wasn't some groupie or some jet-setting rich girl who didn't have a care in the world—I was just, *me*. A girl with dreams and responsibilities of my own.

He used his thumbs to wipe away the liquid running down my cheeks. "Baby. You fit right here." He grasped my hand and placed it over his heart. "You are all that matters. You're the most important person in my life, and if I haven't shown you that, I'm sorry. Only you, *More Jade*. Please don't give up on me."

"I'll never give up on you. That's not what this is about. I just need you to be okay. I worry about you all the time. And things are changing so much and so fast. It scares me."

"What's changing?" He searched my gaze.

"You're a famous rock star now. People are obsessed with you. They follow you around. They want to take you away from me, and I feel like I'm fighting against a current that's too strong. The lifestyle and the fans. It's just gotten overwhelming."

I'd had all of this bottled up for far too long, and the floodgates had opened, and I couldn't stop the sobs that followed.

"Jade." He pulled me back on his lap and wrapped his arms around me tight. I melted into the safe, little cocoon that was Cruz Winslow. "No one is ever going to take me away from you. Ever. You're all I think about. We'll get through this. Just a few more months. I'll talk to Luke and make it so I can come home more often, okay?"

I sucked in a few long, slow breaths to calm my breathing. "You can't change the band's schedule. We'll just have to get through these next few months. I just want to go back to our simple life, you know?"

"Yeah, I do. It's a lot. But I don't want you to worry. I'm going to cut out hard liquor. I felt like shit after that night. I'll just have an occasional beer or a glass of wine. How does that sound?"

"It sounds like a start. I think you'll be able to handle all of this better if you aren't drunk all the time." I snorted.

"Is that funny?" He tipped me back and laughed when he settled above me.

"It's really not. But it is the truth."

"I agree. No more hard liquor, okay? You don't need to worry about me. We have a little over three months to go and then you'll be with me for the last portion of the tour. We're almost there, baby."

"Okay," I said, tangling my fingers into his hair.

I wanted to believe him. I wanted to believe everything would be okay.

"And Luke's meeting with those two guys this week, right? The ones that might replace you?"

"Yes. He has a meeting with each of them. It's going to happen, baby."

"And I'm staying through Valentine's Day. I'll get to see your presentation too."

"How'd you pull that off?"

"I know some people," he teased. "I missed you, baby."

"Missed you, too."

"Isn't that new opening act starting with you next week? I thought you had to rehearse with them this week?" I said.

"Yeah. Tia. They'll have to figure it out without me."

"I never trust anyone who just uses one name. *Tia*. I googled her. She's pretty," I said, studying his reaction.

He laughed. "She's not as pretty as you. No one is."

His mouth came over mine. I knew in my gut that we'd just put a bandage on our issues, this wasn't a solution. Maybe it would be enough to get us through the next three months. But right now—I couldn't see beyond this moment. Beyond us being together.

And wasn't that the problem?

I never could.

twelve

. . .

Cruz

I HADN'T SLEPT much because my body had obviously grown accustomed to taking an Ambien these last few weeks for sleep. I sure as shit wasn't about to take it while I was with Jade. I'd flushed the pills before I left London. I needed to get my shit together, or I was going to lose her. I'd come just in time because she'd had enough. But being back here, being together—we just picked up where we left off. I was still taking a little Adderall because I was a moody fucker when I wasn't taking it. But I hadn't taken Xanax in the three days since I'd been back with my girl. When I was with her, I didn't need much of anything else. No booze, aside from an occasional glass of wine at dinner. It was the best I'd felt in weeks. Jade was feeling better too. We were good for each other.

I watched her sleep, which I'd normally find creepy, but not with Jade. I loved it. Loved to watch the way her eyebrows pinched together like she was trying to solve the world's problems while she slept. She talked a shit ton in her sleep too, which always made me laugh. I propped myself up on one elbow and studied her pretty features. The dark circles under her eyes had lightened. We'd spent a lot of time in bed the last few days, and I wrote music while she studied. We both needed some downtime, and I was glad to be here with her. Exiled had a break in our tour, but the guys were out in California rehearsing with our new opening act, Tia. She was an up-and-coming singer, and she was very popular with the younger audience. But I'd spoken to Luke, and he'd made it work for me to stay here this week. I needed it and so did Jade.

"Are you seriously staring at me?" Jade whispered, eyes still closed, and her lips turned up in the corners.

I laughed. "I like watching you all tortured and angry when you sleep."

Her eyes opened and her smile grew wider. "I am not tortured and angry in my sleep."

"How the hell do you know? Have you ever watched *you* sleep?" My voice was all tease.

"No. What do I do?"

"Well, you know how in the movies they always show the princess sleeping and she looks like a peaceful angel? All content, and calm, and shit?"

"Yeah," she said, studying me as she licked her plump lips.

"*You look nothing like that.* You're like a mad superhero on a mission. All pissed off and ready for battle."

We both burst out in laughter and she swatted my shoulder. "I do not. You're making this up."

"I'm not. I just rummaged through your closet to look for your cape just in case you needed it for tonight's mission," I said, pushing the hair back from her gorgeous face.

"Well, I'm probably fighting off all those girls who keep throwing their panties at you."

I leaned down and kissed her. Morning breath and all, the girl was perfection. I couldn't get enough. Ever.

"You're my superhero, *More Jade*."

"Yeah? See, you really do need me," she said, pushing to sit up. "What time is it?"

"Almost eight. You ready for your presentation?" My girl was brilliant, and I loved seeing her shine. I was happy I'd get to see her present this afternoon.

"I am. So, it's going to be a few hours. You're okay just hanging out there? It's probably going to be very boring."

"Of course, I'll be fine. Don't worry about me. I love watching you strut your shit."

"I don't strut my shit. What does that even mean?" She laughed and shook her head.

"It means you're going to show off all your nerdy superpowers today. And then I'm taking you somewhere to celebrate Valentine's Day after. I know you can't travel right now, so we'll be doing it here. In the wonderful state of Illinois." I planned a little staycation for her. Tomorrow was Valentine's Day, and I thought relaxing at a hotel would be nice for her.

"You sure found your way out of the doghouse, Winslow."

"Did I? Well, I did give you that get out of the doghouse free love coupon you gave me. That was supposed to be a free pass. I'm just throwing in all these bells and whistles as a bonus," I said, kissing my way down her neck.

She laughed and arched her back so I could pull the T-shirt over her head.

"What other bells and whistles you got?" she asked, already breathless.

"I've got a lot of bells and whistles for you, baby."

"Ohhhh," she whispered when I slipped her panties down her legs.

My gaze locking with hers as I propped myself above her and settled between her thighs. "I love you."

"Love you more."

Our mouths collided and her fingers tangled in my hair. I pushed forward, owning and claiming her in every way possible. She arched into me, wanting more.

"Slow, baby," I whispered against her ear, as I filled her completely.

We moved together until we were both sweaty, and panting, and desperate with need. She cried out my name with her release, and I tumbled over the edge right along with her. Always with her.

Jade fucking Moore was the real rock star. The girl got up in front of a room full of professors, doctors, researcher's and students and—owned her shit. They fired question after question at her and she never missed a beat. I sat back, watching in awe. She had so much passion when she spoke. Everyone was mesmerized, me included.

She hurried over to me when she finished, and I moved to my feet. She wore a white blouse and the blazer I'd given her for Christmas sans the attachable hoodie and black dress slacks. Her hair was straight and tucked behind her ears, and her jade eyes beamed when they met mine.

"So, what did you think?" she asked, pushing up on her tiptoes to give me a quick kiss.

"You killed it."

"Yeah?"

"Yeah," I said, pulling her closer and wrapping my arms around her.

"This must be the infamous Cruz," a lady said as she approached.

Jade pushed back and smiled. "Yes. Professor Callahan, this is my boyfriend, Cruz."

"So formal today, Jade. Hi, I'm Elaine, nice to meet you." She extended her arm and I shook her hand.

"Hi, Jade speaks very highly of you. It's a pleasure to meet you," I said.

"Same. You must be proud. Jade, you blew me away today. Well done."

"Thank you. I was pretty nervous," Jade said, looking up at me and smiling.

"Well, it didn't show at all. You appeared cool as a cucumber. Maybe you get your stage presence from your boyfriend," Elaine teased.

"That means so much to me. Thank you. I'll see you next week." Jade gave her mentor a hug and reached for my hand.

"Have a nice weekend. Go celebrate. You deserve it."

Jade waved goodbye and we walked back to her house.

"I'm so fucking proud of you. This is why you're here, baby. You're in your element. You kicked so much ass out there," I said.

The wind blustered around us, but the sun was out, and it was a beautiful day.

"I'm so happy you were here for it. I've been so down lately, and just having you here has turned everything around." She looked up at me and bit down on her bottom lip. So vulnerable and honest. I loved the shit out of this girl

"I'd do anything for you. Are you ready to go on a little staycation?"

"Okaaaaay. So, what's this staycation? We're going somewhere?" she asked.

"Yep. Pack an overnight bag. You don't really need any clothes unless you want to leave the room to eat." I teased.

"We're going to a hotel? In the city?"

"Yes. I booked us a suite at the Waldorf for two nights. How does room service, massages, and lots of sex sound?" I wriggled my brows.

She laughed. "You're such a perv. It sounds like heaven."

"Heaven, huh? Who's the perv now?" I said as we walked into her house.

"Maybe I'm a perv when it comes to you," she said, dropping down to sit beside me on her bed.

"Pack your bag, or we'll never leave this room."

She kissed me before pushing up and grabbing her new suitcase from the closet. We threw a few things in her bag and got the hell out of there. We'd needed this time together more than either of us had realized. Spending time without having other people around us. Without all the outside noise and distractions. Just me and Jade. Just the way I liked it.

———

When I landed in Los Angeles, I tried to rally. We had a concert tonight and I was still wishing I was back in the city with my girl.

We'd barely left the room for two days. We'd talked and laughed, shared great food, and spent the rest of our time in bed together. In the shower together. We'd walked down to Oak street beach this morning before I took her home and headed to the hangar. This week solidified that I was doing the right thing. I needed out of this band and this world as soon as possible. Stepping away for a few days showed me how fucked up my reality had become. It was so skewed. I'd spent a few days sleeping normal, eating normal and I'd barely had anything to drink since London. And it felt good.

"You look good. Refreshed. How's our girl?" Luke said when he met me at the back door of the venue.

"She's fucking amazing. Thanks for making that work out with my schedule. We needed it. It was nice to unplug and get away from here for a while."

"Yeah, I get that. Just a few more months, brother, okay?"

"Yep. How's that going? Did you talk to the guys at the label?" I asked.

"I did. They aren't thrilled, but they also don't want to lose Exiled by fighting you on this. They're open to both candidates and Jerry is flying out this week to meet with them. It's a process, but we'll get there. Is your dad still giving you a hard time?" Luke asked.

"Nah. He doesn't have anything to bargain with, so he's backed off."

"Good. Well, I'm glad you're here. Adam and Dex got into it this week. I don't know that they're ever going to get past their issues."

"What happened? Tory was here with Adam, right?"

"Yeah, and Dex kept messing with her, which sent Adam sideways. You know, the usual," Luke said, and I dropped my bag in the back room.

"Did Lennon get involved?"

"He was the peacekeeper. You know your brother. He doesn't like conflict," Luke said, and we both laughed.

"Yeah, I know. But someone needs to put Dex in his place, man. He's such an asshole."

"You're preaching to the choir. But we can't afford to lose him. Not with you transitioning out, Cruz. I think it's ultimately going to happen, because he's out of control. But we're going to have to cross that bridge when we get there. Hopefully the guys can keep it together until then."

Shit. I wanted Dex out, but I wanted myself out more. It sucked because Dex knew he was in a power position and he used it against everyone. Even Luke sounded resolved to the fact that it wouldn't work with Dex long term, but he couldn't do anything about it now.

"I'll talk to Adam. Thanks for putting up with all our shit." I said, slamming a bottle of water.

"No problem. That's what I'm here for. Glad to see you drinking water. You look good, man. Who knew?" he said with a laugh.

"Who knew what?"

"Who knew all you needed was a week with your girl. You look like a new man," he said with a shit-eating grin.

"Yeah. Jade's got that effect on me. So how did it go with Tia? Is she any good?" I asked.

"She's decent. Has a good band that works with her. She shut down Dex the day they met. She doesn't take his shit which is good."

"I like the sound of that. Hopefully he backs off. We don't need to have drama there. They're going to be with us for a while, right?"

"Yeah. We'll see how it goes. She'd like it to be long term, but we need to see how our fans respond to her. See if she brings in a good element with her fan base."

"Alright. Sounds good. Are they out there right now?"

"They are. You've got ten minutes," Luke said, before walking out the door and giving me a little privacy.

I reached in my backpack for my Adderall. Time to get my game face on. We had a long show ahead of us and I needed to get back in work mode. I sent my girl a quick text and told her I missed her.

"Let's go asshole," Lennon shouted before pushing my door open.

"Hello to you too." I rolled my eyes and followed him out.

"Look at you," Lennon said.

"I know. I look fucking good." I walked beside him down the hallway.

"No. You look sober though. It looks good on you."

"Fuck you, very much," I said. "I heard Adam and Dex went at it a little this week. Everything okay now?"

"It's as good as it's going to get. They really hate each other. Dex wouldn't stop messing with Tory. Adam had every right to be pissed off. The dude does it on purpose. He wants to get a reaction."

"Look at you, Dr. Phil. Impressive. And speaking of sober, you seem to be pretty sober yourself," I said, studying him as we walked toward Adam backstage.

"Yeah. Tia's sister, Bailey, tours with her. She's part of the crew, and she's a super cool chick. She's been sober for ten months. We've been hanging out, so you know, just trying to be respectful." He smiled and I couldn't help but laugh. My brother was a sappy bastard and I loved it.

"It's always about a girl, isn't it?" I teased.

"Glass houses, brother. You're the most pussy-whipped mother-fucker I know."

"Touche," I said. Because he was fucking right.

"Tia shut Dex down. You would have loved it. She doesn't take any shit. You're going to like her," Lennon said.

"Did you hear about that cocksucker?" Adam moved to stand beside me, anger radiating from him.

"I did. How you doing with everything? Did Tory head back to school?" I asked.

"Yeah. She was pissed though. Dex was a dick all week. I swear that dude has a death wish. If you weren't so hell-bent on getting out of this band, I'd cut his ass right now. I don't know how long I can work with that asshole," Adam said.

"Is that so? You're over here whining like a little bitch?" Dex walked up behind me. I stiffened at the sound of his voice. I needed to be on guard with this dude.

"Fuck you," Adam spewed.

Lennon and I stood between them. "We're going out in five. We don't have time for this shit. Pull it together. People paid a lot of money to see us play tonight. Sold out show. Let's get our heads in the game," my brother said. Holy shit. Look who'd gone and grown up this year. Lennon was leading this band now, and I was fucking proud of him. I'd been so lost in my own bullshit I hadn't even noticed.

"Lennon's right," Luke said, stepping up to stand beside Adam. "Bury this shit for the next three hours."

My gaze locked with Adam's and he nodded. "Alright. Let's do this."

Dex slammed half the bottle of whiskey and offered it to me. "No. I'm good."

"Another fucking boy scout. Just what this band needs," he said, and jogged out on stage in front of me.

The crowd went crazy.

And just like that, I was back in work mode.

thirteen

. . .

Jade

"I CAN'T BELIEVE how fast this year has gone. It's spring break in a couple weeks," Ari said, pausing to take a bite of her salad.

"I know. Have you and Jace decided yet if you're going to go to Mexico?"

"Yeah. I agreed to go. I just don't want it to be a drunken week with all his friends, you know. But he promised we'd do our own thing too, so we'll see how it goes. And a little sunshine and a few pina colada's does not sound bad right now."

The café was booming, and we were lucky to find a little table in the back corner. The black and white floors and hanging chandeliers gave it a French feel. I liked to come here and study in the mornings when it wasn't busy, but we'd definitely hit the lunch rush now.

"You're going to have so much fun. Just go with the flow and don't overthink it. Jace's friends are cool and they all love you," I said.

"Yeah. And you're going to be out west with Cruz? Will he have shows the whole time?"

"Yeah, I'm excited to spend a week with him. He has a few days off, so we'll sneak away from the band and do our own thing."

"Are you excited to meet Tia for the first time tonight?" she asked.

"I'm curious to see what she's like. Cruz likes her, which is odd since he dislikes most people he meets." I laughed.

"I'm excited for the show tonight. I've never been backstage at a concert before either. We're going to have so much fun," she said.

"Hey, ladies." Brayden walked up to our table. His brown hair was slicked back neatly, and even wearing a T-shirt and jeans, he looked like a politician.

"Oh, hey," Ari and I said in unison and laughed.

"Jace gave me a ticket to the show tonight. Thank your boyfriend for me," he said with a smile.

Cruz wasn't a fan of Brayden's, but he offered Jace ten tickets and he couldn't really control who he gave them to.

"I will." I nodded.

"We'll see you there, but I'll be backstage with the cool people most of the time," Ari said, and she wriggled her brows and chuckled.

"Sweet. Well, I'll see you guys tonight." He walked back to the counter to grab his order from the pick-up window.

Ari and I finished lunch and headed back to class. Cruz would be here in a few hours and I couldn't wait. We'd only have two days together and they'd be busy. But we had spring break right around the corner, and we'd get to spend some quality time together. Those were the visits that got me through the misery of being apart. Things had been better since he'd returned from Europe. He was drinking less and feeling better. And so was I.

———

Ari and I stepped out of the Uber and Cruz came running out the back door. Security chased after him, but he didn't seem to care. He forgot how famous he'd become most of the time and I tried to do the same. A few people had gathered by the door and security held them back.

He scooped me off my feet and spun me around. The air left my lungs and I laughed.

"Hey, baby," his gruff voice said against my ear.

"Hi. I missed you."

"Missed you too," he said, putting me back on my feet and giving Ari a quick hug.

Two security guards hurried us inside and shot Cruz a warning look. Obviously, he'd run out without letting them know and they weren't pleased.

"Sorry, man. Just excited to see my girl," he said and both men nodded.

"I can't believe I'm back-stage at a concert," Ari said, rubbing her hands together and smiling. She wore her Exiled T-shirt, leggings, and Doc Martens. She called this her *rocker-chic* look.

Cruz led us to the back room where a group of people were hanging out. Lennon rushed me and gave me a hug. He then hugged Ari, as they'd met a few times in the past.

"Jade, come meet Bailey. She's the chick I told you about." Lennon called me often for girl advice, and he'd been talking about Bailey for the last two weeks.

"Bailey, this is Jade," Lennon said after he pulled me across the room to find her. Cruz and Ari followed us.

"Hi, Jade. I've heard so much about you. Literally, from everyone. It's the only time I can get Cruz to even speak to me. Apparently, you're his favorite topic," Bailey said with a laugh. She had a blonde pixie haircut, her eyes were large and brown, and she had multiple earrings covering her ear. She was warm and kind, and I instantly liked her.

"She's my favorite—everything," Cruz said, wrapping his arms around my middle, his chest to my back. His chin rested on my shoulder and he kissed my cheek.

"Oh gag. I can't handle you all sappy, Winslow," a voice said from behind me, and I whipped around to see her. Tia.

Tia and Bailey looked nothing alike. Tia had platinum blonde hair that fell down her back and stopped at her waist. Her sapphire blue gaze locked with mine as we assessed one another. She smiled and I did the same. She was a few inches taller than me, much curvier than I was, and she wore a sports bra and skinny jeans. Her boobs filled out the black and white sports bra, but I guessed that was the point. She had on tall black spiked boots, that stopped at her knees. Her makeup was dark and dramatic, almost a bit goth, and she oozed confidence.

"Shut up, asshole," Cruz teased, turning around to face her.

"Takes one to know one." She winked and stopped in front of me. "You must be Jade."

"Yeah, nice to meet you, Tia. This is my friend, Ari," I said.

Tia shook both of our hands. There was a hardness about her, but at the same time, she managed to come off friendly.

"Well, this guy mopes around and talks about you all the time, which is saying a lot because it took us days to get him to actually speak to us," Tia said, punching Cruz in the arm.

I watched them interact and didn't miss the comfort between them. Cruz told me she was cool, and they'd obviously become friends.

"I just don't have much else to say." Cruz leaned down and nuzzled my neck.

"Dude. Get a room. No one needs to see you fawn all over her." Tia's laughter filled the room, and everyone joined in. I couldn't read her yet.

"It's time Tia. The guys are already out there. Let's go," a guy I'd never seen before said as he leaned his head in the room.

"On my way. Just had to meet the infamous Jade. Impressive," she said, looking me up and down.

Cruz laughed. "Told you."

"You sure did. See you out there." She turned and walked out the door.

"I'll catch up with you guys when Exiled goes on. I need to go watch my sister," Bailey said. She gave Lennon a quick kiss, and her cheeks burned red. He slapped her on the ass on her way out the door.

"What do you think?" Lennon asked me the minute she was gone.

"She's super cute. I like her." I smiled at him. I liked grown up Lennon. He was coming into his own. This tour had been good for him.

Adam, Luke, and Dex walked in the room, and Adam did not look happy. Cruz leaned down and talked so only I could hear him. "Don't ask. Those two are going at it."

"Princess, you're back," Dex said, saluting me.

"Ignore that prick," Adam said, hugging me and smiling at Ari.

"Hey, Jade. Good to see you," Luke said, and the hug-fest continued.

"So good to be here. I missed you guys."

"Sam texted me. He'll be here in about thirty minutes. I told him to text you and he and Cara can come through the back door." Cruz and Sam had become good friends, which was great, seeing as they hated each other when they first met.

"That was nice of you. Thank you," I said, pushing up to kiss him. My stomach fluttered when his gaze locked with mine. I loved the way he looked at me. The way he kissed me. The way he made me feel.

"What do you think, Ari? Should I bring you and Jade out on stage so I can sing to her tonight?" My boyfriend asked, his gaze never leaving mine.

"Hell yes." Ari fist pumped her arm in the air, and I laughed.

"Hell no. You have no idea how scary it is out there. Their fans are insane, and they hate me because I'm dating him. I don't need anyone to throw their dirty panties at me," I said.

"I'll guard you. They don't hate me," she teased.

There was a knock at the door, and it was the same guy who'd come to tell Tia she needed to get out on stage.

"They're ready for your guys, Luke," the man said.

"Alright, let's go. Adam and Dex, leave your shit backstage. Lennon, kick some ass. Cruz, try not to stare at your girl all night while you're performing for a crowd who paid money to see you." Luke opened the door and winked at me. "I've got chairs set up for you and your friends, Jade."

"You're the best. Thank you," I said.

"Sit where I can see you, okay?" Cruz asked as he led me down the hall, beside the stage.

"Always." I agreed and dropped down on the stool where I could see him.

Cruz rumpled Ari's hair when she sat beside me, and he picked up my hand and kissed the tattoo on my wrist. "Love you, More Jade."

"Love you." I pushed up to kiss him.

"Have fun, princess," Dex said as he stopped to look at me. His gaze traveled from my feet to my face and chills ran down my spine. He chuckled and jogged on stage.

"What the hell was that? He's so creepy," Ari whispered close to my ear.

"Tell me about it."

Bailey came to sit beside us after her sister jogged off stage. Tia said she'd be right back. She wanted to go get cleaned up.

"So, you both go to school at Northwestern?" she asked us.

"Yep. This one is basically a junior because she's graduating early next year. I'm a sophomore. How about you? Do you go to school?" Ari said.

"Nope. I was going to state school in Oregon, but I left a month ago. Getting to open for Exiled was a big break for my sister, so I promised I'd come with her on tour. I hope to go back at some point."

"That was nice of you. Lennon said you work for the band?" I asked.

"Yeah, I do all the behind the stage stuff. I handle all the drama. And trust me, when Tia's around there's always drama," she said with a laugh. "So, it keeps me busy."

It reminded me that Cruz had agreed to come on tour for his brother. Cruz and Bailey had both left their lives in order to support their siblings. It was honorable. Cruz was not going to finish his courses as quickly as he'd hoped, because his tour schedule was far busier than he'd expected. But he'd finish next year when he was out of the band.

"What are we talking about over here?" Tia asked, pulling up a stool beside me.

"I was just telling them I was in school in Oregon before we came on tour with Exiled," Bailey said.

"Yes. My little sacrificial lamb." Tia chuckled and patted her sister's cheek. Bailey's smile appeared forced. "So, Jade, you're pre-med, graduating next year, and just the most brilliant thing in the world. Why in the hell are you dating Winslow?"

Her tone was all tease, and everyone laughed. Except me. I couldn't read this girl. She was cool and flippant, yet her questions felt more purposeful. Manipulative, maybe? She wanted to know about Cruz and I. And I had no problem talking about it.

"He's the best guy I know." I smiled and sipped the beer that Luke had given me.

"Really? Fascinating. He such a brooding asshole though," Tia said.

"Not with Jade. He's different with her." Ari beamed at me, jumping in to rescue the awkward conversation.

"I can tell. Seriously, when we can get him to speak, he talks about you. It's so *un-Winslow* of him," she said. How close were they? She acted like she knew him really well. They'd been touring for two weeks, and Cruz wasn't easy to get to know.

"Love will do that to you," Bailey said. She was clearly the more soft-spoken, delicate sibling.

"Oh my God. All these people around me in love is nauseating. My sister's as bad as Winslow," Tia scoffed.

"Yeah, Lennon has been talking about you non-stop." I smiled.

"Really?" Bailey's face flushed, and she tried to cover her smile.

"Please. Like you don't know? You two are always all over one another. It's annoyingly cute." Tia winked.

I couldn't tell if she and her sister were close or if they hated one another. The fact that Bailey had come on tour with her told me they must be close. Tia just had an edge to her that I hadn't quite figured out.

"So where are you from?" I directed my question to Tia.

"We're from the Bay Area, and this one tried to escape by moving to Oregon for school." Tia smiled and thrust her thumb at her sister. "We grew up similar to Cruz and Lennon, you know, with the whole silver spoon thing. We're just a couple of spoiled rich girls chasing our dream."

"Chasing *your* dream," Bailey said, staring hard at her sister.

"Fine. I'm definitely the more spoiled one. I begged this one to come with me to chase my dream while she figures out what hers is."

Bailey chuckled. "That's true."

Ari and I locked gazes and I could see how fascinated she was with them.

"Baby." I heard Cruz's voice over the speakers.

Oh my gosh, not again.

I waved, and Tia laughed so hard she fell off her stool. "No wonder he's so crazy about you. You're not caught up in his bullshit at all. You're clearly not after the fame. I kind of love it."

I smiled, but put my focus back on my boyfriend, who was calling me out in front of a packed house.

"They want me to sing to you, Jade. Come on. Ari can come too," he said, and the crowd cheered.

"We so have to do this," Ari said, moving to her feet.

"I really don't want to go out there," I said. My heart raced. Why did he keep doing this to me? I didn't like the attention. The only one I ever wanted attention from was Cruz.

"Oh, hell yes, we're *so* doing this. Let's go, Bailey," Tia said before tugging my hand, as she led me, Ari and Bailey all out on stage. I couldn't make out the crowd because the lights were so bright. Cruz beamed when our eyes locked.

The screams were deafening. The crowd liked that we'd come out in some sort of girl posse, and Tia reached for a mic. "Who wants to see Winslow sing his ass off to his girl?"

Dear God. She wasn't helping. I glanced over at Ari who had a grin spread clear across her face. She was loving this. Bailey looked as horrified as I was, and she kept smiling at Lennon. Before I knew it, Luke had four stools on stage and we all sat down, as Cruz sang "More of Me," and the audience sang along. For a moment I just took it in. The way my boyfriend commanded the attention of everyone in the room. The way he oozed confidence and owned the stage. His words sunk in and my heart exploded. Ari's hand came around my shoulder and I swiped at my cheeks when I realized two tears were streaming down my face. When had I become such a blubbering mess?

When he finished the song, he walked off stage with me. "Happy you're here, baby."

"Me too."

"Did I embarrass you?"

"Yes. You always do," I said before kissing him.

He jogged back out and his fans greeted him with even more cheers. I wondered if it would be hard for him to leave when this all came to an end. Was he leaving for me, or did he hate this lifestyle as much as I did?

"Hey, J-bird, sorry we're late. Got caught in traffic," Sam said when Luke escorted him over to us.

"Who the hell are you?" Tia snarled, and I couldn't help but laugh. This girl was fascinating. I didn't know if she loved me or hated me. But she certainly didn't appreciate Sam giving me a hug.

"This is my best friend, Sam," I said.

"I thought *Ari* was your best friend." She crossed her arms in front of her chest, giving Sam a once over from head to toe.

"I'm the girl best friend. He's the guy best friend," Ari said with a chuckle.

"Okay then. Nice to meet you, Sam." Tia forced a smile, and I introduced her to Cara.

"Nice to meet you too, I guess?" Sam's tone was all tease.

"Sorry about that. Just a little protective over Winslow. Can't imagine what he'd do if this one ever dumped him." She flicked her thumb at me, and Sam's laughter bounced off the walls.

Tia was an enigma.

An enigma who went by one name, had an intimidating edge, and an odd friendship with my boyfriend.

But I liked her.

I think.

fourteen

. . .

Cruz

"SO, is it true? Are you really leaving Exiled?" Tia said, barging into my room on the tour bus. Who the fuck did this chick think she was?

"Have you ever heard of knocking?"

"Don't deflect. Are you leaving the band? Seriously?" She huffed, pulling out the chair at my desk and dropping down to sit, like she owned the place.

"Wow. Make yourself at home." I crossed my arms in front of me and stared at her.

"Dude. Quit avoiding the question."

"*Dude.* It's none of your business," I said, slipping my phone in my back pocket.

Sure, Tia and I had become friends, and I use the term loosely because I'd known her for all of a month. I didn't trust her, so I sure as shit wasn't telling her what I was doing where Exiled was concerned. But I knew exactly where this was coming from. My brother and Bailey were acting like two lovesick teenagers, and I'm sure the asshole opened his big mouth.

"Dude. It is my business. I came on tour with you. My career is riding on this too, Mr. Rock Star. The world doesn't only revolve around you."

"What the hell are you talking about? What I do with my life has nothing to do with you. This is not your business. Stay out of it," I said.

"Are you fucking kidding me? Believe it or not, Winslow, opening for Exiled is my big break. And unfortunately, you are the face of Exiled. People aren't following any of those other dipshits around. They favor dipshit number one, which is you. And if you leave, this whole ship goes down. Where the hell does that leave me?"

"Well, thanks for caring. Nobodies' ship is going down. Do you really think I'd do that to my brother? Or to Adam? Mind your own fucking business, Tia. Keep this to yourself or it's going to blow up in everyone's face," I said.

She stood up and reached in her back pocket and pulled out a baggy with pills in it, tossed two in her mouth and reached for my water bottle. Yes. Tia liked to help herself to my things. The girl had no boundaries. None. And she was getting on my last fucking nerve. She slammed the water and swallowed whatever the hell she just put in her mouth.

"Do you really think I'd leak this to the press? This will bring my career to a screeching halt. So, thanks. Those two Vicodin are because of you, asshole." She dropped back down in the chair.

Why was this my problem? I wasn't responsible for anyone else's career. My goal was to exit the band without hurting my brother and Adam. That's it.

"Mom, is that you?" Sarcasm dripped from my voice, because pill-poppers loved to blame other people for their problems.

"Save your rich boy issues for someone who buys that shit. Your mommy likes the narcs, I get it. Play your violin somewhere else, Winslow. I grew up with it too, and right now Vicodin happens to be my favorite coping mechanism. So, get the hell over it. Tell me what's going on, or I'm going to follow you around day and night and haunt your nightmares."

"Jesus. It's not going to affect you. The label has it under control. They're looking at two guys right now to take my place. If this gets out, I'll fucking know it was you, and I'll get your ass fired."

"If I were you, I'd suspect Dex way before I'd worry about me. He's a devious little shit. I'm a pain in the ass, but I shoot straight. I'm not going to the press, that's the last thing I'd do."

"Dex won't leak it because it would hurt Exiled if it came out now. Keeping it under wraps until we release a statement with the name of the guy taking over is our best shot at a smooth transition. He won't do anything to hurt himself," I said, running a hand over my face.

"So, when is this going down?" she asked.

For some odd reason, I believed Tia wouldn't go to the press with this. Not only because it would hurt her as well, but because she wasn't a malicious person. At least she hadn't been yet. And it would hurt my brother, and I doubted her sister would appreciate that.

"Not for a few months. I gave them a year, and they convinced me to wait until the end of summer. Jade will come on tour with us those last few months, so I agreed to the extension."

Tia and her band had their own piece of shit tour bus, but they were constantly in ours when we traveled during the day because apparently their bus smelled like dirty feet. They slept on their own bus but refused to sit on it when they were awake, for whatever reason.

"Are you quitting for Jade?" she asked.

The girl was as direct as me. She didn't hold back.

"Has anyone ever told you that you're fucking nosy?" I said.

"Yes. Many people have. I just don't give a fuck."

I laughed. "No. I'm not leaving for Jade. I never wanted to do this. I agreed to come on tour for a year, and I've done my part. I'm even staying a few extra months through the summer. I want to finish school and figure out what the hell I want to do with my life. Not that it's any of your business."

"You really want to leave all this?" She put her hands out at her side and chuckled.

"I can't wait. I'm sick of traveling. Sick of Dex. Sick of people being in my business every fucking time I step outside. And I'm sick of being away from my girl. End of story."

"You're a classic psych case, you know that, right?" she said.

I let out a long breath. I really wasn't in the mood to be psycho-analyzed by Tia, with no fucking last name, who'd spent less time in this business than I had and wanted to be famous as much as Dex did.

"Okay, ol' wise one. Let's hear it."

She leaned back in the chair, extended her legs, crossed her feet at the ankles and propped them on my desk. I glared at her, but she ignored me.

"Relax, Winslow. It's a tour bus, not the Four Seasons. This is what I think—since you asked." She chuckled before continuing. "You're a rich boy with mommy and daddy issues. You probably lived in a big mansion, surrounded by lots of people, yet it was unbearably lonely. So, you want the white picket fence, and the lame-ass minivan with lots of seating for all your nerdy little kids. They'll probably be preppy little fuckers with plaid shirts and high-waisted cargo pants, they'll play golf and polo, maybe ride horses—you'll marry Jade who will be the perfect mother and doctor, and you'll do that whole annoying bedtime routine where it takes you two hours to put your over-indulged children to sleep because you have to read them fourteen bedtime stories or they won't be educated enough to attend Princeton in the future—" She paused. Thank fucking Christ, because I don't know how much more I could take. Unfortunately, I laughed. Because she was odd as hell, and a little bit crazy.

"Yeah, you had me at *lonely childhood*, and then the train left the station."

"You know what I mean. You want the dream of a normal, boring life. You're overcompensating for your lack of normalcy as a child. *Typical Millennial*. But guess what, buddy. Most people want what you have. The grass is always greener, you know. Maybe you should just convince Jade to jump ship and come this way instead. You could have a couple little snotty kids running around the tour bus. Kids love that shit."

"You just might be clinically insane. I'm good. But thanks for the advice. No one's having kids or buying minivans. This just isn't what I want to do with my life. But you'll be fine. Exiled will go on, and I'm sure they'll keep your annoying ass around. For what it's worth, you're a kickass opening act," I said.

She put the back of her hand to her forehead. "Winslow, did you just give me a compliment? Be still my beating heart."

"Fuck off. The therapy session is over, and I need to call my girl."

She rolled her eyes. "Don't you have your big interview with Rock the Band tomorrow? Is that why we're rushing to New York?"

"Yes. And the fact that we have a show there," I said.

"Well, don't slip up and tell the legendary rock magazine that you're leaving all this to pursue your education. Groupies and fans frown upon that shit." She stood up and walked toward the door.

"You'll keep this between us?" I reiterated the importance of keeping it quiet.

"Of course, I will. This isn't a secret I'm dying to tell."

The closer it got, the more difficult it would be to keep it quiet. I couldn't wait to put this behind me and move on with my life.

———

Riley Lawson was a legendary reporter for Rock the Band. She'd interviewed every big rock star over the last decade. We were meeting her downtown at a studio for the photo shoot and the interview would follow. Luke had been a nervous wreck all morning, because depending on how it went, it could make or break our future in a lot of ways. Rock the Band had launched newcomers to superstardom, and it had painted ugly pictures of bands that were on top of the world.

"Dex, I'm not fucking around. You need to think before you speak. No one is to bring up Cruz leaving this band, do you understand me? We control his exit right now, and that's how I want to keep it. Do not bring up your dispute with Adam, or with anyone in this band. We clear?"

"Christ, Dude. Relax. I got it," Dex said, running a hand through his long, wavy hair.

"No problem. We've got this," Adam said, dropping to sit on the couch in our hotel suite.

"Okay. We're taking the bus. They may want to snap some pictures of you guys on the tour bus. We'll see when we get there." Luke called the driver and told him to pull up out front.

When we arrived, we were taken back to hair and makeup and pulled into different rooms. I tried not to be annoyed. I sent a text to Jade while I sat in the chair.

> They're making us pretty for the photo shoot. Apparently, my hair and face need some work.

MORE JADE

> You don't need any work. They probably just have to do that, so they don't offend Dex because he needs some help.

> Touche. How are you feeling?

MORE JADE

> So much better. Can't wait for Spring Break. I miss you so much.

> Miss you more.

MORE JADE

> Has Tia kept quiet about you leaving the band?

> Yeah. Haven't heard anything and I think if she were going to leak it, she would have done so by now. She doesn't seem like the type to do it.

MORE JADE

> I agree. I can't wait till this is all behind us.

> Me too.

"Are you texting your girlfriend?" the chick rubbing some kind of hair product into my hair asked.

"Yeah. Sorry." I set my phone down on the counter in front of me.

The room was small, and she and another girl were crammed in here with me.

"Don't be sorry. Just curious. I'm Christy and this is Niki. I do the hair and she does the face," Christy said with a laugh.

"Please tell me you aren't putting makeup on me." I quirked a brow and waited.

"Well, the camera doesn't capture you with the same vibrancy as we see in real life. So, you need to really exaggerate the makeup because it's not as strong through the camera. The light changes the way it looks. Basically, we're just trying to make you look as good as you do in person, but in a photograph," Niki said, and her face burned red.

"I have no idea what that means, so I'll just have to trust you. The other guys better be getting this done too."

"They are. But they wanted the most attention to go on the cover model." Christy chuckled.

I sat forward. My hair looked exactly the same, messy and unruly, but it stayed in place, so I guess they knew how to make it do that.

"The band is going to be on the cover," I said, unsure if I misheard her.

"Oh, really? They told us you were going to be on the cover. They said the band would have a few photos inside with the interview. But maybe we heard wrong?" Niki said, and she and Christy exchanged a look in the mirror.

They took me out to the studio after putting me in a black tailored button-up and a pair of dark fitted jeans. There were a slew of people positioning me where they wanted me and telling me to look every which way while they snapped what had to be thousands of photos. The photographer's name was Mig and he must be a big deal because everyone did what he said. The good news was that Mig didn't ask me to smile all that much, so my natural, pissed off face seemed to meet his approval.

"Can we do a few without your shirt? I know you've got some impressive ink, and I want to have a few to offer the art director. I think that makes for a more interesting cover," Mig asked.

"Sure." I took off my shirt and Christy came out of nowhere to grab it.

He had me lie down, sit up and even took a few of me standing. "Holy shit, these are gorgeous. The tat over your heart is magnificent. What's the meaning there?"

He continued to shoot pictures while he spoke, so I assumed he didn't care if I answered while he shot some more photos. "Jade's my girlfriend. Just a way to keep her with me even when we're apart."

"Fucking beautiful, man."

"Thanks," I said with a laugh. He was passionate, and I admired anyone who took their job that serious.

"Of course, your shirt is off," Lennon said, and he bellowed out in laughter when he, Adam and Dex walked in the room.

"Hey. Don't hate me because I'm beautiful," I said, flipping him the bird.

"Fuck, you photograph well," Mig gushed as he continued to take shots. "Alright, let's get you guys in here. Take some group shots."

"Here's your shirt back," Christy said, handing me the button up.

"Thank Christ. I'm a little pale right now, so a shirtless photo shoot is not in the cards," Adam said, and we all laughed.

Mig snapped pictures for the next thirty minutes, and I was over it. Riley met us in the conference room where we sat around a large table. She was a petite woman with shoulder-length black hair. She wore jeans with a white button-up and a blazer.

"So, tell me how you all met," she said, setting her phone down to record our conversation.

"These assholes all knew one another, and then they discovered my talent. The missing piece," Dex said, with a shit-eating grin across his face. I made a conscious decision not to roll my eyes in front of her.

"Cruz and I are brothers, so obviously we've known one another since birth," Lennon said with a laugh, before continuing. "Cruz and Adam were best friends growing up, so Adam and I started playing together and sort of forced my brother to sing in the band because neither of us could hold a tune. And then we met Dex in high school and Exiled was formed."

"Who chose the name?" she asked.

"I did. You know, at the time it really fit. Probably still does. We were always getting into trouble at school. We definitely pushed the envelope when we were young, so the name sort of picked us," Adam said.

"I like that," Riley said, staring at me and waiting for me to chime in. She hadn't asked me anything specific and Adam and Lennon had answered the questions well.

"So, you sort of forced Cruz to sing in the band? He didn't want to?" she asked.

My brother looked over at me and smiled. My chest squeezed. Why the fuck did the kid always make me soft. I hated it.

"I wasn't a great singer, but I was better than these assholes," I said with a laugh.

"And then you came into your own and found your talent?" Riley said.

"I wouldn't say that. I still don't think I'm all that strong of a singer. I'm average at best. But I write good lyrics, and these guys kind of mask my lack of singing talent with their music." I took a swig of water, anxious for a smoke. It had been a long day and I was in need of some nicotine.

Riley laughed and continued her questioning for the next hour. We kept all our dirty little secrets to ourselves and I don't think she noticed the animosity that lived between all of us and Dex.

"So, Cruz, I'd like to do a solo interview with you if you don't mind," Riley said as everyone got up from the table.

"Yeah, that's fine. Can I go grab a smoke?" I asked.

"How about we walk next door to my favorite coffee shop. You can smoke while we walk, and we can grab a bite to eat. You must be starving."

"Yeah, I could eat. Sounds good."

Riley told Luke they had all the pictures they needed of the group, and she'd bring me back to the hotel when we were done, so they could head out. I didn't know what else we had to talk about, but I lit up a cig and we walked down the street. A few people snapped pictures of us on their phone.

"Does that ever get old?" she asked.

"When people take my picture? Nah. It doesn't bother me. I don't like when they write things that aren't true, that bothers me." I snubbed out my smoke, and we stepped inside. She'd obviously called ahead because they took us to a private table in the back of the restaurant.

"Good to know. Let's make sure I get my story straight. Is there anything that's off limits?" she asked with a laugh.

"I don't think so. Can I let you know as we go?" I didn't have a clue what she wanted to know, and I certainly wasn't going to talk about Lennon's overdose or anything like that, but I doubted she knew about it.

"Absolutely."

We sat down and ordered lunch before she started recording our conversation.

"So, Cruz. People report all sorts of things about your relationship, are you or aren't you in one, and if it's on or off, so let's start there. Are you in a relationship with one girl?" she teased.

I nodded. "Yeah. Have been for over a year. With the same girl. I don't know why it's such a mystery. Most of the songs I've written are for her. I've sung to her on stage a couple times and talked about her at our concerts repeatedly. She's with me as often as she can be, because she's going to school."

"I assume we're talking about Jade Moore. So, when that story from Farrah Clearwater came out that she was with you in Miami, it wasn't true?"

"A blatant lie. I don't fuck around on Jade. I was with my girl the weekend Farrah claimed she was with me. I've never even met the chick. I have no idea why she made it up," I said, taking a sip of my water.

"Why didn't you come out and defend yourself?" she asked.

"Because it feeds the flame. I don't need to justify lies with a response. As long as Jade knows the truth, that's all that matters to me."

Riley smiled and leaned back in her chair. "I like that."

I laughed. "Thanks."

"So, tell me, where do you see yourself in five years?" she asked.

I took a minute to think about it. I answered honestly without saying much about the band. This interview was more personal. It wasn't about Exiled. She wanted to know about me, and I gave her what she wanted.

fifteen

. . .

Jade

I ARRIVED IN NASHVILLE LATE, as I had work to do with Elaine before I left on spring break. I went straight to the hotel, as I'd missed the show. Cruz was on his way back to the hotel when the car dropped me off. I found Tia and Bailey in the lobby when I stepped inside.

"Jade," Bailey called out and waved me over.

"Hey, what are you guys doing here? You left early?" I asked.

"Yeah, we just got here on our piece of shit bus. The guys are right behind us," Tia said. "Cruz is in a notably better mood today, which I can only assume is because you're here."

I laughed. "Well, that's good to know. I can't wait to see him." I took a seat beside them and stared at the front door of the lobby.

"So, you two are going somewhere for a few days in between shows, right? He's being all secretive about it." Tia rolled her eyes.

"Yeah. He just told me to bring a few bathing suits. That's all I know," I said.

"I think that's sweet." Bailey smiled.

"No dude is going to plan my vacation for me. I find it annoying and sexist." Tia pushed to her feet and walked toward the bar. "You guys want a drink?"

Bailey and I both said we were okay.

"Ignore her. She doesn't do romance. And she's like a bull in a china shop, but she's harmless," Bailey said.

I laughed. "She's funny. She doesn't bother me."

"Good, she actually likes you, which is very rare," Bailey said with a laugh.

"What's so funny over here?" Cruz came up behind me and tipped my head back so he could kiss me.

"Jesus, get a room, Winslow," Tia said as she dropped down in the chair across from me with her martini in hand. She pulled a baggy out of her pocket and tossed a few pills back in her mouth. She didn't even try to hide it. She caught me staring, maybe even gaping as I watched her.

"*Vicodin*. Want one?" she asked.

"Um, no. I, er, sorry." I stuttered.

"You're adorable when you're nervous, Jade. This just takes the edge off. You might really benefit from it." Tia chugged her martini in one long sip.

"Don't offer her that shit. And it clearly doesn't work for you because you're acting fucking crazy," Cruz said, pulling me to my feet and wrapping his arms around me.

"I'm not crazy, asshole."

I hugged Lennon, Adam, and Luke as they walked over to join us. Dex stared at me, and I ignored him.

"Okay, we're out of here. Catch you guys in a few days," Cruz said.

"Yeah, enjoy your time off. You deserve it, buddy," Luke said, clapping Cruz on the shoulder.

I waved at the group as Cruz led me to the elevator. When we stepped on, he pressed me up against the wall and kissed me hard.

"Where are we going," I said, already breathless.

He pulled back to look at me. "It's a surprise. You brought your bathing suit, right? Although we could just skinny dip the whole time."

I shook my head and laughed as we stepped in his hotel room.

"Yes, I brought my suit. Are we spending the night here tonight?" I asked.

"No. Although now I'm questioning my decision to leave tonight because I finally have you all to myself."

"What's the hurry?" I teased, running my fingers through his hair, and pushing up on my tiptoes to kiss him.

Cruz had just finished his show, and his hair was a disheveled mess. His black fitted T-shirt accentuated every line of his defined abs and I wanted to appreciate every inch of him.

"Fuck," he muttered under his breath. I didn't miss his frustration when he pulled away. "We have a car waiting for us downstairs. Ponch is doing me a solid agreeing to fly us this late."

"We're leaving tonight?"

"Yeah. If I stick around here, those assholes will ask me about something for the band. Or Tia will need me to listen to a demo. I want to spend time alone with you. Uninterrupted. But right now, I want to strip you naked and have my way with you," he said, and his mouth came over mine again.

"There's time for that. Come on. Let's get out of here while we can." I laughed.

He grabbed his bag and we made our way out to the car without anyone recognizing or stopping him. It was a rarity. I didn't go anywhere with him anymore that he wasn't recognized. I was happy for Exiled, but I'd be lying if I didn't admit to hating it at times. We had no privacy when we were out in public. Especially in big cities. Back at school wasn't bad for some reason. Maybe because it was a college town. Sure people stared and took pictures, but they didn't interrupt our dinners or stop him on the street for selfies.

We were at the hangar in no time, and we greeted Ponch and took our seats.

"Are you going to tell me where we're going now? How long of a flight?"

"A few hours. Sleep, baby. I'll tell you when we get there." He kissed the top of my head, and I settled my cheek against his chest. His arms came around me, and I was the most content I'd been in a while. My eyes were heavy, and exhaustion set in.

———

I slept the entire flight and apologized for not sitting copilot with Ponch, for the landing. He didn't seem to mind. There was a car waiting for us when we landed, and then we got on a boat to take us *God knows where.*

"We can't get there in a car?" I asked, as the wind whipped past us, and the boat glided through the ocean like it was sliding on silk.

"Nope. There are no cars on the island. No grocery stores or restaurants. It's very slow and peaceful. I thought we could both use it. A couple uninterrupted days," Cruz said, his arms were wrapped around me and my back rested against his chest as I looked out at the water. I tucked my hair behind my ears as the wind whipped around us.

"Really?" I asked, turning to face him. "Just me and you, huh? Where are we?"

"It's called Little Gasparilla Island, on the west coast of Florida between Sarasota and Ft. Myers. You can only get to the island by private boat or water taxi. My grandfather has a home here that hardly ever gets used, because you know my dad, he likes a crowd and a lot of attention. The thought of privacy probably scares the shit out of him." Cruz laughed and pulled me back down against him.

"That's so cool. When was the last time you were here?" I asked. Water droplets danced across my cheeks as we sped through the water.

"Man, Lennon and I loved this place when we were kids. We came with Mom a few times when my grandfather was out here vacationing. I haven't been here in years, but I always loved it. It's peaceful. No one will bother us. The house is at the end of the island, so it's very private, even for Little Gasparilla."

"Oh my gosh, I'm excited."

"Me too." He kissed the top of my head, and we pulled into a dock in front of a large house on stilts that sat back a few feet from the water.

"Thank you for the ride. We'll see you in a few days," Cruz said, handing the man who drove the boat some cash.

"Yep. If you need anything before then, just call my cell," he said before he pulled away.

The yellow house was two levels, raised on stilts with baby blue shutters and a white wrap-around porch. The lower level had white stairs leading down to the ground, and we wheeled our bags toward the house. A large boat sat beside the dock, and Cruz said we could take it out later.

He grabbed my bag and carried both of our suitcases up the stairs. The muscles in his back flexed as I walked behind him, and I couldn't look away.

"You checking me out, Jade?" He set our bags down and wheeled them inside.

I laughed. "I guess I'm busted."

As soon as we were inside, Cruz pushed me back against the door and kissed me. "God, I missed you, baby."

"I missed you too. I'm so happy we get to spend a few days alone," I said, against his mouth. He had a dusting of scruff peppering his chin, and I ran my fingertips along his jaw.

He pulled away. "You must be starving. My mom had the house-keeper stock the place with food. She was really happy we were coming here."

"That was sweet of her. And, of course I can always eat." I scanned the room. Light colored wood floors ran throughout the main floor, as far as I could see. There were floor-to-ceiling windows every which way I looked, and crystal blue water sparkled in the distance. It was breathtaking.

Two white over-sized couches took up most of the family room. Navy and white striped pillows with red anchors sat on the sofas. The beach-themed home was large yet managed to feel cozy at the same time. The kitchen was all white. White cabinets, white shiny counters, and a large white chandelier hung over the breakfast nook table.

Cruz pulled out some deli meat, pre-made pasta and potato salad, and two bottles of water. I grabbed some plates and we took it all out on the porch to eat. There were two tables on the deck and a porch swing with white throw pillows which hung beside the table.

The view was incredible. Turquoise water shimmering in the sunlight surrounded by white sandy beaches. The air smelled like salt and sunshine and I breathed it in.

"This is unbelievable," I said, taking a seat beside him.

"Yeah. I've always liked it here. Away from the chaos, right?"

I smiled, and the way he looked at me had my stomach doing all sorts of little flips.

I moved to settle on his lap. I needed to be close to him, and I knew he needed it too. He rolled up a piece of turkey and handed it to me.

"You're feeding me now?" I laughed.

"You need fuel, woman. I plan on giving you quite the workout while we're here," he said before he leaned down to kiss my neck.

"Is that so? What do you have in mind?" My cheeks heated at the thought. It had been a few weeks since we'd seen one another, and I'd missed him.

"You know, lots of long walks and kayaking," he teased, and I swatted his shoulder.

He lifted me out of the seat and stood, holding me like some kind of baby.

"You know you don't have to carry me around. I do have legs." My head fell back, and I chuckled as he dropped me on the couch.

"How about we go for a swim first. Cool off. Wait till you see how nice this water is." He reached for my shirt and pulled it over my head.

"Sounds like a plan. I need to go grab my suit," I said, my voice breathless and gravelly.

"Why? I'm just going to take it off you as soon as we get out there."

"No way. I'm not walking out there naked. It's broad daylight." We'd flown through the night and the sun had just come up when we arrived. I was not prancing outside naked for everyone on the island to see.

He pushed up and walked across the room. "Stay put."

"So bossy," I said.

He handed me a robe and pulled me to my feet. He tossed two

towels on the couch and dropped down on his knees, pushing my jeans and panties down and helping me when I stepped out of them. Goosebumps spread across my skin, and I pulled the robe on. Cruz yanked his T-shirt off and dropped his pants, without a care in the world. I couldn't look away, and he laughed when he caught me staring.

"Someone's excited to see me, huh?" I teased.

"Oh, you think that's funny, do you?" He slipped his hand beneath my robe and stroked between my thighs, causing me to gasp. "I think someone's equally excited."

I pushed his hand away and laughed, burying my face in my hands. He grabbed a towel, wrapping it around his waist, before leading me outside.

"I can't believe you still get embarrassed with me. I love to see how much I turn you on, baby."

We walked down to the water and I was surprised that there wasn't a soul in sight. I looked both ways, and the beach was completely desolate.

"Wow. You weren't kidding. It is private."

He reached for the belt on my robe and tugged it open. "I told you. Come on, let's go in."

He dropped his towel and I looked around once more to make sure no one would see us, before dropping my robe. I let go of his hand and ran in the water. I needed to find cover fast. I wasn't as confident strutting around naked on the beach as my boyfriend was. His laughter bellowed out behind me and I dropped down in the water and blanketed myself in a sea of turquoise. The water was cold, but it felt good. I was hot and sweaty, and it was refreshing. Cruz walked up beside me, taking my hand and pulling me out deeper. He stood and the water came to the top of his chest. I pointed my toes barely able to find the bottom.

"I'll hold you, shorty," he said, smiling as he pulled me against him, and I wrapped my legs around his waist.

"I'm not short. You're just tall." My arms came around his neck and his honey-brown gaze sparkled with gold and orange flecks where the sun hit him from above.

"Ah, this feels good. I'm so glad we're here. God, I fucking missed you. Can't wait for this long-distance bullshit to be over," he said.

"Me too. We're almost there. And I'll be with you all summer, so that will help."

I arched my back and dipped my hair in the water, pushing it away from my face with my hands before I returned them to his neck.

"You're so fucking beautiful," he whispered.

"Stop. I look horrible. I haven't even looked in a mirror since yesterday." I laughed.

"You're so pretty, baby."

His mouth found mine, and I sighed against his lips. We'd get to spend four days just being together, and it felt damn good. My fingers tangled in his hair, and he held my face in his hands. His tongue found mine, and my body started to grind against his of its own volition. The water slapped against all his hardness. Every inch of him was strong and firm. His desire throbbed beneath me, driving me mad with need. His hands were on my hips, shifting me just above him. I gasped, as we moved together in perfect rhythm. His hands moved up my back, tangling in my hair, and his gaze locked with mine.

"I want to watch you come apart for me, baby," he said.

His words undid me. My head fell back, and I cried out my release as he followed me over the edge.

"Oh my gosh," I panted, burying my head in his neck.

"Not a bad way to start our vacation, right?" He laughed before kissing me again. "I always need, *more Jade*."

I pushed his wild hair back from his face, studying his features. I'd never seen a more perfect person. I ran my fingers over his scruff, admiring his chiseled jaw. "I always need more Cruz Winslow, too."

"I'm all yours. Always."

The water lapped against our bodies and I bobbed up and down a little. "Good to know. What do you want to do now? Should we take that kayak out?" I asked. Dad and I loved to kayak, and I was looking forward to showing off my skills.

"Yeah. I'm down. Can we do it naked or are you going to insist on wearing clothing?"

"We're not kayaking naked," I said with a laugh. "Let's grab our suits. We can go adventure around the island."

He carried me all the way in and set me down when we reached the shore. As I wrapped myself in the robe, I watched Cruz as he gazed out at the water. I never wanted this moment to end.

———

"Are you even rowing?" I panted, glancing over my shoulder, shooting daggers at him.

My boyfriend sat back, his legs were crossed at the ankles and hanging off the side of the kayak. I was determined to paddle out to this little alcove I spotted up ahead, but it was further away than I anticipated. We'd kayaked every day since we'd arrived, and I loved it. Cruz definitely preferred to sit back and enjoy the scenery.

"Baby, I don't need to. You're treating this like an Olympic sport. I'm just here to watch my girl go for the gold."

I used my paddle to shovel water in his face. He laughed, before grabbing me from behind and tipping our kayak. We both went under, and his hands were on me as we surged to the surface.

"I can't believe you tipped us over. We'll never get there now that you capsized us," I said, pushing the hair back from my face and trying to hide my smile, while treading water to stay afloat.

"I wish we could stay here forever." Cruz kissed me before flipping our boat over and helping me back in. He jumped up and flopped into the kayak and I tried my best to steady us so we didn't fall over again.

We'd spent the last few days in the water, lounging on the beach, and playing board games. Just me and Cruz. We'd talked about the future, and pretty much had sex in every room in the house as well as multiple times in the water. I'd never been so relaxed. We were going to be fine. Summer was just around the corner and this was exactly what we needed. Cruz barely drank the entire time we were here, and the only prescription he was taking was the Adderall. He promised he'd stop taking it as soon as he was done touring. He'd kept his promise to cut back on the drinking and I was proud of him.

"I wish we didn't have to go back either. This is my new favorite place. It's so peaceful."

"Yeah, we only saw the one couple yesterday. It's been so quiet. I love it," he said.

"Are you referring to the couple we smoked in the kayak race?" I teased.

"Yeah. That eighty-year-old couple with a cooler on the back of their kayak, who had no idea we were in a race. They were out for a picnic and you fucking left them in your wake." He laughed hysterically and I couldn't help but join in.

"That guy bowed up when we pulled along-side him. It was *go-time*. I can't help it if I smoked him. And no thanks to you. I don't even think you put your paddle in the water once," I said, rolling my eyes.

I stopped and moved to sit between his legs. I took in the beautiful surroundings. The water glistened in the light shining down, and the sound of the water lapping against the shore filled the space around us. Tranquility at its finest. All of our hard work to stay together had paid off. We were in the final stretch, and we were closer than ever.

And I'd never been happier.

sixteen

. . .

Cruz

"YOU'VE BEEN in a perpetual bad mood since your trip to Gilligan's Island, Winslow," Tia said as we exited the tour bus and made our way into the hotel.

"It's called Little Gasparilla Island." I rolled my eyes and stepped on the elevator. She was right though. I was being a dick. Spending those days with Jade reminded me of what I was missing. Not only my fucking amazing girl but the normalcy she brought to my life. Stepping away from this chaos proved how much pressure I'd been under. The label was up my ass for more lyrics. Luke still hadn't locked either of the two dudes they were considering down. The hours were brutal. I was trying not to drink and had cut back on my pill intake, and I was miserable. I never knew what day it was, or when it was time to sleep. I was a walking zombie. And Tia was annoying as hell as she insisted on reminding me daily how grumpy I was.

Lennon was crazy fucking in love with Bailey, and I was happy for him. My brother was in a good place. I could finally step away without carrying the weight of the world and the fear that I might be hurting him. But for now, I was stuck in this limbo state and I hated it. Adam was the only one I really talked to about it, because he understood my misery. He loved the band, but he wasn't like Lennon. He could see a life beyond it. For now, it was his livelihood, and he kicked ass at it, but I could see him stepping away in a few years. And Dex—that little prick was on my last fucking nerve. He brought chicks back to our suite continually. All of us had girls now, yet he continued to push these girls on us. It pissed me off. He was drunk more than he was sober, in fact, I couldn't remember the last time I'd seen Dex sober. Not since we'd been out on tour.

"Ah, so that's what you're crabby about. My lack of knowledge in geography?" she grumbled in the elevator.

"I'm fucking tired. We've been traveling more than usual, and I'm burned out."

"Yeah. I'm ready for a weekend off, too." She walked beside me down to her room and pulled her baggy out of her back pocket and popped a few pills in her mouth.

"You sure are taking that shit a lot," I said.

"Are you a doctor now?"

"Nope. Suit yourself. Just know a pill popper when I see one," I said, stopping at my door and swiping the keycard.

"Fuck you, Winslow." She stormed to her room.

Jesus, I needed a break from all these people. I dropped on my bed and called Jade. She answered the phone groggily, and the sound of her voice calmed me.

"Hey, baby," I said. Her room was dark, but I could see the outline of her pretty face.

"How was the show?"

"Good. Crazy. Long," I said, tugging my shirt over my head.

"You sound tired. You okay?" She turned on her side, and the light from her phone illuminated her, allowing me to make out her features.

"Yeah. Just need a shower and some sleep. I love you."

"Love you, more. I'll call you in the morning, okay?" she said, and her sleepy smile did crazy shit to me.

"Yep. Talk to you in the morning."

"Good night," she said before we disconnected the call.

After I rinsed off, I climbed into bed, desperate for sleep. My head hit the pillow and I was gone.

———

A banging on my bedroom door startled me from sleep. The room was still dark, so I knew it wasn't morning yet. I was going to kick someone's ass for waking me up.

"Cruz," Luke shouted through the door.

I stumbled across the room and flipped on a light. What the fuck was going on? This wasn't like him at all. The dude didn't party, and he wasn't an asshole.

I yanked the door open.

Luke stood on the other side, and the look on his face made my heart race.

"What's wrong?"

"It's your mom. She's in the hospital. I need to get you and Lennon on a plane now."

He stepped inside and shut the door. I dropped to sit on the edge of the bed. "What happened? Is she okay?

"I don't know Cruz. Your dad said she never woke up. She's in a coma."

"A coma? How the fuck is she in a coma? Was there an accident?"

"That's all I know. It's not good. Your dad is a mess," Luke said.

I pulled on some joggers, a T-shirt, and a hoodie. I grabbed my phone and my Adderall and dropped it in my backpack. I was going to need to be coherent today.

"Where's Lennon?"

"He's getting dressed and meeting us downstairs in ten minutes. See you down there," Luke said as he answered his phone and stepped out in the hall.

———

We made it to Los Angeles in two hours and found Dad sitting beside Mom's bed. He looked the way I felt. Like he couldn't figure out what the fuck was going on. I stared at my mother, hooked up to tubes and machines, looking lifeless. Lennon dropped down on Mom's bed and sobbed. I didn't cry. For some reason I couldn't access that emotion. I'd been through this before, with my brother. Maybe I'd lost my ability to feel the devastation of what was happening. Or maybe I didn't want to believe another family member had numbed themselves into a fucking coma. That's what we'd been told. She'd taken too many pills. Mixed all sorts of prescriptions and washed it all down with half a bottle of vodka. And she never woke up.

"She's going to be fine, boys. We have the best doctors in the world working on her. This was a terrible accident." My father met my gaze as the words left his mouth.

"A terrible accident?" I repeated his words.

"Yes."

"We sure have a lot of those in our family, huh?" I said.

"What the fuck does that mean? This was an accident, Cruz. She's going to be fine." My father pushed to his feet and started to pace the length of the room.

The beeping in the background from the monitors irritated me. A reminder of where we were.

"By definition, an accident means that something occurs unintentionally. Popping a shit ton of pills is an intentional act," I said, and my gaze locked with his.

He pointed his finger in my face. "I don't want to hear your psycho-babble right now. Show some fucking respect."

Respect? I didn't have any for this man. He was the reason my mom was here. He was the reason Lennon had been here not so long ago.

Lennon gasped from where he sat on the bed as he stared at his phone screen. His words broke on a sob, "You motherfucker."

I moved to my feet as my brother charged my father, slamming him up against the wall across from Mom's bed. I scrambled to maneuver between them, shoving them apart. As much as I wanted to kick my father's ass, this wasn't the time or the place. It was also very unlike Lennon to stand up to my father, so I was on edge as I held my brother back while my father straightened his dress shirt.

"You fucking did this. You piece of shit," Lennon spat. He shook his arms, breaking free of me and moved to the bed to grab his phone. He held the screen in front of my face. "He fucking cheated on her."

Fuck me.

I did not see this coming. The only normal thing I'd ever had in my life—my parents actually loved one another. Almost obsessively. My mother gave up all her dreams to follow my father. Hell, she gave up being a mother to Lennon and me during our childhood, all to support this man. I'd never understood it. But now, we didn't even have that? The final nail in the coffin for the world's most fucked up family.

I didn't charge him. Didn't speak. There was nothing to say.

"We're fine. It was a mistake. It's already taken care of," Dad said, dropping to sit in the chair beside Mom. He ran a hand down his face, and his hair was a rumpled mess.

For the first time in my life, he actually looked broken. He hadn't been affected when Lennon overdosed and nearly died. But today, it was all catching up to him. And I was fucking glad. I wanted that motherfucker to feel what we all felt in the wake of his selfish, narcissistic behavior. He was a destructive prick and karma was a bitch, and she was paying him one hell of a visit.

"It's taken care of. Meaning you paid off your whore and now everyone should just get over it? I don't think anyone's fine here, old man. This is anything but fine. Look at your fucking wife. She's lying in a bed after trying to take her own life because the man she loves betrayed her," I said.

I grabbed his chin between my thumb and my finger and yanked it in the direction of my mother. I wanted him to acknowledge what he'd done. To actually own something for one time in his miserable fucking life.

He didn't push my hand away. He didn't fight me at all. Instead he wept. His sobs vibrated off the walls, and I dropped my hand and stormed out of the room. Luke stood in the waiting room along with our security team of four men. Yeah, Exiled traveled with security now, which meant I never got a fucking minute to myself.

"Cruz, how is she?" Luke asked.

"Not good. No news. Has the story broke yet?" I said, shoving my hands in my pockets. Lennon had seen something on the internet, so I assumed it was out there now.

"Yeah, it's still early so we have a few hours to get in front of it. We'll have you and Lennon release a statement this afternoon and ask your fans to respect your privacy. But, honestly Cruz, your father's a public figure and people love a cheating scandal, and with the band's popularity right now, I think it's going to be a social media nightmare," Luke said, pausing to clear his throat.

A blur in my peripheral had me turning, and Jade rushed into my arms. I buried my head in her neck and took in her scent.

Sunshine and goodness.

"I got here as soon as I could." She dropped her backpack on the chair beside us and studied me. I'd called her from the plane, but I'd told her not to come. Jade had a shit ton of tests this week, and she didn't need to deal with my bullshit.

"I told you to stay at school. There's nothing you can do here. She's in a coma," I said, wrapping my arms around her and kissing the top of her head.

"I want to be here for you." She hugged me tighter.

Lennon stepped out in the lobby. "Cruz, the doctor's in the room. Do you want to speak to him?"

"Yeah. I'm coming." I kissed Jade on the forehead, and she dropped down to sit beside Luke.

Dr. Song proceeded to fill us in on all the unknowns. This wasn't new for me. I'd heard all of this when Lennon was in the hospital; however, Lennon hadn't been in a coma. There were a lot of factors that were unknown as my mother was currently not responsive. Injury to the brain can occur during overdose. He filled us in on hypoxic brain injury, which is a lack of oxygen to the brain, not uncommon after overdose. We wouldn't know the extent of the damage until she was awake. The paramedics had administered Naxolene, which is used after an opioid overdose, in an attempt to revive her. Jesus Christ. This was my family. This was our norm now.

"Any way of knowing when she'll wake up?" I asked.

"Unfortunately, it's impossible to say. It could be hours, months or years," Dr. Song said, flipping some papers on his clipboard and meeting my gaze.

"Unacceptable. We brought her here because you're supposed to be the best. You've got to have a better answer than that. You need to fix her," my father shouted, startling everyone in the room. He hadn't heard a word Dr. Song had just said. The man was on *send*. He didn't listen. He just demanded. And this time his money couldn't fix the situation.

"Mr. Winslow, I understand your frustration. Unfortunately, there isn't a doctor in the world who could tell you when your wife will wake up. We are doing everything on our end to make that happen, but it's up to her now."

"Didn't you go to Harvard Medical School?" My father continued his tirade, pacing the room as he barked at the doctor.

"Yes, I did. And if you don't feel comfortable with me as her physician, feel free to bring in someone else. I can only tell you what I know." Dr. Song shook mine and my brother's hands, before nodding at my father and exiting the room.

"You're an asshole," I said when it was just Dad, Lennon, and me. And my lifeless mother who was hanging on by a thread while her cheating husband berated everyone for trying to help her.

"She will get the best medical care out there," Dad said, his hands fisted at his sides as he stared out the window.

"Do you know who he had the affair with?" My brother's voice was just above a whisper.

"Not now, Lennon." My father huffed and moved back to his chair beside my mother.

"Does it matter? I don't give a shit who she is." I stared out the window. A little girl walked between a man and a woman, who I assumed were her parents. They each held one of her little hands and swung her between them. Her small feet barely touched the ground and her head fell back in a fit of giggles. I'd never walked like that with my parents. Couldn't remember a time I'd ever held my father's hand. Or giggled in his presence. Even as a little boy. He'd never been that guy.

"He's been seeing Victoria Regate. He tried to end it and she decided to tell Mom." My brother stared at my father with disgust as the words left his mouth.

I wasn't hearing him correctly. He must mean Victoria's mother, Lana Regate. "Victoria or Lana?"

"Victoria." Lennon pushed to his feet and stormed over to stand beside me.

Victoria was the daughter of my father's attorney and closest friend, David Regate. She and Lennon had dated on and off for a few years.

"What the fuck. What is she, twenty?" I stared at my father in disbelief.

"Nineteen," Lennon said, his arms folded over his chest and absolute hatred poured from him.

"Enough. It was a mistake. Let's call it my mid-life crisis."

I shook my head. Unbelievable. "Your entire life has been a mid-life crisis. You've been seeing a teenager. Cheating on your wife and betraying your best friend. Not to mention your son used to date her. This is all kinds of fucked up. Even for you. The press is going to have a field day with this. She's younger than Lennon and I. How could you do that to Mom? To David and Lana? Do you have no shame?"

"Trust me. I'm not proud of my actions. But I don't need my sons judging me." He stood and shoved his hands in his pockets.

"Why not? I'm older than your girlfriend." I snorted.

Lennon left the room. Bailey had just arrived, and he'd had enough.

"I screwed up. I get it. Your mother's going to be fine. She has to be. And I'll spend the rest of my life making it up to her. That's why I ended it with Victoria, because your mother is the best thing that ever happened to me."

"You don't get brownie points for breaking up with your teenage girlfriend. You know that, right? Cause it feels like you think you should be applauded."

"Listen, Cruz. The shit's about to hit the fan. The story is going to go public. I've offered a lot of money to stop it, but Victoria is telling anyone who will listen. That's why I filled Lennon in on the situation. Right now, they just know I had an affair. Fuck. When they find out it's with David's daughter, I'm fucked."

"I mean, your wife is fighting for her life, but by all means, let's worry about your image. You're an asshole. Focus on Mom right now," I hissed.

He was right though. Our lives were about to become a media frenzy. All while my mom lies there in a coma. What the actual fuck was wrong with my family? I stepped out of the room and stood in the hallway. From where I stood, I could see Jade. She sat on one side of Lennon, while Bailey sat on the other. Lennon's girlfriend had just flown in to be with him. I wanted my girl as far from this shit as she could get.

Jade's books were spread out on the waiting room table. She was going to try to study, take care of me, and herself. She'd barely recovered from having mono, and here I was dragging her back down again. She didn't have a clue the shitstorm that was coming. She would be hounded by the press, too. All because she was dating me. The light coming from behind her shone around her like some sort of halo.

I spoke to Luke and texted Ponch to make arrangements. Jade looked up and met my gaze as I walked toward her. I stopped at the table and grabbed her books and started shoving them in her backpack.

"What are you doing?" She rose to her feet and wrapped her delicate fingers around my bicep.

"Ponch is taking you home. I have a car coming to get you in fifteen minutes," I said, closing her laptop and sliding it into the backpack as well.

"What? No. I want to be here with you," she said, her tone more frantic than I'd ever heard it.

"Jade, you don't need to be here. Shit's about to explode in our faces. My mom may not wake up for months. There's nothing for you to do here. You need to be back at school, kicking ass."

"I don't care. This is where I want to be." She crossed her arms over her chest and held her ground. I normally liked Jade's strength, but I wasn't in the mood for it today. I needed her to go home, needed her to remove herself from this situation. Unfortunately, this situation was my life.

I took her hand and led her to the far corner of the waiting room. "Listen to me. My father had an affair with a nineteen-year-old girl. A family friend. His best friend's daughter, actually. The story is about to break. I need to get you out of here. They will probably bombard you for a few days. But at least if you're back at home you can focus on school. I need to deal with this."

"Why won't you let me help you?" she said, and when I met her gaze my chest squeezed. Her green eyes welled with emotion. Sadness. Devastation. The Winslow family was like a wrecking ball. Taking out everyone in their path.

"Baby, I appreciate that you came here *so much*. But it will help me more if you go home. I don't want to take you from school, from your research, you know? I promise to keep you posted, okay? Please, please just do this for me."

She let out a long sigh, and she used the butt of her hand to swipe at the tears running down her face. "Okay."

"Luke has the driver pulling up at the side entrance. Apparently, the press is camped out downstairs. I can't imagine how bad it'll be when the whole story comes out." I led her down a long corridor.

Jade was quiet when I pushed the door open and saw the car in the back alley.

"Hey," I said, lifting her chin to meet my gaze.

"Okay, then. Keep me posted."

She was wounded. I got it. But I was protecting her whether she liked it or not. She didn't know how bad this would get. I worried about Jade all the time, and right now I needed to focus on my mom and my brother. Make sure my mother would pull out of this and Lennon wouldn't get pulled into the abyss of hell. I could feel everything slipping away, maybe it symbolized my life. I had no control over anything, but the one thing I could do is save my girlfriend from going down with me.

"I love you, baby. You know that," I whispered against her ear, when I wrapped my arms around her.

The driver walked to our side of the car and took her bag for her.

"I love you, more." She held her head high and backed away before stepping in the car. My eyes locked with hers through the window, and tears streamed down her pretty face.

A piece of me broke as I watched her drive away. It felt more final than I meant it to. Maybe I was preparing for the inevitable.

I'd always feared that I'd taint her in some way.

Jade was so good, and my family was so fucked up. And whether I liked it or not, I was a part of them. A part of something ugly. And I didn't want Jade anywhere near it. I'd seen what the press would do when they had a story like this. And the Regates were going to crucify my father. And they were justified in doing so, but it meant we were going to be dragged through the mud by the media.

I picked up my phone and called Dr. Grove. "Hey. I'm going to need a new prescription of Xanax. Maybe you can up the dose."

"Sure. I'll call it in now. Text me your location and I'll find a pharmacy."

"Thanks," I said before ending the call.

And I couldn't wait to stop feeling all the shit that was threatening to pull me under.

For the first time in my life—I really felt like a Winslow.

seventeen

. . .

Jade

IT HAD BEEN two days since I'd been home and I'd barely heard from Cruz. I wished I hadn't left. He was pulling away from me. I could feel it in every bone in my body. He sounded weird on the phone, and I knew in my gut he was using something to cope. I didn't know if it was booze or pills, but he was so distant and short with me. I asked him if he was taking something, and he ripped my head off. Said he was fine and now wasn't the time to question him.

I sent texts and called several times a day. He'd only responded twice. The texts were short. I knew he was going through a lot, but it was more than that. It was like everything had piled up and he was done fighting it. Maybe he was done fighting for us. Fighting for me.

I knew it had to be an outside factor, because Cruz and I had been through a lot and he'd never stopped fighting for us. Why now? What was different? There was no emotion there when we spoke. He was completely detached.

The story had come out, and I don't think anyone could have prepared for what followed. Steven Winslow's affair with his best friend's teenage daughter took on a life of its own. Photos of Cruz's parents and their family were on every news channel, splashed all over the internet, and the topic of almost every conversation I overheard. Lennon's overdose had come out in the story, and his photo was splashed all over social media as well. Victoria had spilled a lot of details about Cruz's family. She was clearly determined to take Steven Winslow down, and she had succeeded in destroying his reputation, and his family was left in the crosshairs.

"Jade," Ari called out when she stepped inside. "Are you home?"

"Yeah. I'm back here." I moved to my feet, leaving my bedroom to meet her in the living room.

"There're four dudes camped out front. Did they follow you when you went to class?" My roommate set her backpack on the couch and dropped to sit.

"Yep. I'm just ignoring them."

"I should try that. I told them to fuck off. Probably not the best thing to do." Ari laughed, and I forced a smile.

"I'm sorry you have to deal with this," I said, reaching for my phone in my back pocket when it vibrated.

"Don't be silly. It's not your fault. Is that Cruz?"

"Yeah."

CRUZ

She's awake and she seems okay. She's talking normal and is pissed at my dad, so she must remember what happened.

Oh my gosh, I'm so happy she's awake.

Tears ran down my face and relief flooded. Thank God she was okay. I watched the three little dots disappear. He wasn't going to respond again. That was all I was going to get. I swiped at my cheeks.

"What did he say?" Ari asked, concern filled her blue eyes.

"She's awake and she seems to be okay." I smiled, but I still couldn't shake the sinking feeling that something was going on with Cruz.

My roommate hugged me and ran off to take a shower. I ordered a pizza for us, and we'd both hunker down and study. Hopefully the press would back off now that Juliette was awake, and they'd let

Cruz's family heal in private. I called my dad and Sam and filled them in.

My dad sent a police officer friend to drive by a couple times to scare off the men huddled out front, but it was public property and they could park themselves on the sidewalk if they wanted to.

My phone buzzed a little past two o'clock in the morning and I reached for it.

Cruz.

I was happy he'd FaceTimed me. I hadn't seen his face in a few days, and I missed him terribly. I sat up in bed, anxious to finally talk to him. See how he was handling everything. Hear how his mom was doing.

"Hey," he said, his eyes looking everywhere but at me. My stomach twisted. Cruz never avoided my gaze.

"Hey. How are you? How's your mom?" I tucked my hair behind my ear.

"She's doing well. She kicked my dad out of the hospital, so her memory is intact." He chuckled, but his smile didn't reach his eyes.

"How long will they keep her there?" I hated how distant we were being.

"I don't know. She doesn't want to go home with my dad. She's talking about living on her own, getting a divorce, possibly going into a program. God, Jade. My family is so fucked up," he whispered, and my chest ached.

"Every family has issues. No one is perfect, Cruz."

"Really? Drugs and overdoses. Affairs with teenagers. Now probably divorce and years of fighting over money. Lennon isn't speaking to my father either. So, the man calls me every five fucking seconds. Wants to know what's happening with Mom. Wants me to speak to her. We can't leave the hospital without being bombarded by the press. Luke bought us time, but we have to be back in California for five shows next week," he said. He finally looked up to meet my gaze, and my heart sank. He looked sad.

Anxious.

Broken.

"Do you want me to come there? I could come tonight. Tomorrow. Whatever you need." The urgency and desperation in my voice surprised me. He was pulling away and I was holding on for dear life.

"Listen, Jade, I um, I think I should distance myself from you for a while." He looked away after the words left his mouth.

"What? No. Why would you distance yourself from me?" My voice broke on a sob.

"Because this isn't good for you. Hell, it isn't good for me, but I have no choice but to deal with it. You can separate yourself from this. You have so much going on in your life, and you don't need my shit," he said.

"Oh my God, you're breaking up with me, aren't you? At least have the balls to say it." My heart raced as the realization that he didn't want to be with me set in.

"Fuck, baby, I'm sorry. I can't be with you right now. I can't be with anyone. I'm doing this for you." He looked up at me, but his honey-brown gaze was so distant that a piece of my heart shattered as I took him in. He wasn't there. He showed no emotion. Like he was empty.

"You're doing this for me? Stop lying. Are you taking something, you don't seem like yourself. Are you back on Xanax?" I asked, concern taking over.

He rolled his eyes. "I'm doing what I need to do right now. I'm trying to keep it together, and I don't need to be judged. Nor do I need a babysitter. This is exactly why I need to let you go right now. I need to figure things out."

Wow. Was he really choosing pills over me? He'd called me a babysitter. This wasn't the Cruz that I knew. I was hurt and pissed at the same time. I couldn't believe this was happening.

"So, you're going to numb yourself just like your mom did because that worked out so well for her?" I croaked.

"You're right, baby. I'm a fuck up. Always will be. You can do a lot better than me." He smirked. His gaze cold and distant. My chest squeezed and my bottom lip betrayed me when it trembled so much it was difficult to talk.

"Don't say that. I've never thought that."

"I can't do this anymore," he said, his voice shook, but he kept his mask in place.

"You can't do what? You can't fight for us? For me?"

"I'm tired of fighting." He looked up, and his gaze was wet with emotion. Was he still in there, somewhere?

"I'll fight for both of us," I said, sounding like a pathetic beggar as I tried to cover my mouth when another sob escaped.

"That's the thing—I don't want you to." His face gave away nothing, and he stared at me. All the emotion left his eyes, and he shrugged. "I want you to let me go."

"Okay. Got it," I said, taking long, labored breaths between my words.

"I do love you, Jade. Goodbye." He ended the call.

I sat there in complete shock for a few minutes as the tears streamed down my face. I couldn't see a future without Cruz in it. I didn't want to. He may have left me—but he took my heart with him.

"So, my family does this crazy thing. We've never told anyone what it was before now, but I ran it past my mom, dad, and brother and they all agreed you are part of the family and I should share it with you," Ari said.

She stood in front of me where I sat on the couch in our living room. I'd only left the house for class and research over the last three days since Cruz had broken up with me. The guys who'd been camped out had moved on since there was no story here. I'd never spoken to them, and they'd gotten the message. If they only knew Cruz and I weren't dating anymore, they'd have a whole new slew of questions. And I didn't hold any of the answers.

"And what is this crazy thing your family does?" I asked, setting my book aside.

Mono had been physically exhausting for me, but nothing could prepare me for a broken heart. Broken hearts could kick mono's ass any day of the week. There was an ache in my chest that never went away. I couldn't eat, couldn't sleep, and I cried every time I was alone. I hated being that girl. The one who fell apart when her boyfriend had no use for her anymore. I'd been tossed aside like I'd never meant anything to him. And it hurt so bad it was hard to wrap my head around. I hadn't told my dad or Sam that Cruz and I weren't together anymore. Only Ari knew that he'd broken up with me. Dad would worry, and Sam would be pissed. I didn't have the energy for either. I leaned on Ari the most. She understood what I was going through. Cruz had gone radio silent on me. I'd not heard from him since our FaceTime call when he told me he was done and he wanted me to let him go. I'd broken down and called him the next day, but he didn't pick up nor respond. I'd sent a few texts asking if we could talk about it—and nothing. Not even a response. He'd erased me from his world. Like I never existed. And I didn't know how to fight for him. How do you fight for someone that wants nothing to do with you?

"Get up and come to the bathroom with me." Ari offered her hand and led me to our little powder room off the living room.

"What are we doing in here?" I rolled my eyes, too tired to think. We were crammed in the small space with beadboard covering the bottom half of the white walls.

"Are you ready to feel better?" She eyed me curiously.

"I don't think it's possible."

"I'm not promising to cure you overnight, but you'll feel better than you do right now, I promise." Her blonde hair was tied back, and she grabbed my hands.

"I'm waiting…" I yawned.

"Okay, so I'm going to count to three, and then you and I are going to say these words: *fuck those bitches*. We're going to repeat it, louder and louder until you feel better."

"You're kidding me, right?"

"Do you trust me?" she asked.

"Unfortunately, yes."

"Let's do this. One, two, three—*fuck those bitches*," we shouted together. She held both of my hands and we repeated it over and over. Louder and louder. *"Fuck those bitches. Fuck those bitches. Fuck those bitches."*

We must have said it a dozen times before we both burst out in hysterics. I hadn't laughed in days. I laughed until I doubled over and dropped to the floor. I couldn't tell if I was laughing or crying, because I was doing both. And it felt good. And it felt terrible at the same time. Ari dropped down next to me.

"Just let it out, Jade." She rubbed my back and hugged me close to her. My laughter turned to sobs and the sounds that wracked my body weren't recognizable. Everything hurt. My arms and my legs. My throat and my chest. My eyes burned and my chapped lips stung. Everything was broken. I was broken. Cruz Winslow had broken me.

We sat on the bathroom floor for over an hour. We didn't speak. I sobbed and Ari held me.

"Who are the bitches?" I finally whispered. My breathing still labored.

"What?" She sat forward and turned to face me.

"Fuck those bitches. Who are the bitches?"

She burst out in laughter. "My bestie is such a little intellect. I don't know. My dad made it up. It's the world. It's whoever hurt you. For me, it was Blane Davenport my junior year in high school. The little wanker cheated on me and dumped me for Carrie Blank. Apparently, she put out. Then it was Mrs. Hiney for giving me the first and only '*B*' I've ever received in my life."

I forced a smile and wiped at my face. "And for me, it's Cruz. I just can't believe I'm sitting here on the floor crying over him. After everything we've been through. I never saw this coming."

"I know. I do think he's going through a lot, but I'm not here to defend him. He owed you more than what you got, that's for sure. So, *fuck those bitches.* It's his loss. He will rule the day he left you," she fist-bumped the air.

I laughed. "I think you mean rue the day. We don't need him ruling the day he dumped me."

I pushed to my feet and helped her up. "That makes more sense. Do you feel any better?"

"I actually do," I said.

I didn't. But I'd deal with it. The least I could do was put on a brave face and fake it.

———

The next few days I went through the motions. I went to class, worked long hours with Elaine doing research and even agreed to meet my dad and his girlfriend Sara for dinner. Sara worked with him and she'd always been more like family to me. They'd made it official, and I was happy that Dad wasn't alone anymore.

Cruz's family was still a daily topic on the internet and social media. His mother had been released and Cruz and Lennon had returned to their tour. There were divorce rumors, and rumors that Cruz and I were no longer together because I'd been MIA since everything happened.

But they were wrong. I wasn't MIA. I'd been erased. Like a faint, unimportant memory. I still cried myself to sleep every night, but I'd grown angry with each passing day. I'd texted him a few more times and he'd never responded to any of my texts and I wanted to kick myself for looking so desperate. I'd lost my boyfriend and my best friend in the blink of an eye. He'd been my person. My everything. And he'd wiped me away—like I'd never existed.

"Hey, Jady bug. You hungry?" Dad asked when I walked up to our favorite Italian restaurant and I found him and Sara standing outside waiting for me.

"Hey, guys." I hugged them both before walking inside.

We sat at a table in the back, and I tried to push thoughts of Cruz out of my head. We'd eaten here so many times together. Everything reminded me of him.

"So, what's happening?" Sara asked. "How's Cruz doing?"

I bit down on my bottom lip. Not telling them hadn't felt like a lie, but pretending Cruz and I were still together now, would definitely be a lie.

"Cruz and I aren't together anymore," I said as the waiter

approached, and we quickly placed our order. Dad stared at me with surprise and hurried the waiter away.

"What happened?" he asked.

"I don't really know. He said he wanted to distance himself from me. I guess I don't fit into his life anymore. He broke up with me." I shrugged, fighting hard to keep it together. *Fuck those bitches*, I whispered in my head over and over, in an attempt to act unaffected.

"Sweetie, I'm sorry. When did this happen?" Sara asked, scooting her chair closer to me.

I sat up straight, making it known I wasn't going to fall apart. I was done with all of that. Well, maybe not when I was alone, but I wouldn't break down in public.

"It's been a week now." I reached for the bread and forced myself to eat a bite. I'd been nauseous for days. Obviously, my heart and my appetite worked together, because I hadn't been hungry since the day Cruz dumped me.

"Why didn't you tell me? Are you okay?" Dad asked, taking my hand and squeezing it.

Oh, please don't do that. Please don't make me feel vulnerable.

"Please, Dad." A lump formed in my throat, and I stared up at the ceiling, exhaling slow breaths as I tried to stay in control.

"You don't always have to be tough, kiddo. It's okay to ask for help," he said.

"You can't help me with this. It's just something I have to deal with," I said.

Dad and Sara exchanged a look, and my father nodded at me. "Okay, but I'm here for you. Always. You know that, right? I'm much cooler than you think I am."

Sara and I laughed at the same time, and I swiped at the single tear that managed to get through my stoic front.

"Thanks, Dad. I'll keep that in mind." I forced a smile.

But just like every other day, my mind wandered back to Cruz. I wondered if he thought of me anymore or if he'd moved on already. If I was that easy to replace.

And then I remembered my new mantra.

Fuck those bitches.

And I pulled myself together.

———

When I got home that night, I pulled out Mom's journal. It somehow made me feel less alone.

April 3rd

Dear Journal,

I've been so overwhelmed lately. I have so much going on with school, and my job at the studio has turned in to a lot more hours than I ever expected. I'm not complaining. It's what I wanted. I need to focus and work hard if I'm ever going to get there.

Jack and I met for a quick cup of coffee today because I've barely had time to see him. He's busy at the fire academy, and my time is so limited, that I honestly feel like the crappiest girlfriend. I asked him if he was going to break up with me, because things wouldn't be slowing down for me until after finals. My heart ached at the thought of it, but I'd also get it if he wanted someone who could give him more.

He laughed. He said he'd never give up that easily, and he'd never give up on me. Not sure how I got so lucky to have the sweetest boyfriend, but I'm thankful for him. Okay, that's all the time I have today.

Ciao for now,

J.E.

I stared at Mom's words and my chest squeezed. I was happy my father had been supportive. Cruz had always supported me. He just wasn't willing to fight for me.

And nothing had ever hurt me more.

eighteen

. . .

Cruz

I TIPPED BACK the whiskey and relished the liquid as it burned the back of my throat. The days had bled together since we'd gone back on tour after our brief leave for *personal reasons*. You get a whole week off when your mom tries to take her own life to escape your father's cheating ass. I suppose I had Vicodin to thank for my current state of numbness. Tia was giving me a few pills a day, and when I mixed them with all the other shit I was taking and swallowed it all down with a shit ton of bourbon—I was able to forget for a while.

I had this ache in my chest that hadn't left since the last time I'd spoken to Jade. But sometimes doing the right thing sucked ass. I'd manned up and did what needed to be done. For her sake. Unlike my selfish prick of a father, I thought of my girl before myself. She could do a hell of a lot better than me. We both knew it. She was just too fucking loyal to admit it. Fuck, even that boy scout Brayden was better for her than I was. That's probably why I hated the preppy asshole.

The funny thing about numbing yourself is that the pain is always there when the buzz wears off. It meant you had to stay consistently fucked up. Lucky for me, I was pretty good at consumption. I was an overachieving asshole. It must run in the family.

I was basically surviving on booze and pills. I had no appetite anymore. I rarely slept. And I fucking hated everyone around me. I went through the motions when I performed. Everything a blur. The one thing that had come out of this was that I was writing a shit ton of music. Apparently, when you rip your fucking heart from your chest—the words tend to flow.

Who knew?

"Let's go, Cruz," my brother said from my doorway, studying the bottle in my hand like he hadn't been a drunk asshole for years who I'd taken care of before. Now he was a dickhead, judging my every move.

I wiped my mouth with the back of my sleeve. "I'm ready."

"You look like shit."

I rolled my eyes. "Do I look like I care?"

"No, you sure as fuck don't. Did you know Mom went into a program today? Checked herself in and everything." My brother walked beside me as he spoke, and it took all my strength not to stop and punch him in the face. He thought he was my moral compass now? Was he fucking kidding me?

"Why are you telling me like there's some kind of life lesson in it for me? I'm the fucking one who has put up with this entire family's bullshit for years. Don't come at me like you have a clue what I'm going through. You don't. I've been taking care of your ass for years, or have you forgotten?" I spewed. My anger was at an all-time high. I'd always been a moody fucker, but I was explosive now. And you know what? It felt fucking good. It was about time I told him how I felt.

"And I'm trying to be there for you now." Lennon paused and leaned against the wall as Tia finished up her set.

Bailey stood across from us, watching Lennon like she couldn't stand to be apart from him for a second. Fuck them. I didn't want to be around it.

"Okay, Let's go," Luke said, his gaze locked with mine.

Luke was the one person who hadn't turned on me yet. He respected my space and I appreciated it. But I felt like he was getting close to crossing the line just like Lennon and Adam had the last two weeks since Jade and I had broken up. Since my parents had separated. Since my mother had admitted she had a problem. Since the media had dragged my family through the fucking mud. Every dirty little secret had come out. This wasn't my father's first affair, and Victoria wasn't even his youngest prey. My parents apparently had a sex tape, and it had been leaked to the world for everyone's viewing pleasure. My brother's overdose was now common knowledge.

And everyone wanted to let me know how to feel about it. Adam had gotten in my face several times telling me I was out of control. Lennon was all over my case. And I didn't give a fuck what any of them thought.

I did, however, think of Jade's father over the last few weeks, and how relieved he must be that his daughter was no longer with me. I hated that my family was part of my story. They defined who I was. I was certainly judged for it. Photo's of me were splashed all over magazines like the poster boy for my parent's sins. People wondered when I'd snap and fuck up like everyone else in my family. Rumors had spread that Jade and I had broken up, but neither of us had made a statement. Hell, it wasn't like I wanted someone else. I wished it were that simple. I'd love to fuck other girls to get Jade out of my head. But it wasn't happening. I had no desire to be with anyone else. And I couldn't be with her. Setting Jade Moore free was the one decent thing I'd done in my life. I'd ignored her texts and calls after our breakup. What was the point in dragging the inevitable out? Nothing worth fighting for here. Dex patted me on the back as we walked toward the stage. Surprisingly, he bothered me the least right now. He stayed out of my business, or he was too fucked up to care. I respected it. He did his own thing. Not sure why that bothered me so much before. But I got it now.

"Let's go kick some ass," Dex said as I jogged out on stage.

Tia started to move our way and paused, jumped on me, wrapping her legs around my waist and kissed me before I could even process what was happening. She tasted like whiskey and lemons. Her fingers were tangled in my hair and I bit down on her bottom lip to cut off the kiss. My arms grabbed her hard and pushed her down.

"What the fuck was that," I shouted in her ear over the screaming cheers that came from the crowd.

"You can thank me later." She smiled and jogged off stage.

Christ. I shook my head and started the show. Everyone had lost their fucking minds.

I faked my way through the first set. I avoided all songs that had been written for Jade, which meant we were performing a lot of our old shit. When we finished up our show, I walked backstage.

"Don't ever pull that shit again." I pointed my finger at Tia.

"Relax, Winslow. You're single, I'm single. It makes for good press." She handed me two pills and I threw them back, chasing them down with a long pull of whiskey.

"I don't give a shit. I'll embarrass your ass the next time you pull a stunt like that."

"It's time to get back on the horse. Move on. You're a fucking rock star who broke up with his girlfriend. Why don't you act like it?" She rolled her eyes.

"Mind your own fucking business, Tia." I got in her face, and Adam and Lennon moved between us.

The crowd chanted. Of course, they wanted *More of Me,* which I refused to sing. I'd sang it too many times to Jade, and I couldn't get her face out of my head. I didn't care what they paid me, I wasn't doing it.

"Okay. You've got to pick something new, Cruz." Luke put a hand on my shoulder.

"How about, *'Bleeding Out,'*" Adam said. I'd written it last week, and we hadn't performed it yet. And yes, it was for Jade, but the audience didn't know that. And after Tia's bullshit stunt, people would assume Jade and I weren't together anymore.

"Fucking fine." I stormed back out on stage.

"We've got something new we want to sing for you," I said. I hated that I had to give this to them. Expose myself this way. I fucking hated it. I was a slave to this fucking life.

The music started, and I closed my eyes for a minute, gaining my composure.

Sunshine's gone, ain't no doubt,

Skies are gray, heart's torn out.
Numb and empty, don't want to feel,
Pills and booze, that's the deal.
Now there's darkness, clouds of rain,
Anything, to avoid the pain.
All the good is gone somehow,
Sins piled high upon me now.
Bleeding out, since you've been gone,
Don't sleep, don't eat, the days are long.
But knowing you are shining bright,
Is worth my battles day and night.
Spread your wings and fly away,
Little bird with eyes of jade.
Beautiful girl with lots of dreams,
You will always be my queen.
Took off the chains and set you free,
The most unselfish act by me.
Find your happiness, out on your own,
Leave me here to wallow alone.
Bleeding out, since you've been gone,
Don't sleep, don't eat, the days are long.
But knowing you are shining bright,
Is worth my battles day and night.
Time will heal, you will see,
But you'll remain a part of me.
Life isn't fair, it's so unkind,
My heart I just can't seem to find.
It will forever belong to you,
No matter what I say or do.
Find your happiness, out on your own,
Leave me here to wallow alone.
Bleeding out, since you've been gone,
Don't sleep, don't eat, the days are long.
But knowing you are shining bright,
Is worth my battles day and night.

The crowd went crazy, just like they always did when they got another piece of my soul.

———

The next few days were brutal. News that my mother had filed for divorce from my father and checked into rehab had spread, along with photos of Tia with her legs wrapped around me, mauling me like a fucking vulture. The headlines were cruel, saying I'd kicked Jade to the curb, one said, *out with the old—in with the new*, and a few dubbed Tia and I a rock-and-roll power couple. My gut wrenched when I thought of Jade. I thought of texting her to let her know it was all bull-shit, but what was the point? We both needed to move on. She hadn't reached out to me again, so I could only assume that's what she was doing. The thought of her with someone else did something to me. My chest ached and no amount of pills or booze could make it go away.

We were loaded on the tour bus and headed back east, and I dropped down on my bed to write. I had a nice buzz, which is when I wrote best. There was a knock on the door, because these fuckers never left me alone.

"What?" I said, no humor in my voice.

"Hey, what's up?" Lennon said, stepping inside my room and closing the door behind him.

"Not much. Where's your shadow?" I snarked. Lennon and Bailey were attached at the hip these days.

"She's taking a nap. I wanted to see if you'd go with me to visit Mom next week. There's a family day, and I think it's important we support her right now."

I ran a hand over my face. "I don't think going fucked up to rehab is a good idea, so I'll skip *Kumbaya* with the Brady Bunch this time around."

"You're an asshole. You could just try sobering up for a few days, ever thought of that?"

"Sure. But I choose not to. It's your turn to lead this family for a while. We'll see how long you stay sober," I said.

I hated myself as the words left my mouth, but what the fuck was new. There wasn't much to like about me these days. I was proud of my brother for all he'd overcome and berating him for it wasn't cool. But I was an asshole, and I wasn't in the mood to celebrate anyone.

"Have you been on the internet today?" he asked while he scanned his phone.

"Believe it or not, Lennon. Some of us have to work. I'm writing lyrics so the label will let me the fuck out of this band. I don't have the same luxuries as you to sit around surfing the net."

He shook his head at me. "You're out in a few months. Why are you still bitching and complaining? Not sure why you're trying to get out of the band anymore, when you dumped the only thing that was actually good in your life. And what the fuck will you have to do when you leave Exiled now? You going to sit alone in a house and drink yourself to death? Look in the mirror, Cruz. You've become everything you hate. You're a pill-popping, drunk who goes through the motions, all while being a dick to everyone around you. And for the record, yes, *you write the lyrics*. But you don't do shit to keep this band together otherwise. You separate yourself from everyone, hiding away in your room all the time. You're a sloppy, drunk asshole when you are around. I write the music to go to your fucking lyrics, genius. I'm the one who makes sure we're all at practice, who gets our shows organized, who's been flying all over the fucking globe to meet with your future replacement, all so you could go live this normal life with Jade. And go fucking figure, you dumped her before we got you out. You couldn't make it one fucking year. You threw it all away, because, why? Because Dad's an asshole? Guess what, brother—Dad's always been an asshole. Mom's always been a mess. Welcome to life. Get the fuck over it and pull yourself together." Lennon pushed to his feet, and my mouth hung open as I stared at him.

I was equal parts impressed and annoyed. Who the fuck did Lennon think he was? After all the shit he'd put me through. But at the same time—holy fucking shit. My brother was behaving like a grownup, and I couldn't help but be proud of him.

"Okay, good talk. Is that what you came here to tell me? That I'm a worthless prick? Thanks for the memo," I said before turning to stare at my laptop like I didn't have time for him. The truth was, I couldn't look at my brother right now, because I knew he was right. I just didn't know if I cared enough to do anything about it.

He opened the door, but before he stepped out, he turned around to face me. "I actually came to see if you saw Jade's statement. Even with what you did to her, she still has your back."

I waited until he left and quickly googled Jade's name to see what the fuck he was talking about. She'd given her first statement ever. Jade had always avoided the press even when we were together and never gave them anything. She'd obviously been hounded since the photo of Tia and I had gone viral. My chest squeezed and I closed my eyes for a minute. She was the one person I hadn't wanted to disappoint, and I'd failed her in so many ways. Ultimately, I'd set her free, which was the only unselfish thing I'd ever done. But I doubted she saw it that way.

She gave them enough to make them go away. I knew the process all too well.

The article stated that Jade had been asked if we'd broken up, or if I'd cheated on her. Her statement was brief, but it pained me to read her words.

Cruz and I did not break up because of any third party. He will always be my best friend, and though we aren't together anymore, I want him to be happy. He deserves that.

A lump formed in the back of my throat, and my eyes stung, so I squeezed them closed. I moved to my feet and grabbed a bottle of whiskey from my closet and chugged it until the lump in my throat disintegrated. I reached for my phone to send a text.

Hey. I need some Vicodin.

TIA

I'm not giving you more unless you start speaking to me again. Get over it. It was a kiss. It helped us both out. Don't flatter yourself. It didn't mean anything to me either.

> This IS me speaking to you.

TIA

> No. This is you using me.

> And that's a problem because??

TIA

> You're an asshole, Winslow.

> Tell me something I don't know. You used me when you mauled me on stage, right? You owe me one.

TIA

> Touche. See you at the next stop.

I typed one more text to get things in motion.

> Hey. Can we pull over soon? I need to get some air and get off this bus.

LUKE

> Yes. I will have him get off at the next exit.

That was easy. Tia's bus was behind ours, so they'd pull over with us. My addiction was calling the shots now, and after reading Jade's statement, I needed to check out for a while. It was all about survival now, and I was doing what needed to be done.

nineteen

. . .

Jade

"AT LEAST THERE'S no one following us anymore," Ari said as we walked to class.

"That's definitely a bright side."

I'd finally made a statement that Cruz and I were no longer together, and just like that, I didn't exist anymore in that world. I wasn't complaining. I hated that aspect of dating Cruz. There were parts of me that felt freer than I had in a long time. Like the constraints had been cut, and I wasn't being analyzed by everyone around me. My relationship under a microscope.

But my heart—it wasn't okay.

It probably never would be.

There was a constant ache in my chest, accompanied by a permanent lump in my throat. I still had no appetite, and I was going through the motions in life. Trying to act like everything was okay when I was far from okay. I still cried myself to sleep at night. I actually looked forward to it each day, because it was the only time when I could let it all out. It was my ritual, and I felt both tortured and relieved when I sobbed myself to sleep. Sadness enveloped me like a blanket, and I didn't know if I'd ever be free of it. This feeling like something was missing. Because it was.

I was a logical girl. I wanted to believe this would pass. But somehow, deep in my soul, I knew it wouldn't. Cruz Winslow was the love of my life, whether that was a good thing or not, he was. I'd never felt that kind of connection with another person, and I missed it.

I missed him.

I was used to speaking to him multiple times a day. FaceTiming and talking. Visiting one another as often as we could. And now it was all just—over. I told him everything. And now I felt incredibly alone. Even surrounded by so many people—I was alone.

Seeing the photos of Cruz and Tia hurt more than I could ever put into words. It made me physically ill. Her legs were wrapped around his waist just like mine had always been. I couldn't see his face in any of the pictures, as her head blocked it, but I was thankful for that. I didn't want to see the desire in his eyes. The smile on his lips. I wanted to hate him, I really did. But I couldn't. I loved him too much.

"If you want to come to Jace's for pizza and football tonight, text me," Ari said when we approached Winslow hall. There were reminders of him everywhere, including the building donated by his father.

"I have research today, and I'll probably work late. But I'll text you when I'm heading home." I turned to walk in the building. I hadn't been out since Cruz and I had broken up, and before that I'd had mono, so to say I'd been a dud this semester was an understatement. Thankfully Ari stopped trying to get me to go out. That's the last thing I felt like doing. Mixing alcohol with heartache would be disastrous.

"Jade," Brayden said, waving at me when I walked into the room.

A group of guys smiled and nodded as I walked past them to take my seat. The other downside to dating someone in the public eye—everyone knew we'd broken up, and the vultures were circling. I'd been hit on more in the last week than I had been in my entire life. Ever since I addressed our breakup in the press, guys were coming out of the woodwork. And trust me, it wasn't because I was looking good. I'd lost weight on my already too skinny frame, I had dark circles beneath my swollen eyes, I was lacking sleep and I had no energy to do my hair or makeup. I was fairly convinced that all these guys just wanted to say they were dating Cruz Winslow's ex-girlfriend. The whole thing disgusted me.

I assumed Cruz was experiencing this on a much grander scale. Unless he'd moved on to a serious relationship with Tia already. Nothing would surprise me anymore. Not since Cruz broke up with me at least. But I'd never seen anything suspicious between Cruz and Tia when we were together. Maybe I'd had blinders on, and something had been going on under my nose. Maybe that's the real reason he broke up with me.

"Hey, how are you?" I asked when I took my seat.

"Good. How about you? You okay?" Brayden had proven to be nothing but a good friend.

"I'm good."

I pulled out my notebook, lined up my pens, and submerged myself in class. Anything to stop thinking about Cruz.

Class moved quickly, and I took several pages of notes and actually spent the last hour thinking more about the human body than my broken heart.

"Hey, why don't you come to Jace's tonight for some pizza and football? Just get out a little and have some fun," Brayden said when we stepped outside.

"I have research. And then I need to study after."

His brows pinched together. "I don't want to pry, Jade. I know you're sad. I've been there myself. But sometimes just being around people, and having some fun helps you forget for a little bit, you know? You should come. Plus, you haven't met Sage yet, and I think you two would hit it off."

Sage was Brayden's girlfriend, and I'd heard only good things about her. Maybe he was right. How else would I ever pull out of this slump?

"Yeah. Maybe. I'll think about it. Thank you."

"Okay, see ya later." He waved, and I walked to research.

Elaine and I worked late, and it was dark when I left her office. I had several messages from Ari and Brayden insisting I come by. I responded and said I was on my way. What did I have to lose? My bed and my tears would both be waiting for me afterward.

"I'm so happy you're here," Ari said, meeting me at the door when I stepped inside. She wrapped an arm around me and offered me a beer.

"No thanks. I'll take a water though."

"You got it. And you have to try this pizza. It's deep dish and— To. Die. For." She handed me a water and a plate, and I grabbed a slice of pizza. She led me into the living room where everyone was watching the game.

"Jade, hey. So glad you're here." Jace gave me a hug, and Brayden pushed to his feet.

"Hi, thanks for inviting me." I hugged him and then gave Brayden an awkward half hug, as his girlfriend stood beside him.

"Hi, I'm Jade," I said, offering her my hand.

"Hey, I'm Sage. I've heard lots about you. It's nice to meet you."

Just then Lucas and Mila walked in and I hadn't seen them in months. Lucas was a good friend of Jace's and I'd met his girlfriend, Mila last year, and we'd hit it off. She pulled me into a hug and shook me around, causing us both to laugh.

"Girl, I've missed you. So good to see you out. Where have you been hiding?" Mila said, pulling away to look at me.

"It's just been a crazy semester. I'm so happy to see you." And I meant it. I liked this group a lot, and it was time to start finding other things to fill my time aside from school and sadness.

Mila, Ari, Sage and I sat on one side of the couch so we could visit. They all drank wine, and I sipped my water and forced myself to eat a few bites of pizza.

"So, you're a pre-med too, right?" Sage asked me, as her boyfriend and I shared the same major.

"Yes. Brayden and I have some tough classes this semester."

"Yeah, that's what he said. And you're graduating early?"

"Yep. I'm set to graduate next year. So, I'm technically a junior, I guess, but it's only my second year of college, so I still feel like I'm just navigating through it all," I said.

"She's a freaking genius, trust me." Ari refilled her glass with wine and dropped back down beside me.

"Okay, so I know we're avoiding the elephant in the room but, how are you?" Mila asked. I guess everyone knew, and they were probably afraid to bring it up.

"I'm okay," I said, trying to keep my composure. "Not my favorite topic."

"You and your boyfriend just broke up?" Sage asked, with a sad frown. She was sweet and I already liked her. She was perfect for Brayden. Her auburn hair rested on her shoulders and her blue gaze was filled with empathy and kindness.

"Yeah, it's been a couple weeks." I sipped my water, avoiding their gaze.

"It sucks ass, doesn't it? But, girl, that's what your friends are for. Let us be there for you," Mila said.

"I'm proud of you for coming tonight. I know you didn't feel like it, but you're here. And we love you." Ari put an arm around me, and I rested my head on her shoulder.

"Thanks. I'm glad I came too."

"And when you're ready, we are going to set you up with the hottest guy out there. Fuck Cruz Winslow," Mila said, her black bob framing her pretty face.

I chuckled along with them, though nothing about it was funny to me. I didn't want to meet someone else. And I didn't see a time when I would hate Cruz. As much as he hurt me, I loved him. Always would.

That night when I got in bed, I couldn't help myself. I searched his name on my phone. I just wanted to see his face. There was a photo of Cruz walking behind Lennon as they entered a rehab facility in Utah. The caption read: The Winslow Boys Stand Beside Their Mother.

I could only see Cruz's profile, and he didn't look any better than I did. I wondered if he hurt the same as me. He had a baseball cap on, his messy hair peeking out the sides. He looked down at the ground as he walked so I couldn't see his face. I ran my finger over the screen, itching to touch him. Feel him. I was proud of him for going to support his mother. I wondered what was going on with their family. According to the news, Juliette had filed for divorce. I wondered how Cruz felt about it. If he felt as alone as I did. If he hurt the way I did.

I lie on my side and played the single voicemail I'd saved from him. For whatever reason, I'd never deleted it, and now I was thankful. It was probably not healthy to play an old voicemail over and over to feel close to him, but right now, I was in survival mode and it helped me.

"Hey, baby. Just missing you bad right now. Can't wait to see you this weekend. You're taking your anatomy test at the moment, and I know you're killing it. So, fucking proud of you. Call me when you're done. Always need *more Jade*. Love you more."

Tears streamed down my face and I hugged my phone to my chest. When would it stop hurting so much? A sob escaped and I held my fist over my mouth and tried to muffle it. My door creaked open, and I stayed completely still. I felt the mattress shift.

"You're not alone, Jade. I'm here." Ari wrapped an arm around me. My back to her chest and she hugged me tight. I let it all out. I didn't try to muffle my tears or my sobs. I just cried.

I was sad. And broken. But I wasn't alone. And it felt good to lean on someone.

"I'm so sad." My words were hard to make out through my sobs.

"I know you are. But it will get a little easier every day. I promise," Ari whispered.

"It's been weeks. It hasn't gotten easier. I feel like I'm drowning in it. I miss him, Ari. I miss him so much." I pushed to sit up, gasping for breaths. I covered my face with my hands.

"I know you do, sweetie. I know how much you love him. And I know he loves you too. I don't know why he did this. Just give it time, okay. I promise it will get better."

"Okay," I said, nodding my head, though I doubted it was true.

"It's okay to be sad, Jade. I'm here for you."

"Thank you."

I realized that this is how I'd always handled things. I was used to locking myself away and dealing with things on my own. But it helped to talk to someone. To admit that I was hurting. And it was okay to say it aloud.

———

The next few weeks were busy, and I was thankful for it. I'd gotten my groove back a little bit. Last night was the first night in over a month that I'd slept for seven solid hours. I'd been functioning on no sleep, and my body finally gave in.

I attended the medical brigade meeting and even took the information about the next few brigades. I still wasn't ready to commit to anything. A part of me was still holding out for spending the summer with Cruz. As sick and twisted as that sounded, I wasn't ready to give up on everything just yet. But maybe the fact that I was actually looking into it was a good sign. I'd not heard a single word from Cruz. Not since our last phone call. Lennon and I had cut off communication as well. Obviously, we didn't want to put the other in an uncomfortable situation, but I missed my friend, too.

I stepped in my favorite café, and Mila waved at me from the back table. Ari and Sage were already sitting beside her, and I made my way over to them.

"Sorry I'm late. The medical brigade meeting went over." I dropped down in my seat and glanced at the menu.

"Are you going to do it next year?" Ari asked as the waitress approached our table and took our order.

"I think so. I got all the info for the summer, fall and spring brigades. It's such an amazing program. I definitely want to do it." It was the first time in a while that I was actually excited about something. Yes, my heart still hurt. Sadness still clung to me like a freaking second skin. But I was looking forward to doing this, and that was a good thing.

"Oh my gosh, this is so *you*," Ari said as she flipped through the brochure and looked at all the photos.

"Girl, I give you credit. I'm more of a five-star hotel chick. I don't know if I could hack this," Mila said, looking over Ari's shoulder.

"It's a third world country. You don't stay at the Four Seasons." Ari rolled her eyes.

"Hashtag, no judgment. To each their own." Mila huffed, and we all laughed.

"I'm proud of you," Ari said, bumping me with her shoulder and handing the brochure back to me.

"Thanks." It felt good to feel good. As crazy as that sounds. I felt a moment of joy, something I hadn't felt in weeks. I'd take what I could get.

"I think it's amazing you want to do it, Jade," Sage said. We'd become friends over the last few weeks, as all three of them had really rallied around me.

"Thank you. So, how did meeting Brayden's parents go?" I changed the subject, and not because I was trying to cover up anything. I truly cared. I guess I was finally living a little again.

"They were so nice. I was nervous, but after a few minutes, they totally put me at ease." Sage snagged a French-fry off my plate and winked.

"I knew they'd love you," I said.

"Well, consider yourself lucky. Lucas' parents don't like me," Mila said before reaching for her sandwich and taking a bite like this was just common knowledge.

We all chuckled.

"I'm sure they do. What's not to love," Ari said.

"No. I'm literally not making this up. His mom actually said, '*I don't like her*' to Lucas when I was in the next room. They have very thin walls in that house." She shrugged. "She said I was crass or an ass? I'm not sure which one. Maybe both?"

My head fell back in laughter. Yep. I'd entered the land of the living again. And maybe I was just surviving for now. But that was okay. It would get a little better every day.

twenty

. . .

Cruz

ANOTHER FAMILY MEETING at the rehab center where my
mother and brother seemed to psycho-analyze *me* a hell of a lot more
than Mom. This time I'd come sober. After Dr. Roberts had called me
out at our first visit, and basically said if I couldn't come clean and
sober, not to bother coming at all. When a rehab facility shames you
for being too fucked up, that's a red fucking flag.

I'd cut the booze out for the last two weeks, and I had to admit
that I felt better. I'd been a self-destructive asshole for weeks, and I
certainly wasn't out of the woods, but I was reeling things in. It
wasn't easy. Not with the constant ache in my chest. I fucking missed
my girl. I'd tried a few times to just fuck someone else so I could
forget about her, but I couldn't stand a single other chick. None.
Hadn't even kissed anyone else. Well, not since Tia's dumb fucking
kiss on stage, which had disgusted me.

Jade had ruined me for all other women. And now I was fucked.
Because I didn't want anyone else, and I couldn't have her. So, I'd
either need to become a monk or be okay with dying of a bad case of
blue balls. The latter was more likely as I doubted the monks would
take me.

"Thank you for coming sober today, Cruz," Dr. Roberts said. She was a no-nonsense woman. Most people took my shit. This lady did not.

"Well, you basically told me I couldn't visit, so you didn't give me much of a choice." I folded my arms over my chest and met her steely blue gaze.

"Yeah. We're funny about sobriety here. It's kind of our sticking point." She was so snarky, but I kind of dug it. I liked people who called me out.

Jade.

She was the one person who got me. And I'd lost her. And I guess I'd lost myself along the way too.

"He's been sober for two weeks now. And he stopped taking that shit Tia was feeding him," Lennon said.

When did my brother become a fucking nark? All the years I had his back. He wasn't good at being the caretaker. He was much easier to deal with when he was the fuck-up.

"And, what shit is that?" my mother asked.

Um, pot, this is kettle.

In all fairness, Mom had transformed. The woman I'd seen brief glimpses of my entire life had emerged. Stronger than ever. Over just a matter of weeks. And if I was capable of being happy, I'd be happy for her.

But I wasn't.

I was bitter and angry at life. Obviously, I was still an entitled prick. Being sober hadn't changed that.

"I was taking Vicodin for a few weeks," I admitted, shifting in my seat.

Mom looked over at Dr. Roberts and she nodded like my mother should speak her mind. How much had Dad fucked her up that she needed approval to speak her mind? Thank Christ I'd never needed anyone to tell me whether or not I could say what the fuck I wanted. I just always had.

"Why would you do something that you despised? Of everyone in this family, you've always been the most outspoken about my abuse of prescription pills, and Lennon's struggle with drug abuse. Why would you, in turn, start doing the same?" My mother sat up straight. Her blonde hair was pulled into some sort of fancy knot at the back of her neck. She wore a cream-colored blouse and dress slacks. The woman looked like she was going shopping on Rodeo Drive, not attending a family support group meeting in rehab. But I liked it. She was coming into her own, and my chest squeezed with something. Pride? Joy? I don't even know. It was short lived, and I shook it off.

"I don't know. Dr. Roberts, you want to take that one?" I asked.

Dr. Roberts a.k.a. the ice queen actually laughed. Well, her head tipped back just slightly, and a little chuckle escaped. "You want me to tell you why I think you've been acting this way? After always being the one in the family that called everyone out for it?"

"I can't wait to hear it." I rolled my eyes and smirked.

"Quit being a dick," Lennon whispered, but everyone heard, and Dr. Roberts smiled. A very brief smile of course.

"Well, Cruz, I believe that whether you like it or not, your mom's overdose and your father's affair shook you to the core. You act like you're completely detached from your family, but in truth, you aren't. You wouldn't be here if you were. You wouldn't have spiraled when your family fell apart, so to speak. You broke up with a girl you claim to love, you numbed yourself with booze and prescription meds, and you punished yourself. You feel undeserving of happiness for whatever reason, and you sabotaged your own happiness." She crossed her arms in front of her chest and stared at me.

Jesus. Tell me how you really feel, Doc.

Before I could respond, a sob came from my mother, and I watched as she fell apart. With her face buried in her hands, she lost her shit.

"I'm sorry, Cruz. You carried so much on your shoulders for such a long time. You were bound to break at some point." She wailed. Lennon grabbed some tissue and handed it to her.

"No one is broken, Mom. I'm fine. I'm figuring it out."

"You're not fine, Cruz. You're far from fine. You all are. But this is part of healing," Dr. Roberts said.

"Christ. Who shit in your Cheerios this morning?" I hissed, pushing to my feet and storming to the window. Why the fuck did I agree to come here again? To be reminded of how fucked up my family is.

She laughed. This time it was a full belly laugh, and Mom and Lennon joined in. Who knew calling her out would get such a reaction?

"It's okay to break, you know. So, let's take this apart a little, shall we?" she said.

Lennon glared at me and pointed at my chair. I took my seat so he wouldn't have a hissy fit. Everyone was losing their shit in this office and I was over it.

"Ah, yes please. You want to take it apart? Let's go over the obvious. My father is a selfish, narcissistic, drug abusing, womanizing, rich, entitled asshole. My mother behaved like a fucking Stockholm victim most of my childhood, doing as she was told by her captor, numbing herself and leaving her children with nannies to raise them. My brother is a talented, sensitive motherfucker, who couldn't handle the insanity of our household, so he used drugs to cope. And after all these years I have come to realize that my family is a part of me, and the fewer people I bring into this fucked up situation, the better. So yeah, I spent a couple weeks staying consistently shitfaced with alcohol and prescription drugs, because it was easier to deal with life that way. *Shoot me.* And now everyone decides to get sober and wants to analyze me? I've been holding this whole family's shit together my entire life. They don't get to judge me for a few bad weeks."

The room fell silent. Tears streamed from my mother's eyes, and Lennon looked visibly shaken. What the fuck? Was this news to them?

"Good, Cruz. That's a fair statement. You've kept it together all this time. Enough is enough. You hit your breaking point." She nods.

"Fucking, right. Yes. You got it, Dr. Roberts." Fucking finally.

"So, when your mom overdosed, that was a turning point for you, yes?"

"I suppose. I'm not exactly sure why. I'd been there before. It wasn't my first rodeo," I said, looking over at Lennon. I hated to bring up his overdose, but we were here, and I was doing this.

"Right. Because you were there when Lennon overdosed, correct?" Dr. Roberts asked.

"Yes."

"And where were your parents?" she asked.

Mom broke on a sob again. As much as I believed in tough love, I didn't want to be cruel. She was trying to get her shit together. We didn't need to kick her when she was down.

"Steven and I were in Europe. He didn't think it was that bad. But I knew better." Mom paused and used a tissue to blow her nose. "He didn't want to fly home right away. The doctors said they had it under control. I knew we should leave. It wasn't right to let Cruz deal with everything, nor for Lennon to think we didn't care. But I chose to go along with your father. I always did."

"You've shared with me that Lennon's overdose was when your drug abuse worsened, correct?" Dr. Roberts asked Mom.

"Yes." Mom looked at me with so much sorrow, and a sharp pain hit my chest.

"So, Cruz. You said your mother's overdose wasn't all that shocking for you because you'd been there before. With your brother. So, what about that experience caused you to spiral. You've called your father a, what was it? A narcissistic asshole?" Dr. Roberts said with a smirk.

"I believe it was a *selfish, narcissistic, drug abusing, womanizing, rich, entitled asshole*," I clarified.

"Ah, yes. Thank you for the clarification. So did his affair surprise you?" she pressed.

I thought about it. "Yeah. That's the one thing I didn't think he was. A cheater. I justified their selfishness my entire life," I paused and winced at Mom in apology. She motioned for me to go on. "I thought they were in love. It was the only normal thing we had going for our family."

"Well, we can decide what's normal a million different ways. Obviously, you didn't have a traditional upbringing, but it was *your normal*. It doesn't make it wrong or right, Cruz."

"Okay. If you say so," I muttered.

"So, you find out your dad is having an affair and your mom has overdosed. What makes you storm out to the lobby and pack up Jade's books and send her home, only later to break up with her?" Dr. Roberts asked.

I look over at my brother. *Fucking traitor.* I've not told this woman about how or why Jade and I broke up. It's none of her business. I assumed my mother mentioned our breakup in her session, but this is very detailed information. It had to come from my brother, because I sure as shit didn't tell her.

"Dr. Roberts and I have had a few phone consults," Lennon said sheepishly.

Fucker.

"I see. So, you left out another piece of the amazing puzzle that is the Winslow family, Dr. Roberts. My father had an affair with a *fucking teenager,* who also happened to be his best friend's daughter. *Fucked. Up.*"

"Agreed. But what does that have to do with you and Jade?" Dr. Roberts asked, tucking a pen behind her ear, and adjusting her notebook on her lap.

"Why are we talking about me and Jade? Aren't we here for my mother?" I pushed to my feet again and walked to the window, rubbing the back of my neck, and moving my head from side to side. I was ready to get out of this place.

"Well, Cruz, your mother and your brother are worried about you. And these meetings are for your family. You're part of the family, right?"

I rolled my eyes and sat back down. "Yeah. Alright. You want to know why I broke up with Jade? Is that where this is going?"

"Sure. I think it's important." Dr. Roberts stood and reached for her water before returning to her seat.

"So, I'm looking at my girl sitting in the waiting room. Her books are all spread out. My shit pulled her away from class, once again. Jade was always sacrificing for me. Hell, she even battled mono because she was pushing herself so hard. And my dad's shit was about to come out in the press, you know, an affair with a teenager, typical Winslow bullshit. I'm at the hospital because another family member overdosed, no offense," I said, shrugging at my mother and my brother.

"None taken," Lennon said.

"Jade's good, you know. She's everything that's good. And the world I live in, with my family, with the band, it's not normal. She deserves normal." I fumbled on my words as I tried to explain myself. "She deserves better."

"You keep speaking of this 'normal' or this idea of what you think is 'normal'. But what does that even mean?" Dr. Roberts asks.

I ran a hand over my face. I don't even know anymore, and I'm tired. "I have no idea. I guess something that's not fucked up. I'm fucked up and so is my family."

"Well, isn't everyone a little messed up? I mean, no one's perfect. Were you unfaithful to Jade?" she asked.

Where the fuck does this woman get off?

"No. And fuck you for asking that. I'm not my father," I said.

"Well, you weren't your mother either, and that didn't stop you from taking pills," she said.

I pointed my finger at her. "You need to back the fuck off."

"Cruz," my mother and Lennon both said in unison.

"It's okay." Dr. Roberts holds her hand up to them. "I hit a nerve. That's okay."

"I never cheated on Jade. Hell, we aren't even together, and I have no desire to fuck anyone else now," I said.

"Why is that?"

"Aren't you the doctor? Why are you asking me all the fucking questions? Obviously, I love her. I always will. It's not rocket science, doc." I shift in my seat.

"Shouldn't it have been up to Jade to decide if your life was too much for her? Did she tell you she disapproved of your family?"

"No. She's not like that. She loves Lennon and my mom."

"Did she push you to get out of the band? Did she have a problem with you being on the road?" Dr. Roberts asked.

"She actually wanted to come on tour with us. Cruz was the one who really pushed her not to come, and ultimately, she remained at school. But she is very supportive of Exiled," Lennon said.

"I think she was talking to me, dickhead," I mumbled. "Jade wanted us to be together. Whether I left the band, or she came on tour. She just wanted us to be together. She didn't like the lack of privacy or the distance, but she supported me. Always. I'm the one who wants to leave the band. It's not for me."

"So, Jade is supportive of your family and your music, but you decided you had to break up with her because your family and your life isn't normal?" Dr. Roberts pressed.

"Do they pay you extra if you're condescending?" I asked.

She chuckled. "It's necessary sometimes, Cruz. Answer the question."

"Yeah. I decided. I decided I wasn't good enough for her."

"Because your family is…" She paused.

"Fucked up," I chimed in.

"And then you went on a bender and punished yourself for doing so?"

"I guess, if that's how you want to look at it. I did the right thing. Doesn't mean I was happy about it," I admitted.

"The right thing for whom?" she asked.

"For Jade."

"So, let me get this straight. You both work hard to make the distance work, because you don't like being apart. She supports your music and your family. She comes to the hospital as soon as she finds out about your mother, because she wants to be there for you. You're at the tail end of your long-distance obstacle, and you decided the best thing *for her* was to break up with her?"

I drop my head back and let out a long breath. I'm tired of the questions. I could use a stiff drink right about now. Oh, that's right. I'm fucking sober at the moment.

"Yep."

"Sounds more like it was the best thing for you," she said, squaring her shoulders and meeting my gaze.

"Best thing for me? I'm fucking miserable. And apparently breaking up with Jade means I have a broken dick, so I can't even have sex anymore. How is this better for me?"

"Only you know the answer to that. But it wasn't for her. She was there for you when you needed her. Maybe you couldn't handle someone making *you* a priority? Maybe you prefer to be the one holding everyone together, not the one in need of help? Maybe you don't feel like you deserve to be happy? Maybe you wanted to check out and go on a bender and breaking up with Jade allowed you to do so? You couldn't have done that if you were with her, correct?" Dr. Roberts said as I processed her words. That was a fucking lot of *maybes* she tossed out there. Both rage and sadness coursed my veins. Was she insane? Was there truth to her words?

"Jade would have kicked his ass if she'd been around this last month to see him behave like an idiot. No, he couldn't have pulled that off if they'd been together," Lennon, a.k.a. Benedict Arnold, said. Christ, this kid was pissing me off.

"Fuck you, Lennon." I pushed to my feet again. Was there a timer or something we were waiting for to end this therapy session from hell? How long had we been here?

"Why are you angry at Lennon? Is he right? Would Jade have called you out for your reckless behavior?"

"Yep. Lennon's right. Should we throw him a ticker tape parade?" I asked, pacing the room.

"Nope. But now you have something to think about until we meet again. Maybe it's time you stop punishing yourself and allow yourself some happiness, huh? That's what your mom and your brother are working on." Dr. Roberts pushed to her feet.

Thank fucking Christ. There was an end in sight.

We all said our goodbyes and we walked Mom back to her room.

She dropped in the chair beside her bed and looked up at Lennon and me. Her honey brown gaze wet with emotion. "I'm sorry, boys. I failed you, but I'm going to do what I can to make things right."

Too much. It was all too much. I hated the way I felt. The heaviness in my chest. The sting behind my eyes. I wanted to go back to just accepting my fucked-up family. It was so much easier to be angry.

"Thanks, Mom. Love you," Lennon said, leaning down to hug her.

"I love you both." Mom smiled up at me.

"Okay. We'll be back in a few weeks. Love you," I said.

She reached for my hand and didn't let it go. She waited until I met her gaze. "I love you, Cruz."

I nodded.

Lennon and I were silent until we got back on the plane and buckled up. I needed to sleep. Needed to stop thinking. I couldn't get drunk, so sleep was the next best thing.

"Hey," Lennon said from the seat beside me.

"What?" I was still angry at how much he'd shared with Dr. Roberts, and I wasn't in the mood to get into it right now.

"You're a good brother, Cruz. The best. You're also a good son. A good friend. And a good boyfriend."

I rolled my eyes before closing them to let him know I was done. "Thank you, Dr. Phil."

"It's okay to let yourself be happy, you know. You deserve it. More than anyone, you deserve it," Lennon said, his voice cracked a little at the end.

I peeked one eye open, just enough to look at him. He watched me. "Thanks." It sounded more like a croak.

I squeezed my eyes closed and swiped when a single tear ran down my cheek. My brother put a hand on my shoulder, and I lost it.

I don't know why.

Wasn't sure what my breaking point was.

But I lost it.

I buried my face in my hands and I sobbed. My brother patted me on the back as I let it all out.

I didn't know what any of it meant.

But it felt fucking good.

twenty-one

. . .

Jade

I SPENT the weekend with Dad and Sara. Hanging out in Bucktown always made me feel better. Something about being home, I guess. I took the train back to school and pulled my phone from my back pocket when it vibrated.

My heart raced as I took in the screen.

CRUZ

Hey. Can you talk?

Should I even answer him? He hadn't responded to my calls or texts weeks ago, so why was he reaching out now? He'd kicked me to the curb. He'd made out with another girl on stage in front of the world.

Yes, I missed him terribly. My heart ached all the time. All the freaking time. I still cried myself to sleep every night, but I was finally sleeping again. My appetite was starting to come back. I'd basically spent the last few weeks trying to pull myself up from the lowest place I'd ever been.

No. He didn't get a response. I wasn't going back down that rabbit hole. Fool me once, shame on me—and all that stuff.

My chest squeezed when another text came through.

CRUZ

You still have your 'read receipts' on, so I
know you read the message. I get that you
don't want to talk to me, but I'd like to
explain things to you.

No. No. No. He doesn't get to do this now.

CRUZ

I've been seeing a therapist at my mom's
rehab center. I'm figuring things out.

CRUZ

I haven't been with anyone since you. I
promise, Jade. That shit with Tia was a
stupid ass stunt. She did it for the publicity.
You couldn't tell in the picture, but I didn't
kiss her back. I bit her actually. I was pissed.
Fuck. I don't want to do this over text.
Please, let me call you, baby.

Tears ran down my face and I swiped at them quickly. Relief flooded that he wasn't dating Tia, which made me crazy, because we weren't together either. Why was he calling me baby? He hadn't spoken to me in weeks, and now he wanted to act like nothing was wrong? One text from Cruz and I was a blubbering mess. This wasn't good for me. He wasn't good for me. Isn't that why he broke up with me? He couldn't change his mind every time he felt lonely. No. I silenced my phone and tucked it in my back pocket.

I stopped at home to drop off my duffle bag before heading to research. Elaine and I were making some serious breakthroughs. I was proud of the work I was doing with her, and the thought of being published in a medical journal thrilled me. I'd found my purpose again, and though I didn't have my mojo back just yet, I was surviving. And I wasn't going backward just because Cruz felt like reaching out to me today. But of course, my mind was completely preoccupied now. What did he want to talk about? Did he want to explain why he'd ended things with me? What was there to even say? Maybe he just wanted closure? Too bad. He hadn't given me closure, and I wasn't going to help him get it either. I wasn't the one who'd walked away. That was on him.

On my walk home from research, I turned my phone back on. Typical Cruz. He didn't give up easily. But I'd prepared for that. Deep down, I knew I wanted to hear what he had to say. But I wasn't ready yet. Wasn't ready to let my guard down with him again. I read through his texts.

CRUZ

> I fucked up. I pushed you away. I don't know why. I thought you deserved better. Hell, I still do. But I'm miserable without you, baby. So, fucking miserable.

CRUZ

> I spent the last few weeks being a fucking idiot, Jade. You would have been disgusted with me. I was pretty much drunk every waking minute, and I took a lot of pills. I don't know why I did it. I just didn't like feeling so much. Feeling ashamed of my family. Sad about not being with you. But I felt it all. Even when I was numb, I felt it, Jade. I couldn't escape it.

Tears ran down my face as I read his words. When I got to my house, I dropped down on the couch and continued reading. He'd all but sent me a novel.

CRUZ

> I've been sober for three weeks now. I'm only taking the Adderall prescription once a day, and I've quit everything else. I'm getting my shit together.

CRUZ

> My mom filed for divorce. She's doing well in rehab. Lennon and I go for family therapy sessions every week. It's helping me sort through all the shit that's been piling up.

CRUZ

Luke and the label finally agreed on my replacement. It's going to happen, Jade. I'm going to walk away from Exiled.

CRUZ

Please talk to me. Please, baby. I just want to talk to you.

I released a long breath I hadn't even realized I'd been holding. My fingers shook above the keyboard.

Hey. I'm really glad you're doing well.

CRUZ

Hey, More Jade. Can I FaceTime you?

No.

CRUZ

Can I call you?

No. I'm not ready to talk to you, Cruz. You can text me.

CRUZ

Whatever you need. I love you. I love you so fucking much.

I didn't respond. I moved to my bedroom and curled up in a ball and cried. All these feelings I have for him are terrifying. I'm in too deep. I'd just found a way to survive without him, and I couldn't just jump back in. No way. He could change his mind tomorrow. Why was it so hard to stay away from him? Why did loving him have to hurt so much?

"Jade," Ari called out when she got home.

I pushed to sit up and swiped at my tears. No one wanted to see me fall apart again. Even I was sick of it. Enough is enough.

"Hey," I said, meeting her in the kitchen.

"What happened?" She dropped her backpack on the table and studied me with concern.

"Nothing. I just got home."

"And your eyes are all puffy from research?" She laughed. "Spill it."

I handed her my phone and dropped to sit at the kitchen table.

She scanned through the texts. "Wow."

"Right? No word from him for weeks and now he wants to talk."

"I believe him about Tia. I never thought he ended it because he wanted someone else. Hell, I couldn't figure out for the life of me why he did it. That guy is obsessed with you," she said, shaking her head.

"Well, he cut me off without a care in the world. I'd be wise to remember that."

"I get it. I would be cautious too. He needs to grovel for a while." Ari pushed up and grabbed an apple from the fridge.

"Definitely. I just don't want to get hurt again, you know?"

"I know. Love sucks, sometimes." She huffed.

"Not for you."

"Jace and I had a fight today. He's graduating next year, and I'm not. So, what then?" Ari's eyes grew wide and she shrugged.

I laughed. "You have a whole other year to figure it out. It's way too soon to worry about that."

"If I were brilliant like you, I could have graduated in three years. Now I'll have another year after he's done. He's not going to want to stick around a college town and wait for me. He said I was being ridiculous."

"That's because he will absolutely be waiting for you. He's crazy about you," I said.

"You know what we need?"

"What?"

"Let's go get a couple tubs of ice cream and have a girl's night. We can watch chick flicks and forget our boy problems for the night. Drown our sorrows in dairy and sugar. Sound good?" Ari said, pushing to her feet.

"It sounds perfect."

On our way out the door, she grabbed my hand and pulled me into the bathroom.

"We need a quick round of *fuck-those-bitches* first. After all, the love of your life just reached out to you after torturing you for weeks. My boyfriend is going to move on without me while I'm stuck here at school. Get ready to scream," Ari said, and I couldn't help but laugh.

Because she was right.

———

One week had passed, and Cruz had upped his game. He was texting me non-stop and sending me selfies on the hour. I rarely responded, but my resolve was weakening. I studied every photo. I missed his face. Missed his body. Missed everything about him. Three floral arrangements had arrived at the house with my favorite flowers. Hydrangeas and peonies. He remembered.

I still wasn't ready to talk to him. I had finals coming up and I needed to focus right now. But I checked my phone constantly, and I read every message he sent me over and over. Loving this boy was deliciously torturous.

I grabbed my mail on the way inside the house and saw a letter addressed to me. I recognized the writing immediately. I tore the envelope open to find a letter from Cruz.

Dear Jade,

I know you aren't speaking to me right now, so I wanted to write you. The texts cut me off when I go on too long, and I wanted to send you some lyrics I wrote since we've been apart. I've written you so many songs. I'm hoping this will help you understand what I was going through.

I love you most.

I love you always.

I love you more.

Cruz

The storm is coming, and it's time to prepare,

I look at the destruction and try not to care.

Always taking cover, staying one step ahead,

Knowing shit will follow, I sense impending dread.
So many mistakes I've made along the way.
I don't really care what I do or what I say.
And like a bright light, you come to me one day,
The only one that ever made me feel I was okay.
I want to keep you safe, shield you from the pain,
But you stand beside me, come sunshine or rain.
I'm about to tumble down, the weight is too much,
I need to let you go but I'll miss your sweet touch.
The world's a dark place when I am not with you,
I numb myself to survive, at least I believe that's true.
But when you love someone, you do what must be done,
I want to set you free, let you bask out in the sun.
Not drown you in my storm, where the days are cold and gray,
And watch your tender heart as the edges start to fray.
But I can't stay away, can't take a breath without you,
Our hearts beat together, no matter what we say or what we do.
I'll ask you to forgive me, and trust me once again,
To try to remember that you are my best friend.
My faults are heavy, it's something that I dread,
Drawn to a girl with a halo around her head.
I'll splinter and I'll falter, yet always stay true,
Because you were meant for me and I was meant for you.

My back is against the wall and I slide down until my bottom is on the floor. I read his words over and over, trying to see through my tears. I reach for my phone and I FaceTime Cruz.

I was ready to talk.

twenty-two

. . .

Cruz

WE'D JUST FINISHED rehearsals and I was walking back to my hotel room when my phone vibrated. FaceTime call from More Jade moved across my screen and I nearly fumbled to answer it. I pushed in my suite and walked to my room as I waited for the phone to zoom in on her pretty face.

My heart raced.

Knees weak.

Palms sweaty.

I immediately thought of the Eminem song and wanted to say, "Mom's spaghetti", but I'd waited so long to talk to her I wasn't going to be an asshole now.

"Hey," I said, studying every one of her gorgeous features. Her eyes were puffy which immediately had me on edge.

"Hi. How are you?" She was sitting on the floor in her living room, and she held up my letter. "So, I got this today."

She swiped at her cheeks, and my chest squeezed.

"I'm actually good. Didn't mean to make you cry. Just wanted you to know what I was feeling."

"Yes, you did," she said. Her lips turned up in the corners and her glossy gaze met mine.

"Well, maybe a little. You wouldn't talk to me. I had to pull out the big guns."

She laughed a little before tilting her head and studying me. "You look good."

"You look fucking good, baby."

"Shut up." She smiled and rolled her eyes. "Don't one-up me."

"Never," I said.

"Okay."

She let out a long breath, and I dropped down to sit on my bed. "I was an asshole. I know I screwed up. I'm sorry. I'm working on it. I swear to you it won't ever happen again."

She nodded. Still quiet. We sat like that for at least two or three minutes.

"I miss you," she whispered, finally.

"Yeah?"

"Yeah."

"When can I see you?" I asked. I wanted to fly there tonight. I had a show tomorrow, so that wasn't going to happen, but I needed to see her. Hold her.

"No, Cruz. I'm about to go into finals. We need to take this slow. Where are you?" she asked.

"I'm in New York for the next week. Maybe I could come there?"

She sighed. "Maybe. It's your birthday next week. I didn't get you anything because I didn't think we'd be speaking. You ignored me for weeks, Cruz."

"All I want for my birthday is you. I want to explain everything to you. Why I did what I did," I said.

"I'm listening."

She wasn't going to wait until I saw her. That wasn't Jade. She had questions and she wanted answers. Hell, she deserved them.

"I freaked out. My dad was having an affair with a fucking teenager. My mom took enough pills to put herself in a coma. I knew it was all going to be very public. I was embarrassed. Ashamed." I paused and scrubbed a hand over my jaw. "I didn't want to pull you into it. I thought you deserved better."

"So, what's changed?"

"Well, I still think you deserve better, I just don't fucking care. I can't live without you. So, I'll just do better. Be better," I said.

"I don't want you to do or be better. I love you exactly how you are. Sure, I don't want you to use booze and pills to deal with life, that's what we have each other for. But I've never had a problem with who you are, or where you come from. I'm not perfect, Cruz. I'm human too."

"You're perfect to me." My gaze locked with hers.

"Maybe that's part of our problem. You hide things from me because you think I can't handle them. I'm stronger than you think."

"I know you are. I don't doubt that. I just don't want to disappoint you," I admitted.

"The only time you've ever disappointed me was when you walked away from me. Shut me out of your life. You can't do that. I need to trust you, and right now, I don't."

"Baby, you can trust me. I just lost my shit for a while. I checked out. It won't happen again." I wasn't backing down. I'd fucked up, but I'd learned from it.

"You don't get to decide when I trust you or when I don't. You broke me, Cruz. I never saw it coming. And it has been a really rough couple weeks for me." She paused when a sob escaped, and my chest squeezed.

"I know. I'll do whatever you need. If you don't want to see me for a while, I'll wait. I'm just happy you're finally speaking to me again."

She wiped her face with the sleeve of her sweatshirt. Her cheeks were rosy, jade eyes wet with emotion, lips plump, and I fucking itched to touch her.

"Let's just take this slow, okay?" She twirled the ring around her finger, and I was happy to see she still wore it. She hadn't completely given up on me, had she?

"You're still wearing the promise ring I gave you?"

She held up her hand and rolled her eyes. "Yes."

"So, you didn't totally give up on me," I said.

"I don't think that's possible."

"I love you," I told her.

She paused for a few seconds, studying me through the phone. "I love you, more."

I spent the next two hours on the phone with Jade. Hearing about her classes and her research. We talked about the incident with Tia, and though she was still hesitant with me, I knew she loved me. I knew we were going to be okay. I agreed to take it slow, though that went against every instinct I had. I wanted to fly her here. I wanted her with me now. I was an impatient bastard, and I needed to work on that if I wanted Jade to trust me again.

———

Shit was falling into place. I dropped down in a chair in the studio, meeting my replacement, Zach Balsecky, for the first time. He was a cool dude, but all I could think about was the fact that his last name sounded a hell of a lot like *ball sack*. The kid must have been brutalized growing up. I shook it off and focused on the obvious—transitioning out of Exiled and back into a normal life.

I'd dropped the ball on my classes, so I planned on taking the last two courses I needed this summer. I was hoping Jade would still spend the summer with me on tour, but since we were still technically *'taking it slow'*, I didn't want to push her. We were back to talking a dozen times a day, and I would take what I could get right now.

"So, Zach's going to make a few appearances this summer with you guys on stage. We'll be planting the seed of him joining the band, but no one will know the capacity until we need them to," Luke said, running a hand through his hair. The guy had aged a lot this past year, as Exiled had definitely had its ups and downs.

"So, you don't write music then? *You just sing*?" Dex asked, sitting all high and mighty on a bar stool, like he owned the place.

Zach didn't write music, which was the reason the label was hesitant to choose him. But the dude was talented as fuck in every other way. His voice was kickass, and he played both the electric guitar and the drums. He wrote music, not lyrics, and Luke thought that Zach and Lennon would work well together in that area. The label had agreed to let me continue to write for the band after I left, and I was open to that. Hell, I liked writing. Liked creating something. So why did Dex feel the need to fuck with the dude?

"I also play a mean electric guitar." Zach smirked, and my head fell back with a laugh.

I already liked him. Dex was being an asshole and Zach wasn't going to take his shit. He'd fit right in.

"I've seen you play Dude, and I'd say your vocals are your strong suit." Dex raised one brow before slamming a beer.

"Ignore him. He's the staple dickhead in the group. He's never heard you play, because he doesn't have the attention span to go online and check you out, and he hasn't seen you live," Adam said, rolling his eyes.

"Whatever, asshole. I'm just giving him shit. It's part of the initiation. Please tell me you don't have a girlfriend. If I have to deal with one more bandmate with a chick, I'm going to lose my shit. We're on the road. We're fucking rock stars. We're supposed to be acting like it." Dex stood and dropped his bottle in the trash.

"No girlfriend right now," Zach said, studying Dex as he staggered across the room before his gaze locked with mine. "So, Cruz, you sure you're ready to give all this up?"

"Yes." I didn't hesitate and everyone laughed.

"He was ready before we even started," Lennon said.

"Okay. I hear ya. It's not for everyone."

"Whatever. Who wouldn't want this? He's a dumbass," Dex said, glancing over at me. If I cared about the dude, it might bother me. But I didn't. We'd long passed caring. He's an asshole and I don't care what he thinks of my decision. I care about making sure my brother and Adam are okay. I care about making this a smooth transition for Luke as well. He's been there for me. They all have. Dex is here for himself. He's a one-man show.

Tia came barreling through the door and deadpanned on Zach. "Sorry, I'm late. You the new guy?"

"You're not late. You weren't invited." Luke rolled his eyes. Tia inserted herself in our business because she was our opening act and insisted it involved her. She knew everything that was going on because her sister and my brother were inseparable, and he couldn't keep his goddamn mouth closed.

She laughed. "Shit rolls downhill, Luke. I need to prepare for it."

I glanced at my brother and shot him a look. It was going to be difficult to keep this shit quiet, and Tia was a loose cannon.

"We've got this under control. Your job is to do your thing as our opening act, and keep your mouth closed about the changes to come," Luke said.

"Have I opened my mouth once to anyone but you guys? No. So stop telling me to be quiet. Loose lips over here is the one who keeps dropping shit to the press." She flung her thumb at Dex, before turning her attention back to Zach. "Well, you're not as pretty as Cruzie boy is, but you've got that rocker edge thing going for you. I watched a few YouTube videos of your shows, and you're pretty fucking talented. Dex should be scared. You jam on the electric guitar, dude. Phenomenal."

Fucking Tia loved to drop a bomb on the room. She and I had gotten back to normal. I'd been pissed at her for a while after that bullshit stunt she pulled, but I got over it. She wasn't into me, she was into her career.

"Oh, yeah. I'm really nervous. Dickhead over here is leaving, I think my job is pretty safe, but thanks for your concern," Dex said with a laugh.

"It would suck for you if the new lead singer is a better electric guitar player than you, though, wouldn't it?" She taunted. Jesus. Tia had bigger balls than most of the dudes I hung out with.

Dex moved, getting in her face. "It would suck for Exiled to drop your lame ass, wouldn't it? There's a million piece of shit bands dying to open for us, so I'd watch yourself."

Tia held her chin up, and I swear she puffed her chest out. My God, I think this girl would go to blows with him if it came down to that. Adam, Lennon, and I all moved between them within seconds.

"Easy, tiger," I said, wrapping my fingers around her bicep and walking her back a few steps. "Chill the fuck out."

She rolled her eyes. "Okay, good talk. Zach, welcome to the band. I'll see you later."

Tia stormed out of the room and Zach was the first to speak, "That was hot. What a badass chick."

We all laughed, with the exception of Dex. His arms were crossed over his chest and he dropped back down on his stool. Zach was going to fit in just fine. We spent the afternoon rehearsing together before he took off. We wouldn't introduce him to our fans until a few weeks before my departure. He'd perform with us on stage this summer, and I could already tell it would be an easy transition.

———

"Promise me you won't cut it too close. The label's breathing down my back with all the changes coming up, Cruz," Luke said, walking beside me to my waiting car.

"I give you my word, brother. I just need to see her."

"Alright. See you tomorrow." Luke clapped me on the shoulder before walking back into the hotel.

Ponch had agreed to fly me to Chicago to surprise Jade. I needed to see her. Touch her. It had been weeks and I couldn't go another minute. Surprisingly, it wasn't about sex. I didn't expect anything. I knew she needed time, and I'd agreed to take it slow. Which I would still honor. But I wanted to see her.

Thankfully, Ari was a willing participant and always helped me pull off a surprise for Jade. She'd been a little icy to me at first, but after a dozen calls over the last two days, Jade's best friend had warmed up to me. Jade and I were talking all day, every day, but she wasn't expecting me to visit. Our tour schedule was tight, and she was starting finals this week. I'd spoken to her right before I got on the plane, and she didn't have a clue I was coming. It would be a short visit, but I needed to know we were okay.

When I arrived on her doorstep, I texted Ari. She opened the door and laughed.

"You know you're crazy, right? Flying all the way here for five hours," she whispered.

"I've been called worse. Where is she?"

"In her room studying. I hope she doesn't kill me for this. You're supposed to be taking it slow. So, you best work your magic, so I don't get in trouble for helping you." Ari continued to whisper on the front porch like we were conspiring to rob a bank.

I knew Jade wouldn't be pissed that I came. She wanted to see me as much as I wanted to see her. She was just guarding her heart this time around, but she didn't need to. I'd never hurt her again.

"You worry too much," I said, walking past her and heading down the hall.

Jade's door was closed. I knocked lightly.

"Come in," she called out.

I opened the door. She sat in the middle of her bed, papers and books sprawled everywhere. Her hair was tied in a messy knot on top of her head with two pencils sticking out of the bun. She looked like a mad scientist, yet the sight of her almost dropped me to my knees. It had been too long. A knot lodged in the back of my throat, making it difficult to speak. She stared down at her book, assuming Ari had just walked in. Her head turned slightly, and when she caught sight of me, she gasped.

She was on her feet, bed bouncing and papers scattering everywhere. "What are you doing here?"

Before I could answer her, she lunged from the mattress into my arms. Her legs wrapped around my waist, and her face buried in the crook of my neck. Her warm breath tickled against my skin, and I breathed in all her goodness.

Sunshine.

Everything I'd missed.

She quickly slid down my body, like she'd come to her senses and realized she'd wrapped herself around me, now putting a little distance between us.

"It's a short visit. Just a few hours. But I wanted to see you. Tell you to your face how much I love you, and how sorry I am about everything," I said. I held her face in my hands, taking her in. Fuck, I'd missed her.

"I can't believe you're here." She smiled.

"Listen, I know you want to take it slow. I'm not here for anything more than this."

Her gaze locked with mine. "Yeah. I definitely think we need to take it slow." She twirled the ring on her finger. A habit she always did when she was nervous. Hell, I was just happy she was still wearing it.

"I'm fine with that. I just wanted to see you."

Her hands settled on my chest before they came around my middle and she hugged me.

"I'm glad you're here," she whispered.

"Yeah?" I leaned forward and grazed her lips with mine.

"I'm not sleeping with you. You know that, right? We're taking this slow," she said with a chuckle, but I didn't miss the tremble in her voice.

I laughed against her mouth. "Is kissing you off the table?"

"Kissing is as far as it goes, Winslow."

My mouth came over hers. Slow and gentle. My hand moved into her hair, tilting her head back for better access. She moaned into my mouth before cutting off our connection. She took a step back and tucked her hair behind her ears. Her face was flush, and she licked her lips and shook her head with a laugh.

"Okay, we're not going to be taking it slow if we keep that up."

"I missed you so fucking much, Jade." My fingers interlaced with hers.

"I missed you too."

I dropped to sit on her bed, and she settled on my lap. My arms came around her and it was the most content I'd felt in weeks.

"Is it okay that I came?"

"Yeah. I'm glad you're here."

"I know you have to study, and I didn't come here to interrupt your life. So, if you need to work, I'll just sit with you and write," I said, running my fingers through her silky hair.

"I was just about to wrap things up and get some rest." She pushed to her feet and started collecting all the papers on the bed.

"Yeah?"

"Yeah."

"Okay. Good," I said, and for the first time in my life, I was nervous. I didn't want to fuck things up again, so I wasn't sure what to do.

She walked in the bathroom and washed her face and changed into her pajamas, while I leaned against the door frame and watched her. She turned around when she took her top off, and I laughed. As if I hadn't seen her a million times. She was apprehensive with me, and as much as I hated it, I understood it. She stepped back in the bedroom and climbed into bed.

"We can sleep together without *doing the deed*," she said, wriggling her brows.

I laughed. "The deed?"

Her head fell back, and she chuckled. "You know what I mean."

I dropped my jeans and tugged my T-shirt over my head before slipping under the covers with her. She reached and turned off the light, and we both rolled on our sides and faced one another. Our legs were tangled up, as if they had a mind of their own.

"I thought about what we talked about. You know, about spending the summer together on tour."

"Oh, yeah?" I held my breath as I waited for what she had to say.

"I want to go with you. Let's just see how the next few weeks go, okay?"

All the air left my lungs. We were going to be okay. She was giving me a second chance.

"Thank fucking God," I said, moving closer to her and wrapping my arm around her waist. I settled my forehead against hers.

She laughed, and I swear my fucking heart squeezed. "We just need to see how things go. But, I want it to work. You know that."

"I'm happy to hear you say that."

"I just want to make sure you're okay. How do I know this won't happen again?"

"It won't. I was just going through a lot of shit. It's not an excuse. I really thought I was doing what was best for you at the time."

"Breaking my heart is never what's best for me. And you broke it, Cruz. And I don't know if I can trust you. It's not that I don't want to, I'm just nervous now, you know?"

I played with a long strand of hair that broke free from her knot. I twisted it around my finger. "I'm so fucking sorry."

"I know you are," she said.

"I'm going to make it up to you, baby."

"I hope you do," she said, and her eyes closed. I tucked her head beneath my chin, and her breathing lulled me to sleep.

I only had two hours until I had to be back at the hanger, and it was completely worth it to have this time with her.

It was going to take time, but Jade and I were going to figure this out.

Because I'd do whatever it took to win her back.

twenty-three

. . .

Jade

"I'M GOING to the store as soon as it opens to buy as many copies of Rock the Band as I can," I told Cruz, as I brushed my hair.

The phone was propped in the sink while I got ready. We'd only had five hours together, but they'd meant everything to me. And now I missed him even more. It had been a few days since he left, but it felt like forever.

"I'm curious to see the article. I think most of it is about the band, but she did interview me separately, and I ended up talking about you the whole time." Cruz laughed. He was lying on his side in bed as he FaceTimed me.

"Oh, this should be interesting. Do you know if they used you on the cover or the band?" I asked.

"They ended up using a solo picture of me. They included a bunch of group shots on the inside. I'm sure that will piss off Dex, but I had no control over it. I would have preferred a shot of the band on the cover."

"I can't wait to see it. And it's your birthday in seventeen hours. I can't believe I'm not going to be with you," I said, frowning into the phone.

Were we back together? Kind of. We were taking it slow, which basically meant we weren't having sex. Everything else had gone back to normal. We were talking all day, every day, and had picked up where we left off. The truth was—Cruz is my best friend. I'd missed him. Did I trust that he was out of the woods with his battle with alcohol and prescription drugs? No. But I wanted to. I believed we would get there.

"I don't give a shit about my birthday, baby."

"I do. Of course, I do. It's just impossible to get away right now with finals coming up."

"Don't worry. I'll get to see you the following weekend. I just want to spend time with you," he said, pushing to sit up. My gaze locked on his abs as the camera was propped on his bed.

I whistled and he laughed.

He lifted the camera and walked to the bathroom. "You like what you see?"

"Always." I wriggled my brows.

"You have class and research today, right?" he asked as he brushed his teeth.

"Yep. I should be done before you leave for the show. I'll try to call you then. If not, we'll talk right after. I'll be your first call on your birthday, which means we need to talk at 12:01 tonight, or technically tomorrow morning."

"Alright. I love you."

"Love you more," I said before I hung up the phone and grabbed my backpack.

I grabbed several copies of Rock the Band as soon as I got out of class and swooned over the cover on my walk to research. The picture was gorgeous—A closeup of Cruz's bare chest and face. The tattoo script: *more Jade* on full display. He wasn't smiling or posed, it was more of a smoldering gaze. Honey brown eyes that I swore could see into my soul were shimmering with pops of gold and orange. I studied every single inch before sending him a quick text. He had a busy day with meetings and rehearsals before the show.

Oh my gosh. Have you seen it? It's amazing.
I love it so much! Can't wait to read the
article.

CRUZ

Haven't even seen it yet. Been in meetings all
morning. Glad you like it, baby. Yours is the
only opinion I care about.

It's perfect. Love you!

I walked into Elaine's office and she was sitting behind her desk, her glasses were propped on her head and she looked deep in thought.

"Hey," I said as I dropped in the chair across from her.

"Hi. Did you get me a copy?"

I laughed. Elaine and I had grown so close this year. "I did. The cover is gorgeous. I can't wait to read the article."

I handed her a copy.

"Wow. Great cover. And that's the tattoo he got for you, right?" She winked and chuckled.

"Yes," I said, feeling my cheeks heat.

We both opened to the article and read in silence. The first portion was all about how the band met. Cruz hoped that they would be able to hide the discord amongst the band, and as I read it, I didn't sense any tension. The interview with all the guys was short, and the photographs of the four of them together were peppered across the five page spread. There were several more of Cruz solo, and I studied each and every one of them. He looked amazing. Thank God this hadn't come out while we were apart. It would have been torture. I turned the page to read Cruz's interview. They labeled it: Riley Lawson (RL) and Cruz Winslow (CW).

RL - So Cruz, people report all sorts of things about your relationship, are you or aren't you in one, and if it's on or off. So, let's start there. Are you in a relationship with one girl?

CW - Yeah. Have been for over a year. With one girl. I don't know why it's such a mystery. Most of the songs I've written are for her. I've sung to her on stage a couple times and talked about her at our concerts repeatedly. She's with me as often as she can be, because she's going to school.

RL - I assume we're talking about Jade Moore?

CW – Yes.

RL - So, when that story from Farrah Clearwater came out that she was with you in Miami, it was a lie?

CW - A blatant lie. I don't fuck around on Jade. I was with my girl the weekend Farrah claimed she was with me. I have no idea why she made it up.

RL - Why didn't you come out and defend yourself?

CW - Because it feeds the flame. I don't need to justify lies with a response. As long as Jade knows the truth, that's all that matters to me.

RL - I like that.

CW – Thanks.

RL - So, tell me, where do you see yourself in five years?

CW – Honestly…I don't know. I definitely see myself married to Jade. She'll be in med school then. I hope to be writing music, maybe teaching art, traveling, all that good stuff.

RL – Doesn't sound like the life of a rock star.

CW – I think the only way to make it in this business is to have a life outside of it. Or you'll drown in the chaos of it all.

RL – That makes sense. Is it difficult doing the long-distance thing? Especially while being on the road?

CW – It's not fun. Jade's the real deal, you know. She works her ass off. She wants to be a doctor. She's the best person I know. And dating me isn't easy. She's been forced into the public eye, and it's attention she never asked for.

RL – I'm sure that's not easy. You have to trust one another immensely.

CW – There's no problem there. Jade and I are solid.

RL – So if she has years of school left, and you're on tour, how long can you keep this up? You know, being apart?

CW – As long as we need to.

RL – Good answer.

CW – Thanks. (laughs).

RL – So it appears people just really want to know you, and you've been pretty private up until now. We got a ton of questions that our readers sent in. Do you mind if I fire through a few of those?

CW – Sure.

RL – Okay. What do you do for fun?

CW – Hang out with my girl, go to the beach, galleries, travel.

RL – Favorite color?

CW – Black. (laughs)

RL – (laughing from previous answer) Okay. This is a popular one. How did you and Jade meet?

CW – In the dorms. My brother, Adam, and I went to check out the new freshman, and I met her.

RL – Love at first sight?

CW – For me, yes, absolutely. For Jade, no. She hated me before she loved me. (laughs).

RL – You grew up in a Hollywood family, has that helped you deal with fame?

CW – I don't actually know. Possibly. I definitely think it helped to get us here.

RL – This one's a good one. What inspires you to write music. Do songs just come to you?

CW – I think life inspires me. Most of the songs I've written this past year have been inspired by Jade. So, I guess love probably has a lot to do with inspiration.

RL – Wow. I like that. I have to say, I didn't expect you to be so—open and honest.

CW – I try to keep my personal life private, you know? But I don't have anything to hide. It's more to protect those I love. Which is a very small group of people. (laughs).

RL – I get that. What about school? You were attending Northwestern before you went on tour, one of the top academic schools in the country. Have you always been a good student?

CW – Yes. School has always come easy for me, with the exception of science.

RL – That's ironic, huh?

CW – Why's that?

RL – Because your girlfriend wants to be a doctor, I'm guessing she's pretty good at science. (laughs).

CW – Oh, yeah. She is. She actually tutored me, and that's how I wormed my way into her heart. (laughs).

RL – Well, it looks like that was a good thing. You've been together for quite a while now. How does she handle the pressure of the press, and the attention?

CW – Jade puts up with it for me, but she has no desire to be in the spotlight.

RL – She sounds like a keeper.

CW – One hundred percent.

RL – One last question, because I know we're going to get it after some of the photos are printed when this article goes to press.

CW – Okay.

RL – What is the meaning behind your tattoo? More Jade?

CW – Exactly what it says. More Jade. I always want more. (laughs).

RL – Before this interview, I wouldn't have guessed you a romantic. (laughs).

CW – Only with one girl. (laughs).

RL – As it should be. Thank you for talking with me today, Cruz.

CW – Sure. Thanks for having me.

There was a closing paragraph thanking Cruz and the band for taking the time to meet with Rock the Band.

"That was something," Elaine said, fanning her face with the magazine and laughing. "That boy is crazy about you."

My cheeks burned, and I bit down on my bottom lip. "Yeah, that was so nice."

"Nice? You have a rock star pledging his love for you to the world. That's damn sexy," Elaine said.

I laughed and shook my head. I was so glad Cruz and I were back on track. He really did love me. I didn't doubt that. "I know. I wish I could go surprise him tonight for his birthday."

"Why can't you?"

"Well, I have a review session tonight, which is mandatory. I'm working with you tomorrow morning." I chuckled and held my arms up in question. "And I have a review session for my final in anatomy tomorrow afternoon. Why it was scheduled on a weekend is beyond me."

"Okay, I'm going to give you a little unsolicited advice. You've got a long road ahead of you with school, kiddo. Find your balance. Go to your review session tonight and fly out right after. It's not that long of a flight to New York. And I don't even need you tomorrow. You can have someone take notes for you at the review session tomorrow. Do you have anyone you trust in there?" she asked.

I twirled my ring around my finger. "Maybe. I could ask Brayden. But I'd have to book a flight, and it's such short notice."

I wanted to surprise Cruz, and I could probably try to reach Lennon to ask Ponch if he would fly me, but they were in meetings all day and had a show they were getting ready for. And doing it on such short notice would be a lot to ask of Ponch. I'd need to book my own flight. I had a credit card with plenty of room on it. I could do this.

"You text Brayden, and I'll look up the flights. You could get in late tonight and fly home Sunday. You'd technically have two nights there, and it would be the best birthday surprise."

"Okay. Let me text him. Thank you. I can't believe you're helping me with this," I said with a laugh. My mentor had become so much more. She was a friend too.

"Are you kidding? This is the most excitement I've had in years." She smiled while her fingers tapped out the info on her keyboard.

> Hey. Is there any way you could take notes for me at the review session for anatomy tomorrow if I need to miss it?

BRAYDEN

> Of course. Everything okay?

> Yes. Everything is great. I appreciate it so much.

"He said yes," I said, shaking my head. Still surprised I was doing this.

"It's meant to be. What time is your review tonight?"

"Six to eight," I said, moving to the other side of her desk and pulling out my credit card.

"Can you get to the airport for a nine-thirty flight? It will get you into New York a little after midnight with the time change, but hey, you'll be there on his birthday, right?"

"Yes." My hands were shaking as I typed in my credit card info and booked the flight.

This was going to be the best surprise ever.

And it was my way of saying I was ready to jump in with both feet.

twenty-four

. . .

Cruz

I DROPPED down on the couch in our suite. I'd been in rehearsals all day, as this was a new venue we were performing in tonight. Jade had given me bits and pieces about the article, and she seemed pleased with it. I'd had dozens of texts from friends and family. My mom had phoned to say she loved the cover and the article. My father had gone radio silent over the last few days. He hadn't been welcome to join our family therapy sessions yet, and Lennon and Mom were both still not speaking to him. He'd been calling me incessantly up until two days ago. My family was still in the midst of a shit storm, but we were finding our way through it. I was surprised I hadn't heard from my father today, as no one had been more excited about the spread in Rock the Band than him.

I liked Riley Lawson, and the interview was fair and honest. She didn't twist any of my words or make any assumptions. I was thankful for that, because I'd been warned that they could make you appear a certain way if they didn't like you. That wasn't the case here.

I tried to call Jade before I went to grab a bite to eat with the guys on our way to the show. She'd be heading to her review session, but it was worth a try.

It went to voicemail, so I sent her a text.

> Hey. Just leaving for dinner and the show. Hope the review goes well. I'll talk to you at midnight. Love you.

MORE JADE

> Talk to you tonight. Just started review. Love you more!

———

"What the fuck is going on with Luke?" Adam asked as we watched our manager huddled in the corner with his phone. He raised his voice multiple times, which wasn't like Luke.

"The fuck if I know," I said.

"You guys aren't exactly the easiest band to manage. He's always putting out fires. It's probably nothing." Tia stretched her neck from left to right and did a few stretches. The girl did some crazy ass stunts in her act, so it never surprised me that she needed to warm up before she went on.

The crowd was already rowdy and loud—the energy palpable.

"You aren't in this band so keep your ass out of our business," Dex said.

"Okay, chill out, dude. She's just trying to help." Lennon moved between them.

Dex kept wiping his nose and there were remnants of white powder there, because he didn't care to clean himself up. The dude was so out of control, I wondered how he was still functioning.

"Fuck you, Lennon," Dex mumbled before reaching for a bottle of whiskey and tipping his head back.

Tia got called out on stage, and we sat and watched as she warmed up the crowd.

Luke walked over, and he didn't look happy. "You guys ready?"

"What's going on?" Lennon asked.

He let out a long sigh and ran his hand through his hair. "Shit. I didn't want to tell you until after the show, but I don't want you to be blindsided out there if anyone shouts something out to you."

"What is it?" I asked, and my stomach twisted.

He stared at Dex as he spoke. "Fucking Farrah Clearwater is claiming she's pregnant."

Dex laughed with zero emotion.

"She's claiming it's yours, Cruz. She's gone to the press." Luke turned to look at me.

"What? I've never even met this chick," I said.

"I know."

"Is it yours?" Lennon asked Dex. "Why doesn't she just say she banged you?"

"The hell if I know. It can't be mine. I wrap my shit up. She was obsessed with Winslow the night I banged her though," Dex admitted.

What the actual fuck.

"Well, the article in Rock the Band makes it clear that I was never with her. Let people think what they want. I'll demand a paternity test and we can share the results publicly," I said. This girl was a crazy bitch, and I worried about how it would affect Jade. We were barely back on track, and I was trying to earn her trust. I'd talk to her tonight and see how she wanted me to handle it.

"Okay. And maybe you could try to talk to her?" Luke said to Dex.

"I can do that," Dex said, surprising me. Dex wasn't usually the most cooperative guy.

"And FYI dude, you can get a girl pregnant even if you wrap it up. I'd demand a paternity test to make sure it isn't yours since you actually did sleep with her." Luke didn't hide his frustration.

Tia came jogging off stage and high fived me on the way out. We put on one hell of a show and it was fairly drama-free. I was tired and ready to call it a night. Luke was still putting out fires on his phone, and when I stepped on the tour bus, he chucked his cell phone at the wall. Everyone stilled. The dude never lost his cool.

He dropped to sit on the bench and buried his face in his hands.

"Dude, what's going on?" I sat beside him, and Lennon and Adam stared with concern. Dex boarded the bus with three chicks in tow, not a care in the world.

Yeah, dickhead, you might have a kid on the way, but by all means, have some fun.

"Take them in back," Adam said to Dex, shooting him a warning glare.

"Yes, your highness. Will do." He cackled with laughter as he walked toward the back of the bus.

"Your father gave an interview that just came out. It's going viral. He said Cruz was planning to leave the band. He basically blamed Jade for it. She's going to take a shit ton of heat, Cruz. Even if we make a statement and try to clear it up, he planted a seed and put it out there. He also commented on Farrah's claims that you got her pregnant. He said he hoped it was true because it would mean you probably wouldn't leave Exiled if you were with someone else."

I pushed to my feet and kicked the large box sitting on the floor beside Luke. Little pieces of cardboard flew through the air and rolls of toilet paper made their way across the bus.

"Motherfucker," I spewed.

I had some crazy bitch I'd never met claiming she was pregnant with my child, and a father who'd thrown my girlfriend to the wolves along with causing a shit ton of grief for the band.

"Jesus. What is wrong with that man?" Lennon dropped to sit beside Luke on the bench seat.

"Dex," I shouted at the back end of the bus.

Dex stumbled out toward me. "You bellowed?"

"I need you to call that chick and straighten this out. Do you have her number?" I asked.

"I don't know if that's a good idea. We don't want to make things worse," Luke said, running his hands through his hair. "Your dad basically just validated her like it's a real thing."

"Fuck." The voice that left my body was unrecognizable as my anger bounced off the walls.

"I talk to her sometimes. It wouldn't be odd for me to text her," Dex said, and we all turned to look at him with surprise. They were friends? What the actual fuck. How had he not stepped in before now.

"You talk to her? Jesus, Dex. For fuck's sake, call her and get her to change her statement. Get her to tell the fucking truth," Lennon said, pushing to his feet and getting in his face.

"Dude. I don't talk to her daily. We snap and text here and there."

"Then try to clean this mess up. You're the one who brought her into this situation, the least you can do is help fix it," Luke said.

Dex put his hands up defensively. "I'll call her now."

I dropped to sit next to my brother, as we listened to Dex make the call. Unfortunately, we could only hear one end of the conversation, and it was all, uh huh, and mmhmms. I rolled my eyes and Luke mouthed several questions to ask.

Why did she make this up?

What is her beef with Cruz?

Dex listened intently, nodding and smiling the entire time, which made me want to rip his fucking face off. He ended the call as we pulled up to the hotel.

"What did she say?" Lennon asked.

"She said she originally made it up because it got her a shit ton of followers on social media. Hey, at least she's honest." Dex smirked.

"Why not say she banged you? Which is the truth." I said.

"She said she actually liked me and didn't want to do that to me. Plus, she thought with you being the lead singer, it would get her more attention."

"Christ. What is wrong with people? So, what's the deal with the pregnancy?" Luke moved toward the door to exit the bus.

"That's the awkward part..." Dex smiled. It was devious and evil. He enjoyed watching me squirm through this shit show.

"I can't imagine it gets worse." Lennon said, pushing to stand.

"It was your father's idea," Dex said, and we all came to a stop. "Your father reached out to her. He paid her to sell the story about the pregnancy. She isn't even pregnant. He said she can say she had a miscarriage in a few weeks. He even told her she could claim you made her abort it."

My mouth went dry. Limbs numb. The final nail in the coffin for this man. Why? Why would he do this to me? I stared at my brother, and anger filled his gaze. I was speechless. What was there to even say at this point? My father was going to destroy me because I wasn't doing what he wanted. I was quitting the band and he wasn't happy about it. I hadn't gotten him a visit with Mom yet. But what that asshole didn't know was that it wasn't for lack of effort. I was actually trying to help him, because for some fucked up reason, I wanted to repair my broken family. And he'd just guaranteed that would never happen. He'd reached out to some crazy chick and started a shit storm. Jesus. I walked off the bus and dialed Jade. It was midnight. She'd be waiting for my call.

It went to voicemail.

"Baby, I need you to call me. There's a shit storm coming your way, and I'm sorry. You've probably already seen that Farrah is claiming she's pregnant. The whole thing is a lie. I just found out my dad is behind it. He sold a story that I'm quitting the band, *for you*. He also offered Farrah money to say she was pregnant with my kid. Jesus, Jade. What the fuck is wrong with this man? Please call me. I hope you aren't mad. I hope you aren't buying into any of this shit. I need you to call me. You promised to be the first call at midnight, and now you're not picking up. I love you."

I shoved the phone in my back pocket as we made our way into the lobby.

"She said she'll retract it. We might have to throw some cash at her, but it's worth it," Dex said, shoving his hands in his back pockets while his harem of women stood behind him.

Now we were going to pay her to tell the truth. Fuck me.

"Let me think on this. That could look like a payout, we need to be careful. I'm going to stay down here and get a glass of wine and try to clean up this mess," Luke said, studying me.

"Bailey and Tia said we can come hang out in their suite. They're going to order food, watch some movies, whatever. Might be good to take your mind off things," my brother said to me.

"Nah. I'm going to FaceTime Jade and go to sleep. Try to forget about this shit," I said.

"You sure? It's technically your birthday," Lennon said, glancing down at his phone to see the time.

Adam clapped me on the shoulder. "Happy birthday, brother. I'm sorry about this."

"Yeah." I nodded. There wasn't anything more to say.

"Well, me and the ladies are going upstairs for a little fun, if anyone wants to join us." Dex winked and walked toward the elevators.

"I guess that means I'll be sleeping with earplugs tonight," Adam said, forcing a smile as we stepped on the elevator.

My brother hugged me goodbye and asked me another dozen times if I was okay. He was all tore up that it was my birthday. Who gives a shit? I'd never been big on celebrating my birthday. My father was that guy. Acted like it didn't come around every goddamn year and celebrated himself for an entire fucking month. Narcissistic asshole.

We made our way into the room, and Dex dropped down on the couch with a group of giggling, drunk chicks surrounding him.

"You want me to order food? You hungry?" Adam asked from the doorway of my room.

"Nah. I'm fine, dude. Thanks. Go call your girl and get some sleep. I'll see you in the morning."

He knocked on the door frame. "Use your earplugs or you won't get any sleep with the douchebag out there."

I nodded. I was anxious to be alone and take in what just happened. I didn't know if I should call my father and confront him. What was the point? He'd deny it—or worse, he'd admit it and justify his actions. Either way, I was done. I picked up my phone and tried Jade again. I needed to know she didn't believe any of this bullshit. We'd just taken two steps forward, and now we were most likely going to take two steps back. She was probably pissed and over all this bullshit.

Voicemail.

My stomach twisted. Jade was insistent on talking at midnight, so she'd be the first to wish me happy birthday. Something was up. And she wasn't taking my calls. She was mad. My father had fucked me over again. I tossed my phone on the nightstand. It was almost one in the morning now. She obviously wasn't calling and didn't want to talk to me.

I buried my face in my hands and tried to calm my breathing. I couldn't catch a break. Things were finally back on track with Jade, and now she probably hated me again. Jesus.

There was a knock on the door.

"What?"

Dex walked in, looking like a party boy on spring break. He was coked up and high as a fucking kite.

"Dude. I know you're stressed, and I know I'm not your favorite person, but I thought you might need some assistance sleeping tonight." He tossed a prescription bottle at me. "Need a few Ambien to sleep it off?"

I probably wouldn't sleep tonight after everything that had happened. I wouldn't be able to turn my brain off. Couldn't talk to Jade. The only thing that would give me a reprieve was sleep. And nothing knocked me out quite like Ambien and whiskey. Yes, I'd quit. And yes, I'd stop again tomorrow. But life is about moderation, and right now, this would solve my current problem.

"Yeah, that would help," I said, studying the bottle.

"I sent the other chick's home, so it's just me and Lala out there if you want to come out and do a few lines."

Jesus. I hated him. But I was a hypocrite because here I was using him for Ambien when I should be telling him to get the fuck out of my room. I didn't have the energy to go at it with Dex tonight.

"I don't. Thanks for this, though." I moved to the mini bar to grab a small bottle of whiskey.

"Yeah. You got it." He walked out of the room and I pushed the door closed.

I tossed back two Adderall and chased them down with booze. My body tingled immediately, as I'd been sober for a few weeks and hadn't taken Ambien since our European tour. I could feel it hitting my system, numbing me, as my eyes grew heavy. I was barely able to kick off my shoes as I fell back on the bed.

Escape.

I needed an escape. Just for tonight.

Tomorrow I could work on the shit show that was my life.

Happy fucking birthday to me.

twenty-five

. . .

Jade

MY FLIGHT GOT DELAYED due to rain, and we'd circled above New York City for over an hour. Of course, my phone died, as I forgot to charge it before I left for my review session, and I didn't remember to bring the cord to charge it on the plane. I wanted to call Cruz at midnight, but that plan had been an epic fail. But I was here, and that would be a better birthday present than a phone call. I knew he'd be wondering why I hadn't called, and it only made me more excited to surprise him.

I Ubered to the swanky hotel in the city. I stepped into the gorgeous lobby, taking in all the sparkly details that surrounded the entrance. Large chandeliers, glass tables, and white marble floors. Chic and elegant.

I had no idea how I'd figure out what room he was in. I walked to the front desk to beg them to help me out. Worst comes to worst, I'd have to see if they had a cord so I could charge my phone in the lobby and then I'd call Cruz.

"Jade? Everything okay?" a voice said from behind me.

"Luke. Thank God. Yes. I came to surprise Cruz for his birthday, but my phone's dead." I held up my cell and shook it around.

"Glad you're here. The birthday boy is having a tough night. He went up to his room to call you. Are you aware of all that's happened tonight?" he asked. Luke held a glass of wine, and I realized he was a disheveled mess as I took him in.

"No. What happened?" My heart started to race, and my mouth went dry. I could tell he was about to drop a bomb.

"Steven went to the press. Told them Cruz was leaving Exiled, and it was because of you."

"What? Oh my gosh. How could he do that?"

"Oh, it gets better. He paid Farrah Clearwater to lie and say she was pregnant with Cruz's child," Luke said, shaking his head. The veins in his neck bulged. "Steven's got this great kid, you know? And he beats him down. I don't get it."

My eyes filled with tears, and my bottom lip shook.

Cruz.

"I don't get it either. I need to see him. What room are they in?"

Luke reached in his back pocket and handed me a key. "Top floor. Suite at the end of the hall. He went up a while ago. He'll be really happy to see you."

"Thanks, Luke. Have you guys made a statement yet?"

"No. I'm working on it now. I have to figure out how to handle it. If we should just admit that he's leaving or buy more time. How to make it clear that you have nothing to do with it. If we offer Farrah money to out Steven and say it was all a lie, or just pay her to shut it down." He ran a hand through his hair.

"Well, don't worry about me. They hate me for dating Cruz. I can handle them hating me for him leaving if I have to. It's not the end of the world. But you have a mess to clean up, so I'll let you get back to it."

He pulled me in for a hug and held me there for longer than usual. "I'm sorry you and Cruz have to go through this, Jade. I truly am."

I swiped at the tears running down my cheeks when I pulled away. "I know you are. It'll all be okay."

I walked toward the elevator. I waited until I got off on the top floor and tied the bow around myself. I'm sure I looked ridiculous wearing skinny jeans, a blouse and a gigantic hot pink bow around my chest. But it had been a crappy day for him, and maybe this surprise would turn things around.

The suite was the last door at the end of the long hallway. I heard laughter which immediately put me on edge. I knocked first, before swiping the key card. When I pushed the door open, my jaw hit the floor.

Dex sat on the gray couch in the large living room area. There was a pile of white powder on the table. My stomach dipped. Why would he have this around Cruz and Lennon? There was a blonde girl kneeling on the area rug bent over the coffee table. She was mid snort when she realized the door opened. She wiped her nose and laughed.

"Who are you?"

"Hey, I'm Jade," I said, my throat dry.

"Princess Jade returns. Come on over. Join us," Dex said, moving to his feet.

"No thanks. Where's Cruz?"

"The birthday boy is gone for the night. He was sulking over all the shit that went down. Numbed himself with enough shit to be gone till tomorrow, so I'm afraid you're out of luck."

Dex stood in front of me, invading my personal space. I took a step back. He reeked of booze and had remnants of powder on his nose. I didn't want to believe anything he was saying.

"What did you give him? Did you do something to him?" I said, storming through the living space and opening the first door I came to.

"Ah, you're in my room. Was that intentional? You want a little one on one with a real man, do you?"

My heart raced as I shoved him out of my way and hurried toward the next door. The girl on the floor pushed to her feet.

"Come on, Dex. I thought we were getting out of here. I want to go to the club," she said. She was tall and incredibly thin, with blonde hair and a worn face. She wore a backless halter top that was held up by a thin strap behind her neck.

"Sorry doll face. You go on ahead. I don't want to leave Jade alone."

A chill ran down my spine at his words. "I'm fine. Please do us both a favor and *leave*."

He walked to the door along with his date, and I hoped he'd leave with her. I hurried into the next room to find my boyfriend sound asleep. I rushed over to the side of his bed and shook him several times.

"Cruz," I said, shaking his lifeless body. "Cruz, wake up."

What the hell happened? I looked on the nightstand and found a prescription bottle of Ambien in Dex's name and Cruz's prescription for Adderall beside it. Two small empty bottles of whiskey lay on the floor next to the nightstand.

"I told you he was gone. Your boy's going to be out for a long time," Dex said from the doorway.

His white skinny jeans were filthy, and they barely clung to his bony body. He wore a dirty black T-shirt and his hair was overgrown and greasy. Dark circles rimmed his eyes, and he looked gaunt and sickly. But that was how he'd looked since the day I'd met him. Sure, he'd gotten worse, but it wasn't like he took care of himself before Exiled went on tour.

I picked up the bottle of Ambien and chucked it as hard as I could at him. The bottle bounced off his chest and he laughed.

"You're disgusting. You just couldn't help yourself, could you? You had to kick him when he was down, didn't you?" Tears sprung from my eyes. I squeezed my boyfriend's arm, digging my nails into the skin on his forearm in hopes he would wake up.

"He was in a funk. Shocker. The dude's a moody fucker. He was moping around, probably because you weren't here, and his rich daddy fucked him over. What the hell else is new? He was jacked up on too many Adderall, and he needed something to help him sleep. Don't shoot the messenger, Jade. This is all on him." He walked toward me, and I backed as far away as I could without sitting on Cruz. I was barely balancing on the edge of the bed.

"Get the hell out of here." My voice wobbled as my instincts prepared for battle. His dark eyes were crazed.

"I don't think so. It's time you and I had a little talk. You've had a problem with me since the day we met. And now we're going to get to the bottom of that," he said, wrapping his bony fingers around my bicep.

I stomped on his foot and flailed to get away from him, but he was surprisingly strong. He looked weak. He acted weak. But he was bigger than me and apparently stronger than I'd guessed.

"Let go of me. Cruz!" I shouted, slapping Dex's hand away as he dragged me toward the main living space again.

He threw me down on the couch and the back of his knees hit the coffee table, sending the mound of powder all over the floor. I jumped to my feet when he turned to see what he'd done.

"I don't think so, Jade. There's no one here to help you. So, you and me, are going to figure out why you have a big stick up your ass when it comes to me." He pushed me back hard on the couch, and a gush of air left my lungs. I searched the room for a weapon and screamed for my boyfriend again. How could he be that out of it that he couldn't hear me?

"What do you want to know? There's no mystery here. I don't like you. I never have," I said, pushing the hair out of my face. The bow I'd had tied around me was no longer there and must have been torn off in the scuffle. I calmed my breathing, I needed to stay in control. This guy was not playing with a full stack.

There was a large vase on the entry table. I continued to scan the room, desperate for anything I could use to protect myself from him. He sat across from me, but I didn't try to run yet. Maybe if I played nice, he'd settle down and get distracted. His face was flushed, and the veins in his neck bulged. He reached down and scooped up a handful of powder from the floor and held it in front of my face.

"I think you should loosen up a bit. Then you might not be such a bitch," he said, pushing his hand right beneath my nose.

I slapped the back of his hand hard and the powder sailed through the air. I pushed up to run, but he caught the back of my blouse and yanked me back. He flipped me over on the couch and settled above me. I squeezed my eyes closed and flailed my legs, kicking him where I could. It only made him angrier as he brought his face down to mine. The smell of whiskey and cigarettes flooded my system and I twisted and turned and tried to get away. He pinned my arms above my head, using one hand to hold both of my wrists in place.

"Cruz!" I screamed. My voice was not recognizable. It was desperate, and raspy, and panicked.

"He's not coming for you, baby. It's just you and me. And I know exactly what you need."

Fight or flight.

I would always fight.

I pulled one arm free and punched him in the throat as hard as I could. He fell back and I moved to my feet, running for the door. I reached for the handle when he jerked me backward by the hair.

"I don't think so, sweetheart." His evil, maniacal laugh sent a rush of adrenaline through my body.

I wasn't going to get out of here unharmed unless I fought. I swung with everything I had, and I caught a glimpse of his fist coming for me out of the side of my eye. I tried to duck, but his fist made contact before I could react. Pain radiated across my cheek and my feet came out from under me. Like watching a movie, everything blurred before me. I fell hard. My head hit first. I heard the crashing of glass.

And everything went dark.

twenty-six

. . .

Cruz

SHOUTING CAME FROM THE SUITE, and I rubbed my eyes. Jesus. I reached for my phone and it was barely seven in the morning.

"Fuck. Cruz," the voice yelled louder.

Adam? I pushed to my feet, still groggy, I hurried out to see what the problem was.

The air left my lungs, and I dropped to my knees beside Jade.

Jade? What the fuck was happening.

She was on the floor beside the entry table, which was lying on its side with broken glass all around her. I searched her body, but there was no blood. Her cheek was swollen and bruised.

"What is this? What happened?" My voice was unrecognizable as I shook my girlfriend.

"I need an ambulance now," Adam shouted into his phone, giving them the hotel information. "Yes, she's breathing. But she's unconscious."

Tears dripped from my eyes, landing on her beautiful face as I pulled her into my arms.

"Try to wake her, Cruz," Adam said as he continued to listen to the 911 operator.

"Baby, wake up. Jade. Please." A sob escaped as I held her close.

"Her eyes are fluttering open and closed," Adam said into the phone.

"Jade, can you hear me?" I shouted, even though my mouth was next to her ear.

"Okay, okay." Adam hung up the phone and dropped down beside me on the floor. "They're on their way up."

"Dude, what the fuck happened?" I cried, hugging her tighter as she mumbled something.

"I have no fucking clue. I woke up and found her on the floor." Adam's voice trembled as he looked at her. "Jade, can you hear me?"

"Yes," she said, but the word was barely audible.

There was a banging on the door and Adam pushed up to his knees to open it, as we were sprawled on the floor in the entryway.

Why was she on the floor next to the door? How did she get here? When did she get here?

The paramedics stepped in, pushing me back as they moved her to a stretcher.

"Do we know what happened? A time? Are narcotics involved?" The taller man asked, as the other man hooked something up to Jade, and listened to her heart.

"What? No. She doesn't use narcotics. This is my girlfriend. I don't know what happened. We found her on the floor. I don't know when she even got here." I reached for the trash can and vomited into it. Adam moved beside me and put a hand on my back.

"We woke up and found her unconscious." Adam insisted.

"Alright. She's coming in and out. Probably has a bad concussion. We need to take her in, and they'll run some tests."

"A concussion? How?" I asked, and another round of sobs wrenched from my body.

"From a blow to the head. From the bruising on her cheek, it looks like she was struck in the face by something. Something happened here last night." He looked between both of us, and we shook our heads in disbelief.

Luke came charging down the hall as we followed the paramedics out of the room, toward the elevators.

"What's happened? Is that Jade? What the hell happened?" Luke shouted, keeping stride beside us as we entered the employee elevator. Our security team came out of nowhere and I saw two guys take the steps and one stepped on the elevator with us. And the paramedics.

"I want to go home," Jade mumbled, and I reached for her hand.

"Baby, I'm right here. Do you know what happened?" I wiped at my cheeks as I could barely see through the tears that were flowing from me.

She started to sob, and the paramedic told her she didn't need to speak.

Adam filled Luke in behind me.

"You never saw her last night?" Luke asked as we stepped off the elevator and hurried out the front door. Our security along with hotel security kept people back, but it was early in the morning, so the lobby was not crowded.

"No. Did you?"

"Yes. She got in around two in the morning. Wanted to surprise you for your birthday. I gave her a key to the suite," Luke said.

I insisted on riding with her in the ambulance and Luke and Adam caught an Uber and followed us over.

I tried to process what he'd just told me. She'd gotten in a few hours after me. What the hell could have happened? Did someone follow her into the room? Dex was there with a girl.

Dex.

The blood drained from my body, or at least it felt like it did. There's no fucking way he'd touch her. Right? I wanted to call him. Find out what the fuck happened. But I didn't even have a phone. I was in the clothes I'd slept in.

"I want to go home," Jade said again. Her voice was sad and broken.

"I'm here, baby. I'll take you home."

"I want my dad. Can someone call my dad," she sobbed, her eyes opening and closing as the tears flowed.

I didn't have my fucking phone. "I will, baby. I'll fly him here right away."

We pulled up to the ER and they rushed Jade inside, leaving me standing in the lobby. Adam and Luke came running inside.

"I need to call Jade's father. Need to fly him here right away. I don't have my fucking phone." I paced, running my hands through my hair.

Adam handed me a phone. "I grabbed it for you when I got your shoes. I'm trying to reach Dex to see if he knows what the fuck happened. Lennon is on his way."

"Jesus," I said, dropping to my knees in the lobby as I tried to dial Jack Moore.

Adam and Luke lifted me and set me in a chair. Luke took my phone and said he'd call Jack. He said it would be better to hear from him, because my hysteria would scare the shit out of him. He called Ponch and arranged for Jack to leave Chicago immediately. I sat with my face buried in my hands waiting to hear something.

How did Jade get here? What the hell was happening? My brother arrived, and no one had been able to reach Dex, which had alarm bells going off in my head. I'd fucking kill him if he touched her. I'd fucking kill whoever did this. I paced because I could no longer sit.

Minutes turned into hours. The waiting was torture. I asked the front desk to check on her multiple times and they kept insisting they'd taken her back for tests.

"What the hell is going on?" Jack Moore came running into the waiting area, with Ponch beside him.

"I don't know. We found her on the floor in the suite this morning. The entry table was knocked over and a vase was broken beside her. She was unconscious. She'd been struck by something across her cheek. I didn't know she was coming, Jack. I don't know what the fuck happened." I'd never been a hysterical person. Not even with all the shit I'd seen in my life. But I'd lost it now, and I was well past hysteria.

Jack pulled me into a hug. "I know, son. Do we know what time she fell? Who was there? No one heard a scuffle? Shouting? Nothing?"

I pulled away and froze. I fucking froze as I stared at Jade's father. Because he was right. The table was knocked over. There was broken glass. There'd been a fucking struggle. And I'd been near unconscious due to Ambien. I hadn't heard it. I'd fucking let this happen.

Fuck me.

This was my fault.

"Cruz and I had gone to bed. I had my earplugs in because that douchebag, Dex, was partying in the living room. I never heard a thing. I woke up to get a water this morning and found her," Adam said as we all dropped down to sit.

"And she got in at what time?"

"Around two in the morning," Luke said.

"And you found her at seven? Jesus. She may have been unconscious for hours. Has anyone spoken to Dex?"

"We're trying to reach him," Lennon said.

I pushed to my feet, making my way to the restroom, but I only made it across the lobby before I leaned over a garbage can and vomited. Again. The weight of what happened was settling in, and the realization that I'd been just a few feet away while someone attacked Jade—it was a lot to swallow.

It's ironic how last night I thought my world was crashing in around me with my asshole father and fucking Farrah Clearwater and their bullshit rumors. Now none of it mattered. Because all that matters is Jade.

"Are you the family of Jade Moore? I'm Dr. Warble," a woman said when she stepped out clad in scrubs.

I moved next to Jack and prayed to God Jade would be okay.

"So, the good news is, she is going to be fine. Just fine. Her CT scan is normal. She's lucky. She took a blow to the back of her head, which knocked her unconscious, but everything looks good. We're going to keep her overnight just as a precaution, but she's cleared to fly home in the morning. I know she's anxious to get back to school because she has finals on Monday," Dr. Warble said, pausing as everyone nodded in agreement. Of course, Jade was worried about finals. "I would supervise her for another twenty-four hours after she's home, just to be safe."

"Of course, I will. Can I see her?" Jack asked.

"Yes. Just two at a time, please. We want her to rest and take it easy today. I'll take you back."

Jack and I followed Dr. Warble down the hall to Jade's room. When we walked in, she was lying there, tears streaming down her face. Her bruised cheek was more swollen and a darker purple now. I hurried to the side of her bed, while Jack moved to the other side. She didn't look at me. Not once.

"Hey, Jady bug," Jack said, taking her hand in his.

"I'm so sorry, Dad. I'm sorry you had to miss work and come here," Jade said, but it was more of a croak.

Jack studied her. "There's nowhere else I'd want to be. Cruz had Ponch fly me out, so I made it here quickly. Can you tell us what happened?"

She used the back of her hand to swipe at her tears. "I wanted to surprise Cruz for his birthday." She glanced at me for maybe five seconds before turning away. "My flight was delayed, and I got in late. Luke gave me the key to the room, and when I got there, Dex was there with a girl. She ended up leaving, and he—" She closed her eyes and let her head fall back on the pillow.

My hands fisted at my sides. "He what?"

She turned to face me for the first time, jade green eyes nailing my gaze. So angry. Full of despair.

"He was crazed, and said he wanted to know why I never liked him. He was high and acting erratic. He pinned me to the couch, and I fought him off. I tried to run, but he wasn't having it. He yanked me by the hair and punched me in the face. I must have fallen back and hit my head."

"Jesus," Jack said, running a hand through his hair.

Shame enveloped me. I paced around the room. "I'm going to kill him."

"That's not going to help anything, Cruz. He assaulted her, and he *will* suffer the consequences." Jade's father said.

"The police are going to be here in a little bit to talk to me. It's protocol. Will you stay with me, Dad? And we can fly home tomorrow morning. I need to get back for my finals. I never should have come here," she said, tears rolling down her cheeks.

"Of course, I will. You just tell them the truth, and I'll be here with you, okay?" Jack said.

"Okay. Do you mind giving me and Cruz a minute alone?" she asked. My stomach wrenched and heart pounded.

"Yep. I'll go fill in your friends out in the waiting room and call Sara and catch her up to speed. I'll be back in a few minutes."

Once her father left the room, she pushed to sit up and face me.

I'd never seen Jade's gaze as ice cold as it was right now. Anger. Rage. Disappointment. I saw it all.

"Baby, I'm so sorry," I said, reaching for her hand.

"Don't touch me. Not ever again, Cruz," she said through her sobs. She yanked her hand away like I'd burned her.

"Jade, I didn't know you were coming. I would never let anyone hurt you. You know that."

"Do I? I ran to your room. I shook you. I dug my nails into your arm. I begged you to wake up. I screamed for you to help me. And you left me alone with him. I was lying unconscious a few feet from you for hours. Hours." Her words sliced through me in a way I'd never known possible. Like someone had cut me open and ripped out my heart.

Tears streamed down my face and I fell apart. "I'm so sorry. I'm so fucking sorry."

She wiped away the tears and pulled herself together. Stoic and strong. "Give me your hand."

I paused, a moment of hope. I stretched my arm her way, and she turned my hand over, dropping the ring I'd given her in the palm of my hand. "I don't want to be your family. I don't want to be your future. I don't want to be your anything, Cruz. Not anymore. You aren't good for me."

Jesus.

This was really happening.

I had lost the best thing in my life.

I swiped at the tears streaming down my face. "Baby, don't say that."

"Don't call me that. Don't call me anything."

"I'm so sorry," I said as I stared down at the ring.

"I'm not. Please leave."

"Jade," I pleaded. Desperation clinging to me like a second skin.

She hit the button on the side of her bed. "I will have the nurse call security if you don't leave."

I stared at her with disbelief as the nurse entered the room. "Do you need something, sweetie?"

"Yes. I was hoping you could escort him out and ask my father to come back."

The nurse stared at Jade for a moment. "Absolutely."

When I met Jack in the waiting room, I broke down. He pulled me in and hugged me. He didn't know how much his daughter hated me. "It'll be okay, son."

But it wouldn't.

"She wants me to leave. Asked the nurse to escort me out. She doesn't ever want to see me again. She's done." I pulled back and let out a long breath.

"Give her time. She's been through a traumatic experience and she's upset. Look at me," Jack said, waiting for me to meet his gaze. "This is not your fault. It's not your fault."

"Maybe not directly, but I wasn't there to help her when she needed me. Because I'm a fucking piece of shit." I admitted.

"Then figure it out, Cruz. Figure out how to be there for her." He patted me on the shoulder and moved down the hallway toward his daughter.

I walked over to where Luke, Ponch, Lennon, and Adam stood. "Ponch, do you mind sticking around and flying Jack and Jade home in the morning? I will forward you her father's number and you can speak directly to him. She doesn't want me here, and I want to respect that."

"You got it, Cruz. I will make sure they get home safely."

I called an Uber and my brother, Adam, and Luke walked beside me toward the waiting car. "We're leaving?"

"Yes."

"Maybe she's just pissed right now. It might blow over." Lennon sounded like he was convincing himself as much as me.

"She ran to my room for help, and I was knocked out on Ambien. She shook me and screamed for me to wake up while Dex dragged her by the hair and punched her in the face, leaving her unconscious on the floor for hours. While I slept a few feet away. This is not blowing over."

I glanced down and studied the nail mark bruises on my forearm where she'd tried everything she could to wake me.

Everyone walked in silence.

"Where are we going?" Luke finally asked when we got in the Uber.

"I'm going to find Dex before the police get to him. I'm going to beat the living shit out of him, like I should have done a long time ago. And then—then he can go face his consequences." I tried to calm my racing heart. But it wasn't possible. Dex had cost me everything I cared about.

And he was going to pay for it.

twenty-seven

. . .

Jade

"ARE YOU SURE YOU HAVE EVERYTHING?" Dad asked as he and Sara walked me all the way to security.

"Oh, my gosh. Yes. I'm fine. You did not need to come in with me," I said with a laugh. It had been an emotional two weeks, but guess what—I'd survived them.

"This will be the longest we've ever been apart without visiting one another," Dad said, his eyes welled with emotion.

"I'll be back in three months. It's not like Honduras is that far away," I teased, and he forced a smile. "I need to do this, Dad."

My friend, Jessica, stood off to the side waiting for me to say goodbye. She probably thought my family was crazy walking me all the way to security. But I wouldn't change a thing.

I hugged Sara first. "Take care of him for me."

"I will," she promised, and she wiped at her eyes when I pulled away.

"Love you, Jady bug. Be safe," Dad said, hugging me so tight it was difficult to breathe.

"Love you, too. Sam's going to be checking on you guys all summer, okay? And we'll talk once a week," I said.

"And text every other day to let me know you're alive, right?"

"Yep. I will."

I waved at them as I made my way to meet Jessica and get in line.

"Your dad is sweet. He looks so sad about you leaving," she said.

"Yeah, it kind of came up unexpectedly, so I don't think he's had time to prepare for it." I laughed.

I left out the part about the fact that I'd been attacked in New York just two weeks earlier and broken up with the love of my life.

Yeah… good times.

Dex had hired a fancy attorney and he was getting house arrest for what he did to me and he'd move on with his life like nothing happened. Once a rock star, always a rock star, I guess. What he'd done to me had not been leaked to the press and I was grateful for that. Dex had been hospitalized after being beat up pretty bad the very same day I'd been recovering in a hospital bed in New York, and there'd been rumors that Cruz had put him there. Their feud had gone viral on social media and was even being speculated about on news stations and in magazines. Everyone thought it was because Cruz was leaving the band and Dex was angry. Of course, I knew the real story. It had been Cruz who'd put him there. Cruz had texted me to let me know. I hadn't responded to him in two weeks, but he texted me every single day.

Yeah, I could block him. I'd already blocked him from my heart the best I could. But I wasn't ready to block him completely from my life. So, he sent me texts daily. They were short. Respectful. He wasn't begging me to forgive him. He wasn't defending what had happened or making excuses. He said things like:

I'm proud of you.

Dex will get what he has coming.

This will not go unpunished.

I think of you every day.

You deserve better.

I miss you.

It was painful not to respond, but I wouldn't allow myself to go back to that place. Cruz needed help, and I'd come to realize that I couldn't save him. He needed to save himself. And I needed to save myself.

So, I'd signed up for a three-month medical brigade in Honduras. It was time to focus on things bigger than myself. Bigger than my boyfriend and Exiled. Bigger than gossip magazines and rumors. I wanted to do something good with my life, and there was no time like the present. I'd survived finals even after having a concussion and a broken heart. Turns out I was stronger than I realized. And I was proud of that. I'd given everything I had to Cruz Winslow, and it hadn't been enough. And I'd reached for a life vest before he drowned us both.

Turns out love wasn't always enough.

Jessica and I dropped to sit at our gate after meeting up with the others in our group. We had all arrived early, and some went to grab a bite to eat, while others just walked around to stretch their legs before the long flight. I agreed to watch our carry-ons and hold down the fort. I was reading all about the families we'd be working with when I heard my name. I turned around and my jaw hit the ground.

Cruz.

"What are you doing here?" I said, moving to my feet, looking around to see if anyone recognized him yet. He wore a baseball hat and kept his head down. He'd gotten good at blending in and people here seemed to be minding their own business.

"I wanted to say goodbye." He moved close enough that I could feel his warm breath on my face. God, he was beautiful. I wished he were ugly. And had a boring personality. And no charm. And maybe a few warts on his face. That would help.

"How in the world did you get to come to the gate?" I itched to touch him, so I shoved my hands in the back pockets of my jeans.

"I may have bought a ticket I won't be using to fly to Nicaragua, just so I could say goodbye. Too desperate?" He smiled.

My chest squeezed and I couldn't help but laugh. "Not for you."

"So, I wanted you to know that Dex isn't going back to Exiled. I made sure of that. He wasn't going to get away with what he did to you and just return to his life."

Proving what Dex had done was tricky because there were no witnesses, and he found a couple girls to say he'd been with them at the time of the accident. Due to the little bit of physical evidence found at the scene, he was at least slapped with a brief stint of house arrest. I begged Dad to let it go, because I didn't want to drag things out, nor did I want it to become a story for the tabloids.

"Really? What will happen to Exiled?" I asked, because I certainly didn't want the band to suffer for Dex's behavior.

"Zach is going to take his place, and I've agreed to stay on another year," he said, watching me intently as the words left his perfect mouth.

I nodded. We weren't together. There was no reason for him to leave anymore. At least not for me. But my heart still ached when I looked at him. "It's a solution. At least you got him out."

"I did," he said. "And I met with the bigwigs at the label, and they agreed to my terms."

"Which are?"

"Dex is cut from the band, and I agreed to stay on for twelve more months. We take a thirty-day leave from touring so I can enter a program. I've been working with Dr. Roberts, my mom's doctor, doing daily phone consults, and it's important to me that you know I haven't had a sip of liquor nor any prescription meds since the night you were attacked. I flushed everything. I'm sure it doesn't mean much now, but I wanted you to know. I'm going into a program to make sure that I don't slip back into old habits, although, the last two weeks have been the worst in my life, and I haven't numbed myself through them. And it fucking sucks," he said.

"Tell me about it." I met his gaze.

"I'm so sorry, Jade. So, fucking sorry." His eyes filled with moisture and his bottom lip trembled. I didn't doubt for a minute that he'd tortured himself about what happened. But maybe that's part of hitting rock bottom. He needed to take a hard look at his life.

That's how much I loved him. Maybe you could love someone too much. I believed I did. And forcing him to heal was the only thing left to do.

I reached for his hand and squeezed it. "I know you are."

"I love you. I'm going to make things right." He interlaced our fingers and moved closer.

"Don't make promises you can't keep, Cruz," I said, biting down on my bottom lip.

"I never will again."

"You know I'm leaving for three months. I won't be back until school starts." I didn't pull my hand away, but I fought the urge to wrap my arms around him.

"I do. I'll be here fixing myself. Waiting for you." He smiled, and my stomach did little flips.

"We'll see."

"Hey, that's not *no*. I'll take it." He laughed and reached in his pocket. "I have something for you."

"Why?" I asked, my tone skeptical.

"Listen. You gave this back to me. It belongs to you. I get it if you don't want to wear it on your finger, so I put it on a chain. I just want you to keep it with you. You know, a piece of me. So, you won't forget me," he said, his tone was all tease, as he handed me the chain with the beautiful ring hanging from it.

I sighed and held up my wrist to show him my music note tattoo. "Well, I always have a piece of you with me, right?"

He put his hand over his heart. "And you're always right here."

My eyes welled and my breath caught, suddenly overcome with emotion.

"Can I keep texting you?" he asked.

"Yeah. I think there should be some boundaries. How about we text once a week to make sure the other is okay?" I said.

He pulled me in and wrapped his arms around my shoulders, and I was lost in the moment. In his scent, his charm, in his honey-colored eyes and the love I had for this boy.

"That's fine. Whatever you want. I love you so much," he whispered against my ear.

"Sometimes love just isn't enough," I said when I pulled back and looked at him. I swiped at my tears. "Love has never been our problem."

"So, we'll figure it out. There's no one else for me." He held his arms out to the side.

"I'm afraid I'm in the same boat. I'm destined to grow old and gray alone," I said, pulling the chain over my head.

"I won't let that happen. I'll go fix what's broken with me, and I'll be waiting here for you when you're done saving the world, More Jade."

I blinked a couple times to fight back the tears. I wanted to believe him. But old habits die hard for both of us. His ability to convince me he was fine, and my ability to look the other way when I knew things weren't, was something we'd need to overcome if we ever wanted to be together.

"I hope you're right." I smiled.

They called our flight to start boarding and I realized the kids in my group had all returned. Some were on their phones, a few were staring, including Jessica.

"Alright. Time for you to go charge the tundra. Be safe, okay?" he said, pulling me against him one more time.

"You too." I pulled away and reached for my bag when everyone left to get in line.

"I'm sure rehab will be boring as hell, so if you want to actually respond to my texts and fill me in on your exciting life, I'd appreciate it."

I laughed. "I'll keep that in mind."

He held his hand up in a small wave and turned on his heels. I moved to get in line, taking deep, slow breaths to fight the lump in the back of my throat.

"I can't believe he came here," Jessica whispered. "My God, that guy is so crazy about you."

I was crazy about him too.

"Can you hold my bag for a minute?" I asked her, panic setting in that I wouldn't see him again for a long time.

"Of course."

I took off running and spotted him moving down the corridor. I shouted, "Cruz."

He turned around just as I crashed into him. I buried my face in his neck. "I love you, too."

He let out a relieved sigh. "I know you do, baby."

"Do good in rehab, okay? I'm proud of you."

He pulled back to look at me. "I will. I have something to fight for now. Go save the world. I'm not going anywhere."

"Okay," I said, swiping at the tears running down my face.

He wrapped an arm around my shoulder and walked me back toward the gate.

I hugged him goodbye and grabbed my bag from Jessica. Before I boarded the plane, I looked back to see Cruz standing there, watching me board the plane. I waved and he nodded with a smile.

I placed my bag above in the storage compartment and dropped down in my seat. I reached for my phone to turn it off, just as a text came through.

My heart fluttered.

CRUZ

I love you more.

I held the phone to my chest and closed my eyes.

I hoped he meant it.

My heart was counting on it.

THE END

Read More of Us Here:
https://geni.us/MoreOfUs

book 3 ~ sneak peek

. . .

More of Us

WE'D BEEN in Honduras for just a few days, and I was adapting to my new environment. We'd flown into Tegucigalpa, the capital of Honduras, and driven endless miles on dirt roads to our compound. The building was surrounded by a large, cement block wall. There was no TV here, none of the modern conveniences we were all used to, and every evening we all pulled out our pill bottles and took our malaria pills—a daily reminder that we had entered a different world.

It couldn't have come at a better time. I was in desperate need of a change, which is why I'd signed up last minute to spend my summer here. I was sick of the drama that had followed me and Cruz, and I'd come to a fork in the road—and I'd decided to change my course.

My heart ached every day, and I hoped that once I immersed myself in helping those in need, it would hurt a little less. That was the goal. I'd found my rock bottom… it was lying on a hotel room floor after being knocked unconscious by my boyfriend's bandmate, all while Cruz, the love of my life, lie only a hundred feet away unaware because he'd decided to take prescription sleeping pills. Did I mention he chased them down with whiskey? After he'd promised he would stop the pills and the drinking. It could have ended in so many different ways. I could have died if I'd hit my head differently. And no one would have known.

It was time for a fresh start. No more crying over Cruz Winslow. I was sick of myself and sick of who we'd become. I still loved him. There was no denying it. But that didn't mean he was good for me.

He wasn't.

I'd known it for a while, but my traitorous heart had steered me wrong. But I wasn't thinking with my heart anymore. I was thinking with my head. I was a smart girl. It was time I started acting like it.

I'd done well on my MCAT, and I'd be applying to medical school in two weeks, *if* we could find reception out here. My group leader, Richard, would also be applying at the same time, so he said we'd figure it out together, even if it meant driving into the capital to submit our applications.

Cruz had texted me twice since I'd arrived here, letting me know he'd started a thirty-day rehab program in Utah. I didn't have high expectations. He was continuing as the lead singer of Exiled, and I doubted he'd remain in this program for thirty days. Cruz was stubborn and he hadn't thought he had a problem before my accident, so what would make him think differently now? I wanted to trust him, but I knew better.

I needed him to stop texting me every day. I needed this time to figure out who I was and find a new path—and so did he. Love wasn't enough. I'd learned that the hard way. I told him he was free to date other girls and do what he wanted. We were done.

Donezo.

Finit.

The thought of him with someone else made me sick to my stomach. But it was a necessary pain. I needed to get over him, and I couldn't do that if we were still hoping to make things work. This was not our time and the sooner we both got on board, the better.

I shared a room with seventeen other girls from all over the United States. There was a boys' side of the compound and a girls' side. We'd all come on this medical brigade together. There were nine sets of bunk beds in my room, and Jessica and I shared the one in the back corner. I was on the top bunk because apparently Jessica is afraid of heights. I actually laughed when she told me that. She wasn't kidding either. She can't even climb up there to sit and talk. I had to go down to her bunk if we wanted to visit. The window in our room faced the surrounding sugarcane fields, and it calmed me in a weird way. There were no paparazzi waiting outside for me, no gossip magazines spreading lies about me and Cruz, and no drama.

I was here to do something good with my life and help people that were in need.

I stepped in the restroom shared with seventeen other girls, with one shower and one toilet. You weren't allowed to flush the toilet paper in the toilet, and the shower water was cold at all times. It was a perfect daily reminder of my fresh start. Literally and figuratively.

I rinsed my mouth using purified water from my water bottle and quickly washed my face. I pulled my hair into a knot, covered every inch of my body in insect repellant, and slipped into a pair of scrubs.

"You ready to go grab some breakfast before we head out?" I asked Jessica, and she set her journal aside and pushed to her feet.

"Yes. We officially start in our small groups today. I'm so glad we got placed together. And Richard seems pretty cool." Jessica grabbed her water bottle and we made our way to the dining area.

I chose fruit and cereal for breakfast, and we both tucked a peanut butter and jelly sandwich in our backpack for lunch. The food trucks would come out mid-day and provide us with lunch, but Jessica and I gave that food to the kids we were working with, and we brought our own sandwich to hold us over. We were finally breaking into small groups today, and our group would be assisting at a dental clinic for the next few days. I would be working in triage and assisting Dr. Lingy with exams.

"Let's load up," Richard said, and we grabbed our bags and made our way to the bus.

The bus would drop each group at their locations. Ours was the furthest away, and I settled in next to Jesica for the long two-hour commute. The roads were bumpy and Jessica and I laughed a few times as we bounced out of our seats. I pulled out my mom's journal and read today's entry.

May 19th

Dear Journal,

I am working full time at the news station this summer, and I couldn't be happier about it. One of the news anchors told me that this was where he started. I have so many dreams, and I'm so ready to start chasing them. This is definitely the first one, and it's going better than I ever imagined. Sabrina, the lady who set me up with this internship, said that the producer was singing my praises, and she told me to keep up the good work. I definitely plan on it.

Jack and I are going strong. I can't believe how much I love him. Even when he drives me crazy, which of course he does, I love him. We will get to see each other more often now that I'm on summer break. Even working full time, it's better than spending late nights in the library.

We have similar hours as he's training at the fire academy, and he's pretty wiped out at the end of the day. But I'm proud of him for chasing his own dreams. Of course, I will worry once he actually has to run into a burning building, because who wouldn't, right? But we support one another, and I'd never try to stop him from doing what he loves.

I know I'm where I'm supposed to be, and I couldn't be happier. I need to get to work.

Ciao for now,

J.E.

"You two ready to kickass today," Richard said, dropping to sit in the seat in front of us as the bus continued to bobble on the dirt road.

Jonah was asleep beside him, with his head resting against the window.

"Yeah, I'm excited to break into our small groups today," I said.

"Me too." Jessica leaned forward.

"I spoke to the coordinator, Jade, and we can go this weekend and submit our med-school applications. It's going to be a drive into Tegucigalpa, but we'll have wifi there hopefully. So, make sure you have everything completed and ready to upload," Richard said, running a hand through his dark hair. His brown gaze studied me. His white teeth were perfectly straight when he displayed his megawatt smile. He rocked that all-American boy look rather well, and he oozed charm.

"Okay, great. Thank you for setting that up. My applications are all ready to submit, so I can go any time."

"How many schools are you applying to?" he asked.

"Six."

"Six? That's not very many. I'm applying to twenty-eight. You're also young since you're graduating early, you may want to up that number to increase your chances." He smiled, and I straightened in my seat.

"Yeah, I'm pretty set on where I'd like to go, and I'm not *that* young," I said. It came out more defensive than I'd meant it to. The truth was, applying to medical school was expensive. I couldn't ask Dad for more money, because he'd funded my trip to Honduras as it was. Six applications would already be a small fortune, and I'd just have to hope for the best and pray that someone would accept me.

Richard held his hands up. "Sorry, I didn't mean to come off like a dick."

"No, you didn't. Twenty-eight seems like a lot of schools to apply to," I said.

"It's pretty average actually. But you're a rock star, Jade, and I'm sure you could apply to *one* and you'd get in." Richard stared at me with an intensity that made me a little nervous. Was he flirting with me? Was I just out of practice with reading the opposite sex? Seeing as the last thing I was interested in was meeting anyone, I wasn't paying much attention to that.

"Far from a rock star but thank you."

"Don't you date some famous dude in a band?" he asked, and Jessica choked on her water beside me.

"No. We aren't together anymore."

But thanks for asking—this guy was throwing all sorts of salt in my wounds today.

"Ah, good to know," he said with a grin, and pushed to his feet to return to the front of the bus.

"Well, that wasn't very subtle. I think he likes you." Jessica chuckled beside me. "He's super cute too."

"Not interested. Feel free to flirt away with him. He's all yours," I said, leaning back and reaching for my phone when it vibrated in my bag. We went in and out of service as we drove to our destination.

Cruz ~ Just wanted you to know that I sat through a miserable three-hour session with Dr. Roberts, a.k.a. Dr. Evil. She really is a bit sadistic where I'm concerned. She seems to enjoy torturing me. Anyway, she thinks I should respect your wishes to give you space.

I smiled and rolled my eyes at the same time. Why did I have to love him so much?

Me ~ How is this you giving me space?

Cruz ~ You don't see my ass in Honduras, do you?

Me ~ I think we should set some boundaries. We can text once a week for now.

Cruz ~ For now? Until what??

Me ~ Until you meet someone, or we both just move on.

Cruz ~ I'm not going to meet someone, Jade. What, are you on a dating quest in Honduras? I don't want to move on. Are you sure that's what you want?

My chest squeezed. *This* is what I didn't want. He had a way of pulling me back in.

Me ~ Honestly? Yes. I desperately want to move on. But I didn't come here to date. I don't have to be dating someone to move on with my life.

Cruz ~ I'm going to change, Jade. No more booze and no more drugs. I'll prove it to you.

My eyes welled, and it angered me that I wanted to believe him. But I couldn't invest in this relationship anymore. It had all but sucked the life from me.

Me ~ I hope you do. But do it for you, not for me.

Cruz ~ I'll do it for us.

Me ~ I have to go.

Cruz ~ I'll text you in a week. Promise. I love you.

Me ~ I love you. Goodbye, Cruz.

I turned my phone off and dropped it in my backpack. I swiped at the single tear running down my cheek before Jessica noticed. My chest ached. Everything hurt. It was like ripping off the bandage every time I talked to him. I missed him. I loved him.

Focus, Jade.

You can do this.

Getting over Cruz Winslow was not going to be easy. But I'd travelled over eighteen hundred miles away to make it happen.

And I was no quitter.

Do you want more of Jade and Cruz?
Read Book 3, More of Us HERE:
https://geni.us/MoreOfUs

acknowledgments

Greg, thank you for giving me the real-life fairytale. There is no one I'd rather have beside me through this journey. I love you.

Chase, thank you for always making me laugh when I need it. You are such a bright light in my life! Love you always.

Hannah, thank you for the endless encouragement, listening to me when I'm anxious, talking me through plot ideas, and being the best assistant at book events. Love you more.

Pathi, Annette, Natalie, Hannah, Abi, Nicole and Doo, thank you for being the BEST beta readers EVER! Your feedback means the world to me. I would be lost without you!

Thank you, Jena Brignola for bringing yet another gorgeous cover to life!

Sue Grimshaw (Edits by Sue), what a journey we have taken together with this series. I trust you completely, and am so thankful for your guidance and support.

Ellie McLove (My Brother's Editor), thank you for being YOU!! Your comments and feedback make editing so much fun!! Thank you for believing in me and always being so supportive!

Rosa Sharon (My Brother's Editor) thank you for making this book shine!! I love your feedback and appreciate all that you do for me!

Tamara Cribley (The Deliberate Page), thank you for making me feel so good about putting my books out there in the world!! I love every little detail, and all the gorgeous touches you add in!

Jo and Kylie at Give Me Books Promotions, I would be lost without you. Oh my gosh...the disasters that you have saved me from. I appreciate you both so much, and absolutely LOVE working with you!

Ashlee (Ashes & Vellichor), once again…you nailed it! I cannot tell you how much it means to me that you always make time to create the MOST BEAUTIFUL graphics and trailers. I absolutely adore you!!

Dad, Sandy & Mom, Thank you for always supporting me!! Love you!

Eric, thank you for always being the ear that I can bend when I need it.

Lisa, thank you for offering me so much guidance since I started this new venture. #ladyboss

Pathi, it doesn't matter how many rewrites I do, how many errors I make, you are always there ready to dig in and read whatever I give you. Thank you for being the best cheerleader and friend throughout this journey!

Natalie (Head in the Clouds, Nose in a Book), I could never thank you enough for all that you do for me. Thank you for taking on the newsletter, the website, and everything in between. Your support means SO MUCH to me!!

Steph, you are the best book event coordinator around! Thank you for supporting me endlessly, and coordinating our maxi dresses, and all the bundt cakes, and charcuterie boards!

Willow, Thank you for being the best sprinting partner around. You always encourage me, answer my endless questions and I can't even wait to be on Living In The Pages!! I appreciate you so much my sweet friend!

To all of the bloggers and bookstagrammers who have posted, shared and supported me—I can't begin to tell you how much it means to me. I love seeing the graphics that you make, and the gorgeous posts that you share. I am forever grateful for your support!

Lisa, Julie, Eric, Jen and Jim, I am very thankful to have such supportive and encouraging siblings in my life. Love you!

Nicole, Sue, Thompson, Pathi, Bell, Natalie, Annette, Carol, Margy, Steph, Mindy, Kristin, Laura, Anne, Abi, Dina, Kelly, Maggie,

Leigh Anne, Julie, Nancy, Bev, Leslie, Florence, Tina, Renae, Cindy, Kelly & Kate, Darleen, Althea, Jess, Ariel, Heather, Shannon, Brandon, Logan, Brock, Caroline, Liva, Kennedy, all the amazing ladies at d'annata boutique and Bloom boutique, and all of my friends who have supported me along this journey…thank you so much!!

keep up on new releases

other books by laura pavlov

Magnolia Falls Series
Loving Romeo
Wild River
Forbidden King
Beating Heart
Finding Hayes

Cottonwood Cove Series
Into the Tide
Under the Stars
On the Shore
Before the Sunset
After the Storm

Honey Mountain Series
Always Mine
Ever Mine
Make You Mine
Simply Mine
Only Mine

The Willow Springs Series
Frayed
Tangled
Charmed
Sealed
Claimed

follow me

Website laurapavlov.com
Goodreads @laurapavlov
Instagram @laurapavlovauthor
Facebook @laurapavlovauthor
Pav-Love's Readers @pav-love's readers
Amazon @laurapavlov
BookBub @laurapavlov
TikTok @laurapavlovauthor